Tempt

Cloverleigh Farms
Series

Melanie Harlow

Copyright © 2022 by Melanie Harlow

All rights reserved.

No part of this book may be reproduced in any form or by any electronic or mechanical means, including information storage and retrieval systems, without written permission from the author, except for the use of brief quotations in a book review.

For Alice, Crystal, Julia, Kessie, LeAnn, Lauren,
and Kristie.

You brought Millie to life for me, and this book is so much
better because of you.

I am WORTHY, I am FEARLESS, I have CONFIDENCE,
I am BOUNDLESS, I am RESILIENT, I am POWERFUL,
I am ALL ME.
Hunter McGrady

Tempt

One

Millie

September

"**I**t's official," I said to my sister over the phone. "I'm cursed."

Winnie laughed. "You're not cursed."

"Oh no?" I walked over to my hotel room window and peeked out at the city lights, blurred by sheets of rain. Manhattan was under siege. "Let's add things up. A hurricane pummels the East Coast the day I'm supposed to fly home, and my flight is canceled."

"Lots of flights were canceled, not just yours."

"I had to spend a lot of money to stay one more night in this expensive hotel."

"One more night at a four-star hotel is not a curse, it's an unexpected gift. And you can write it off—you're in New York on business. I want to hear how it went today, by the way."

"It was fine," I said grudgingly. "The usual wedding planner expo—noise and chaos. But I did get a few new ideas. Cottagecore weddings are supposedly going to be the trend for a while, and that's a vibe that suits Cloverleigh Farms."

I frowned. *"But the fashion show bothered me, it was not size-inclusive at all."*

"Seriously?"

"Same old, same old. The models were beautiful, but they didn't look like any of the real brides I've ever worked with. Why can't there be some curvy girls in these shows, or short girls, or top-heavy girls, or brides with bigger butts?"

"I don't know."

"I do. Because archaic beauty standards still abound in fashion, and the wedding industry is no exception."

"So do something about it."

"I would, but I'm very busy explaining to you why I'm cursed."

My sister sighed loudly.

"My ex-boyfriend is getting married next month, and I had to plan the wedding."

"You introduced them!"

"I know, but it's still sort of humiliating."

"Think of it as a compliment, Mills." Winnie could always find a bright side when I saw doom and gloom. *"Even though they knew it might be slightly awkward, they still chose you."*

"They chose Cloverleigh Farms because the bride works at the winery and got a discount," I corrected. *"I just happened to be the event planner there. They couldn't have one without the other."*

"Still, discount or not, a lot of brides would have gone with another venue altogether rather than let her fiancé's ex-girlfriend handle the most important day of her life. I think the trust she placed in you is a testament to your professional reputation."

"I guess." I turned away from the window and sprawled across the bed on my belly. *"But this is the third ex of mine who's gone on to propose to the very next girl he dated after me. The third, Winnie."*

"So you're a good luck charm, not a curse!"

"A good luck charm for *them*. What am I doing wrong?"

"Nothing! Be honest, Millie. Did you really want to be Mrs. Mason Holt?"

"No," I admitted. "He's cute, but he was too young for me. I didn't think the four-year age gap would matter that much, but after a few weeks, I knew it was never going to work."

"You knew after a few weeks? You dated Mason for months!"

"I know, but the spark wore off fast. Our relationship was strictly platonic by the end."

"Why didn't you break it off sooner?"

"Because I felt sorry for him. His mom had recently died, his stepdad was out of the picture, he never knew his real father . . . He seemed so vulnerable."

Winnie laughed. "This is your problem. You date lost puppies."

"I can't help it. Lost puppies are so cute. So loving and needy."

"Too needy."

"I *like* being needed. It makes me feel good." Rolling onto my back, I sighed. "It's just really frustrating that I'm thirty-two and still haven't found the one yet. Honestly, I thought I'd have like three kids by now."

"You don't need a man to have a kid, Mills. You just need some genetic material, and I think there's an app for that." She giggled.

"Be serious," I told her, although I'd secretly googled *sperm banks near me* like ten times in the last few months and then immediately deleted my search history.

"I am being serious. You'd be an amazing mom, and if that's what you want, you should go for it."

"I want a *family*," I clarified. "I want a *dad* for my kids, not just someone's genetic material. And I'd like to grow old with someone. You and Felicity managed to find the one. Why can't I?"

"Finding the one isn't something you *manage*, like a project or an event. It takes time. I might be younger than you, but I kissed a lot of frogs before I met Dex. And even he sort of seemed like a frog at first—twelve years older than me, divorced with two young daughters, grumpy as hell and positive he'd never want to be in a relationship."

I snorted. "That didn't last long."

"No, but it wasn't easy. And look at Felicity."

Our middle sister had recently spoken her vows in the orchard at Cloverleigh Farms, after a whirlwind courtship that had involved a fake engagement to her best friend from high school—the one who'd loved her all along. "That *should* have been easy, but they made it complicated."

"*So* complicated," Winnie agreed with a laugh. "But my point is, there are some things you just have to leave up to fate. You can't rush them. And you can't plan them."

"So that's it?" Cranky, I got off the bed and headed for the minibar. "I just while away my days waiting for lightning to strike? That's not me, Winnie. I'm a doer, not a waiter."

"But you keep *doing* the wrong thing. You just have a pattern—you choose guys that need fixing, you solve their problems, part ways with them, and then they go on to meet the love of their lives because you helped them get over their baggage. You need to get out of that rut."

"You're not helping," I told her, perusing the tiny bottles of booze and overpriced snacks in the fridge.

"Want my advice?"

"Maybe," I said, wondering if I had to feel bad that the little sister was the one handing out wisdom to the big sister. Wasn't it supposed to be the other way around? Seemed like yesterday she was wearing footie pajamas and had syrup in her hair. It actually made me smile, thinking about those frantic school mornings where our dad, who'd raised the three of us on his own after our mother left, would scramble to get out the door on time.

We'd lived that way for a few years before he married Frannie, our amazing stepmom, who'd been more of a mother to me in every way than my biological mom. It was from watching my dad and Frannie that I'd learned to believe in real love, the kind that lasts.

I just didn't know where to find it.

"My advice," Winnie went on, "is to change your luck. Get off the hamster wheel."

I shut the minibar door. "How do I do that?"

She thought for a moment. "Do something you wouldn't normally do. I say you put on something cute, go down to the hotel bar, and flirt with a handsome, mysterious stranger."

I laughed. "Are you nuts? It's after nine. That's my bedtime."

"You need to get out of your routine, that's the point! Listen, there must be other people stranded by the storm tonight, and odds are at least one of them is hot, single, and looking for a one-night stand with a bombshell blonde."

"I'm already in my pajamas." But I wandered over to my suitcase and opened it up, rifling through it for something cute. Maybe getting out of my room would help my mood.

"So change out of them! What if downstairs right now is the man of your dreams? One with piercing dark eyes, a chiseled jaw, and a magic dick?"

I laughed as I pulled out a black dress I hadn't worn while I was here. "How am I supposed to spot a magic dick across the room?"

"You won't actually be able to spot it, but judging by the rest of him, it will be *strongly implied*."

Laughing, I held the dress against my body and looked in

the mirror. "I guess I could go down and get a drink. But no promises about a one-night stand."

"I'm not asking for a promise. I'm just asking that you try being a little less predictable, and a little more adventurous. Plot twists are fun."

I felt myself caving. Maybe Winnie was right. "Okay, I'll go down to the bar and see if a plot twist catches my eye."

"Good. But *no* puppies!"

Half an hour later, I walked into the dimly lit bar off the lobby of the small, upscale hotel where I was staying. I'd chosen not to stay at the huge hotel where the expo was being held because by the end of the day, I was done with people and really craved peace, quiet, and a paperback. I also liked to check out more intimate, boutique hotels whenever I traveled, since Cloverleigh Farms was also a small inn and I loved seeing what other places were doing.

I particularly liked the cozy, elegant bar here—its low lighting from vintage brass wall sconces and fringed table lamps, its fern-colored walls and ceiling, the emerald-green leather and brass barstools, the moss-green velvet banquettes along the wall. The vibe was sort of Emerald City meets Restoration Hardware, and I was a sucker for anything with a whiff of a 1920s speakeasy, especially with Amy Winehouse on the speakers.

The place was busy—was I the only person under eighty that went to bed before ten on a Thursday night?—but I spotted one empty barstool and made my way toward it, conscious of eyes that followed me. I wasn't mad about it. I'd curled my long blond hair and given myself a smoky eye. My black dress clung to my plentiful curves, and while it wasn't short or low-cut, it was one-shouldered with a slit on one side that showed some leg. And I was wearing a shade of lipstick called Red Carpet, which you shouldn't really wear if you just want to blend into the wallpaper.

Most days, I was confident in my plus-sized body, although it had taken me a while to embrace it. But once I stopped trying to please other people and learned to love the body I was born into, I'd felt so much relief, and much more at ease in my skin.

Did I always love my thick thighs and rounded belly? No. Did I sometimes get annoyed that shopping was so much easier for my smaller-sized sisters and friends? Yep. Did I secretly feel sort of glad that even Winnie had cellulite that showed when she wore a bathing suit? Maybe.

Okay, yes.

But I admitted it to her, and we both laughed about it.

I certainly remained aware that there would always be people who thought I needed to lose weight to be healthy (not true), who assumed I thought pizza was a vegetable (I have a much better relationship with food now than I *ever* did starving myself to be a ballerina), and never exercised (I work out regularly and enjoy it). But mostly, I just think there are some people who envy the fact that I can cross the room in a badass tight black dress and feel good about myself, even if I don't meet their narrow beauty ideals.

Fuck those people. That's their insecurity talking, not mine.

I reached the empty barstool and slid onto it, setting my clutch on the smooth, mahogany bar. The bartender, a twenty-something with a handlebar mustache, approached me with a smile. "What can I get for you?"

"I'd like a vodka martini, please. Grey Goose, with a twist."

He nodded and set a cocktail napkin in front of me. "Lemon or tangerine?"

Lemon was on the tip of my tongue—my usual choice—but I answered differently. Lemon was the hamster wheel. Tangerine was a plot twist. "Tangerine," I said with a smile.

"You got it."

Although I was tempted to take out my phone, I didn't. It's what I normally would have done, and I wanted to invite a different kind of energy tonight. Maybe by changing a couple small things, I could change my luck.

I watched the bartender shake my drink, pour it into a glass, add the twist. Then I gave him a smile when he placed it in front of me. "Thank you."

"My pleasure. Enjoy."

I was just lifting the glass to my lips when I noticed someone sitting around the curve of the bar to the left. He was broad through the chest and shoulders, wore a black dress shirt with the cuffs rolled up, and sat alone. His hair and beard were short and dark. Our eyes met and my body grew warm. His bone structure was beautiful—his face looked like it was chiseled from granite. He held my gaze for a moment then looked away, and I did as well, focusing on the first cold sips of my martini.

But in seconds, my eyes were drawn to him again, and I noticed the hand holding his glass—wide palm, long, solid fingers, thick wrist. I indulged in a brief and magnificent fantasy that involved those hands in my hair, his beard against my cheek, that brawny chest bare and warm above me. Was it hairy? I'd bet yes. He looked like a man's man. My nipples tingled inside the bustier I wore beneath my dress.

Once more he caught me staring, and I realized too late that I was actually *biting my lip*.

Gawd.

I looked down at the bar, glad it was dark in there—my cheeks had to be flushed pink. Telling myself to be cool, I sipped my drink and concentrated on minding my own business. But I got antsy and self-conscious, and after a couple minutes of listening to other people's conversations—which mostly involved a lot of swearing about the weather and canceled flights—I pulled my phone from my clutch. I had a couple texts from my sister.

> **So how's it going?**
>
> **Any plot twists on the horizon?**
>
> **Maybe one,** I texted back.
>
> **Chiseled jaw?**
>
> **Check.**
>
> **Dark eyes?**
>
> **Check.**
>
> **Magic dick strongly implied?**
>
> **CHECK.**
>
> **Go talk to him. See if you can get under its spell.**
>
> **ITS THICK, THROBBING SPELL.**

I chuckled and took another sip of my martini.

"What's the joke?" asked the guy sitting to my right.

I flipped my phone screen-down on the bar and looked at him. "I'm sorry?"

"You were laughing. What's the joke?" He looked about my age, wearing a white shirt, blue blazer, and cocky grin. His hair was dark blond, and he was incredibly tan, like he'd just gotten off a cruise ship.

"Oh, there's no joke." Nervous, I stuck my cell back into my purse. "I was just texting my sister."

"Your sister, huh?" Then he whistled loudly and yelled at the bartender, "Hey! Can I get another round down here?"

The bartender, who was busy making other drinks, didn't even look over. I didn't blame him.

"The service is so shitty in this place," the guy next to me said. "You need a pair of tits to get any attention." He glanced at my chest. "Yours are fantastic, by the way."

Horrified, I picked up my glass and finished my drink in a couple swallows. I should have thrown it in his face, but it would have been a waste of a good martini. Setting the empty glass down, I reached into my bag for my credit card.

"Hey, don't rush off." The asshole leaned closer. He reeked of cologne. "We're just getting to know each other."

"Not interested," I said, trying to catch the bartender's eye so I could get my check and leave.

"Why not? I'm alone, you're alone." He covered my hand with his. That's when I noticed he wore a wedding band.

I snatched my hand away and slid off my stool, putting it between us. "I'm not alone."

"Oh no?" He laughed and glanced around. "Looks like it to me."

I finally caught the bartender's eye, and he came right over. "Can I get you something?"

"I'll cash out," I said quickly.

The bartender glanced at the asshole. "Everything okay?"

"Everything's fine, I was just waiting for someone, but he couldn't make it, so I—"

"Sorry I'm late." A hand circled my wrist.

Startled, I spun around and saw a black shirt. Wide shoulders. Dark eyes.

The hot stranger and I exchanged a look of understanding before he leaned in and kissed my cheek. His beard was softer than I'd imagined.

"Forgive me?" His voice, by contrast, was deep and gravelly.

"Of—of course," I stammered, my heart pounding. I couldn't stop staring—the guy was *gorgeous*. A little older than I'd thought—there was silver in his hair and beard—but those dark eyes, that deep voice, and the possessive grip on my wrist? The whole package made my knees go weak.

He looked over my head at the bartender. "She's with me."

"Dude, she's not with you," argued the jerk in the blazer. "You were over there by yourself a minute ago. I saw you."

Dropping my wrist, the stranger turned to him and growled, "You should go."

The jerk slid off his barstool and put one palm up. "Listen, I don't want any trouble. I just thought—"

"It's fuckin' obvious what you thought." The stranger's words were laced with fury, but he kept his volume low. Somehow it was even scarier than if he'd yelled. "Now get the fuck out of here, and don't even look in her direction as you walk out, or you'll be trying to do it with two broken legs."

The jerk stood up taller, like he might be thinking of protesting, but he looked like a gerbil facing off against a Doberman. He looked over at the bartender. "Did you hear him threaten me?"

"Yep," said the bartender with a quick nod.

"Aren't you going to do something about it?"

"Nope." The bartender folded his arms over his chest.

Scowling, the jerk adjusted his lapels and moved toward the exit without even glancing my way.

The stranger watched him go with hooded, hawklike eyes before looking down at me again. "You okay?"

"Yes." I was struggling to catch my breath, but it wasn't because of the jerk.

"Can I bring you two another round?" the bartender asked.

The stranger looked at me. "Would you like another drink?"

I took a breath, willing myself to be brave. "Only if you'll stay and have one with me."

He hesitated, rubbing one hand along his jaw. "Okay. Sure."

"Another martini for the lady and a Glenlivet on the rocks, coming right up," said the bartender.

I perched on my barstool again, crossing my legs. "Thanks for coming to my rescue."

"You're welcome." He sat down next to me. "I hope I didn't insult you."

"Insult me?"

"I didn't mean to imply you couldn't handle that jackass on your own."

"Oh! Well, maybe I could have." I laughed a little. "But I liked your way better."

One side of his mouth twitched, setting off a thousand butterflies in my stomach.

"This round is on me," I said as our drinks appeared.

He shook his head. "Not a chance."

I put my Red Carpet lips in a playful pout. "But I'd like to repay you for standing up for me."

"No payment necessary. Any gentleman would have done it."

"Gentleman, huh?" I tilted my head and gave him a playful smile. I was a pretty good flirt when I wanted to be. "So you're saying I'm safe with you?"

He didn't answer right away, and I sat up a little taller in my seat. Slightly arched my back. But his eyes stayed put on mine. "You're safe with me."

Well, damn.

What on earth was I going to do about that?

Two

Zach

SINCE THE MOMENT I SAW HER ENTER THE BAR, I'D BEEN struggling with temptation.

Everything about her was sexy.

That hair—it hung down beyond her shoulders in blond satin waves.

That body—those curves could make a grown man cry for mercy.

That mouth—it was heart-shaped and lush, with her lips painted stop-sign red.

The color was a good reminder. The girl was a knockout, but she looked kind of young, she was alone and vulnerable, and I wasn't that kind of guy. I had literally just fucking told her she was safe with me, and I meant it. Much as I wanted to, I wasn't going to touch her.

I was ninety-nine percent sure of it.

Picking up my whiskey, I took a couple swallows to numb the urge.

"So," she said, her smile seductive. "Can I ask the name of the gallant stranger who rescued me tonight?"

"Zach."

"Nice to meet you, Zach." She held out her hand. "I'm Millie."

I took her much smaller hand in mine—it was soft and pale and smooth. Touching her shot arrows of lust straight to my dick, which had felt like a rocket ready for launch since the moment I locked eyes with her across the bar. I didn't hold her hand a second longer than necessary, immediately picking up my drink again.

"Are you in town on business?" she asked.

"Yes."

After an awkward pause, she laughed. "Are you going to tell me what you do when you're not saving women from creepers in bars?"

"I'm in private security."

"You're a bodyguard?"

"Sometimes."

"What about the other times?"

I cocked a brow and gave her a sideways glance. "You ask a lot of questions."

"I'm curious about you." She took a sip of her drink, and I imagined those red lips rimming something other than her glass.

"I don't like talking about myself."

"Oh. Okay. I can respect that," she said. But I'd disappointed her, I could tell.

We sat in silence for another minute or so, and I was beginning to regret agreeing to one more drink. Every second that ticked by, I noticed something else about her that drove me wild. The curve of her shoulder. The long black lashes. The smell of her perfume. She wasn't even showing off much cleavage, but the silhouette of her breasts in that clingy dress had my mouth watering. I could practically feel the shape of them in my hands, her nipples under my tongue.

What the fuck was the matter with me? Wasn't I too old for this?

Granted, the shitty end of my shitty marriage had me in a pretty long dry spell, but yesterday I hadn't even cared. It was like I'd forgotten what it was like to have such a powerful attraction to someone. To feel desire burning through me. Lately I'd been feeling like maybe those days were over—but sitting here next to her made me feel seventeen again.

"Okay, one more question," she blurted, holding her hands up. "And then I promise I'll leave you alone."

"Shoot."

"What made you come over and save me from that guy?"

A better question was why I'd waited as long as I had. I'd seen the way he was eyeing her, and my protective instincts had kicked in. I knew it was only a matter of time before he made his move. "I know his type."

"But you don't know *my* type." Her voice was teasing. "What if jackasses in blue blazers are my thing?"

"Are they?"

"No." She laughed and took another drink. "I was very happy when you grabbed my wrist." A pause. "For many reasons."

I guzzled some more whiskey.

"I mean, I'd noticed you sitting by yourself over there and . . . I don't know. You intrigued me."

That made me smile. "Yeah?"

"Yes. I couldn't stop staring."

"I noticed."

She laughed again, covering her pink cheeks with her hands. "Was it really that obvious?"

"Yeah, but don't worry about it. I'm someone who's always aware of what people around me are doing."

She picked up her drink and swirled what was left of her

vodka in the glass. "That probably makes you really good at your job."

"Yes."

She sighed. "I'm good at my job too. But you know what?"

"What?"

She finished the martini and set the glass down on the bar. "I don't want to talk about my job tonight."

"Okay."

"And we don't have to talk about your job either."

"Works for me."

"But we have to talk about *something*."

"We do?"

"Yes. I promised my sister I would get out of my comfort zone tonight and talk—no, flirt—with a handsome, mysterious stranger. Guess what?" She gave me an adorably tipsy smile and pointed at my shoulder. "That's you."

A chuckle rumbled in my chest. "Lucky me."

"So how am I doing so far?"

"Oh, I'd say nine out of ten."

"Nine out of ten!" She shrank back, as if she was offended. "What do I have to do to get the last point?"

Everything that came to mind was unspeakable. *Sit on my face. Put your hand in my pants. Let me rub the tip of my cock on that little dimple that appears in your cheek when you smile.*

Tossing back the rest of my drink, I plunked the glass onto the bar. "Nothing. I'll give it to you free—ten out of ten."

"I don't want your pity point, Zach. Tell me what you were thinking."

I rotated my empty glass with one hand, sneaking a sideways look at her. "How old are you?"

"Why? Are your thoughts age-restricted?"

"They should be."

She lifted her chin. "I'm thirty-two. How old are you?"

"Older."

"Older like ninety?"

"Older like forty-seven."

Her eyes raked me over head to foot. "Wow. You're in great shape," she said. "You don't even have suspenders holding up your pants. I mean, you could be wearing sock garters, but who can tell? Maybe I should check your wallet for an AARP card."

I gave her a menacing glare. "I'm taking my pity point back."

She tossed her head back and laughed, while I entertained unholy thoughts about my mouth on her throat and my hand up her dress. "Sorry," she said, trying to compose herself. "I couldn't resist. But I'm not giving back the pity point. I want a perfect ten."

Perfect ten. That described her to a T.

The bartender came over and asked if we'd like another round.

Millie sighed. "I shouldn't. I make very questionable decisions if I have three drinks. And I've got an early flight tomorrow."

"We're all set," I told the bartender. "Just the check." He returned a moment later and set it in front of me.

"Are you sure you won't let me pay?" Millie asked. I wondered if that was a nickname, short for something else.

"I'm sure."

"You know, I really do need to thank you." Her voice was sincere. "I was in a terrible mood earlier. You not only rescued me from a jerk, but you lifted my spirits."

"Why were you in a terrible mood?"

She smiled. "Look at you being curious."

"Forget it." I picked up a pen and signed the check.

"Oh, come on." She poked my arm. "Don't get grouchy on me now. I was just feeling a little unlucky is all. Things haven't been going my way lately."

"Well, if it makes you feel any better, you did not look like you were having a bad night when you walked in here."

"You watched me walk in?"

Words tumbled out before I could stop them. "I couldn't take my eyes off you."

"Why?"

"Why?" I laughed. Did she really not know how beautiful she was?

"Yes." She leaned toward me, placing one hand on my leg. "Why?"

I rubbed the back of my neck, taking a time out. However I answered this would likely determine the rest of the night.

Option A: I could do the right thing—the one that kept her safe with me—and say something complimentary but not provocative. Something that would effectively end this standoff with a polite handshake before I went back to my room alone and jerked off while I fantasized about her.

Option B: I could say something obnoxious about wanting to take her back to my room and fuck her with my tongue.

I looked at her hand on my leg and wanted one thing.

I looked in those sweet amber eyes and felt guilty about it.

In the end, I went for something in between.

"Because it's been a long time since a woman took my breath away."

Her heart-shaped mouth fell open. Her eyes smoldered. "My heart is beating so fast right now," she whispered.

I glanced at her chest—a mistake.

Should I invite her to my room, even after telling her she was safe with me? Would she say yes because she was drunk? A guy had to be fucking careful about that. I didn't know her at all—would she come after me in a month, accusing me publicly of taking advantage of her? In my line of work, I had to keep a spotless record.

But I wanted this perfect ten in my bed tonight.

"Would you like to continue this conversation in my room?" I asked quietly.

"That depends," she said with a coquettish tilt of her head. "Earlier you mentioned I'd be safe with you. If I go up to your room, does that mean you're going to keep your hands to yourself?"

"No. My hands will be all over your body." Leaning closer, I put my lips against her ear. "My hands, my mouth, and my cock. Baby, if you say yes, you're going to be up all fucking night."

She sucked in her breath. "Yes. I say yes. Yes."

For the second time that night, I grabbed her wrist.

The last vestiges of my gentlemanly control went extinct. My manners, which had been on glittering display at the bar, disappeared in a hurry. I shouldered people aside as I pulled her through the crowd. I punched the up arrow button five times in a row, hard. When someone attempted to get on the elevator with us, I stood in their way and growled, "Take the next one." And the second the doors were closed behind us, I turned around and put Millie's back against the wall.

With my mouth hovering less than an inch from hers, I slid one hand into her hair, gripping the back of her neck. I slipped the other hand inside the slit of her dress and ran it up the outside of her thigh. I could feel her breath on my lips.

"You are infuriatingly, *indecently* beautiful," I told her. "And I might never forgive you for making me want you so badly."

She put a hand over my cock, which strained against the denim. "Are you going to punish me for it?"

"Hard and repeatedly."

The elevator dinged, and the doors slid open. I took her

hand and strode down the hallway so fast she could hardly keep up. My key card didn't work the first two times, and I cursed with impatience. Did this fucking door not realize I was about to get laid for the first time in a year by the goddess standing beside me? I knew how to break into a hotel room, and I was about to do it when the light flashed green. I opened the door for Millie, hung the Do Not Disturb sign on the handle, and let it slam behind me.

Inside the room, we rushed for each other, our bodies crashing like lightning. For a few minutes, it was nothing but chaos and heat. My hands on her ass. Her moans against my lips. My tongue in her mouth. Her tits on my chest. My dick growing harder beneath the heat of her palm as she stroked me over my jeans.

I ran my hands all over her body, skimming every delectable, feminine curve. I moved my mouth down her throat, inhaling the scent of her sweetly perfumed skin. "God, you smell so good."

She tugged the bottom of my shirt from my jeans, and I took my hands off her just long enough to wrestle out of it and whip my T-shirt over my head.

Millie murmured sexy little sounds of approval as she swept her hands over my shoulders, down my arms, up my back. She brought her lips to my chest and teased my nipple with her tongue as she slipped her hand in my pants and wrapped her fingers around my cock.

Groaning, I thrust into her fist as long as I could before a warning bell went off in my head, reminding me that coming in her hand would *not* be cool. I needed to slow down. Catch my breath. Focus on her.

Yanking her dress up to her hips, I forced her backward onto the bed. Then I dropped to my knees in front of her and spread her legs.

Braced on her elbows, she watched me lift one ankle and

kiss my way from the strap of her high heel to the inside of her knee to the firm flesh of her thigh. Her skin was soft and smooth. Her breaths came hard and fast. When I reached the apex of her thighs, I placed her leg over my shoulder and used my tongue to caress the scrap of lace covering her pussy. She gasped, her fingernails scratching at the hotel comforter. I hooked one finger around the lace and pulled it aside, licking up the seam at her center slowly, again and again, tasting her, teasing her, fucking her with my tongue. She was sweet and warm, like melted butter.

"Oh my God," she whimpered. "I didn't even have to ask."

"You should never have to ask." I barely took my mouth off her to get the words out.

"That feels so good. Oh, my God. This is—how do you know exactly—fuck, I'm so—"

Her words trailed off, becoming moans as I stroked her clit with long, slow swirls and sucked it into my mouth. I eased a finger inside her, groaning as I imagined sliding my cock deep into the slippery, swollen warmth of her pussy. I added a second finger, gratified when her moans turned into escalating cries of desperate need.

"Yes! Don't stop! I'm so close, please, please, please . . ."

Her begging made me wonder for a second if she'd been with an asshole who not only had to be asked to make her come this way but had stopped before it happened. What the actual fuck was wrong with young guys? It made me even more determined to take her all the way there.

Mere seconds went by before she was coming in quick, fluttering pulses against my tongue, her core muscles contracting around my fingers, her leg tightening against my back, pulling me closer. Greedy for as much as I could get, I continued to devour her until her body relaxed and her cries quieted into breathless pants.

"I want you," she whispered, "now. Please."

"I like hearing you say that word—please." I dragged the black lace thong down her legs and tossed it aside. "It makes you sound like such a good girl. It's almost enough to make me forget what a bad girl you are."

"You think I'm a bad girl?" She sounded sort of impressed with herself.

"Yes." I removed her shoes and stood up, ditching the rest of my clothes. "Walking into the bar tonight looking like that. Putting your eyes on me. Coming up to my hotel room. Letting me taste you. Making my cock so hard it hurts." I wrapped my hand around my dick and gave it several long, slow pulls. "Do you think that was nice?"

Millie's eyes were wide as she watched me. Her red lipstick was smeared around her mouth. She was still ungodly beautiful—like a fallen angel. "No."

"What am I going to do with you?"

She appeared to think about the question somewhat seriously. And it's not easy for people to surprise me, but what she said made my jaw drop.

"Spank me."

Three

Millie

HONESTLY, I HAVE NO IDEA WHAT MADE ME SAY IT.

"Huh?" Zach's hand paused on his dick, which did resemble (as suspected) a thick, hard magic wand. I bet it even vibrated.

"You should spank me," I said, testing out the role. "For being such a bad girl."

"Do you enjoy being spanked?" His tone said he was intrigued.

"I don't know." I'd never been spanked before. I'd read about it in books, but my puppy-dog exes were not the dominant alpha males who starred in my erotic novels.

"Would you like to find out?"

"Yes," I said breathlessly.

"Yes, what?" His voice held a warning tone.

"Yes, please."

He reached for my hand and pulled me to my feet. "I've been thinking about this since the moment I saw you." He grabbed the bunched-up material at my hips and dragged the dress over my head. Underneath, I'd worn a black lace bustier that showed off my hourglass figure.

Zach's eyes popped. "Jesus Christ. Your body should be illegal."

He buried his face in my cleavage, his mouth warm and wet on the spill of my breasts above the lingerie, his beard scratching at my skin. I wove my fingers into his hair, loving the threads of silver among the dark. His capable hands moved from my hips to my ass, filling his palms with my flesh, squeezing hard.

All I could think of was how powerful and masculine he was. I'd never been with anyone whose hands felt so strong, whose voice was so deep, whose body was so muscular and mature. He might have been forty-seven, but he was built like an active-duty Marine. The tattoos. The chest hair. The ripped abdomen and bulging biceps. No wonder he was a bodyguard—every inch of him exuded strength and force and skill. Even his *tongue*. My God, I'd never had an orgasm so fast, not without battery-powered assistance or giving tons of instructions. Not that I minded telling a guy what I liked, but sometimes it felt like I should have provided a map and step-by-step directions to the destination. Maybe a Maglite and a compass. But Zach? Not only did he know the terrain, but he obviously had an internal navigation system.

Would he be just as good during the actual deed? I remembered the heft and length of his cock in my hand and my excitement ratcheted up another notch.

"Zach," I murmured impatiently, reaching between his legs again. "I want you."

"Soon." He lifted his head and spun me around so his erection pressed into my lower back. "But I have to teach you a lesson first," he growled in my ear. "Get on the bed. Hands and knees."

I did what he said, my limbs trembling.

"Just like a good girl." He climbed up on the mattress and knelt behind me. "Now grab on to the headboard."

I moved up farther and placed my palms on the tufted brown leather. My breath was shallow and quick, my chest restricted by the bustier. Fear and anticipation coursed through me. Would he give me any warning? Would it hurt? Those hands could probably do a lot of damage.

It was one thing to hand your body over to a stranger for pleasure. It was quite another to hand it over for pain.

But for some reason, I trusted him.

"So fucking beautiful," he said.

I felt his palms on my butt, rubbing firm, slow circles in opposite directions. More like a massage than anything. Maybe he'd changed his mind. Maybe he—

Smack!

His hand striking my ass set my skin on fire, making me cry out. Immediately he pressed his hand over the sting. "Shhh. Did that hurt?"

"Yes," I whispered through clenched teeth.

"Good." He did it again, cracking his palm across the opposite cheek, then covering them both, rubbing gently. "That's the only way you'll learn."

My eyes were watering, and I imagined my ass was bright red. But my heart was racing, and my nipples were hard— maybe it was just a game, but the idea that he was teaching me a lesson for being too tempting for him to resist made my entire body radiate with desire.

"I've learned," I panted. "I promise. I'm a good girl now. I just want you to fuck me."

He pressed close behind me, and I moaned when I felt his cock trapped between us. I pushed back against it, hoping he wouldn't be able to resist. Instead, he braced one arm on the headboard above mine and reached around my waist with the other hand, dipping his fingers inside me, then rubbing them over my clit. He moaned in my ear, deep and gruff. "Would a good girl get so wet from being spanked? Would a good girl like being punished this way? Would a good girl ask to get fucked?"

I whimpered as he tortured me with his fingers. I didn't know what answers to give to make him want me as badly as I wanted him. I'd never felt so helpless and impatient and frustrated—didn't the guy always want to come as quickly as possible? Was Zach superhuman?

"Tell me what to do," I begged as I neared a second climax. "What will make you say yes?"

"Come for me. Just like this." He plunged his fingers deeper, using the heel of his hand against my clit, and I shamelessly rocked my hips, spiraling higher. In seconds the world turned silver, and my lower body tightened up, every muscle tingling. I cried out as the orgasm tore through me, my body clenching his hand, his teeth sinking into my shoulder, spiking the pleasure with a delicious little sting.

Breathing hard, he took his fingers from me. "I need to see you—all of you," he said, undoing the bustier's hooks at my lower back. It fell open, and I could breathe easier. My chest heaved.

His hands closed over my breasts, lifting and shaping them, teasing their stiff peaks with his fingertips. He put his mouth on one shoulder and moved it up the curve of my neck. Taking my hands from the headboard, I wrapped them around his head, threading my fingers in his hair. Breathing deeply, I told myself to stop racing for the finish—we would get there. No one had ever worshiped my body this way, and I should savor every single, delicious second.

"You are the most beautiful woman I have ever seen," he told me. And maybe it wasn't true, maybe it was just a line, maybe he'd said it to twenty other women before me, but I didn't care. Because he made it *feel* true. All the insecurities that might have taken the shine off this night were nonexistent.

He touched me reverently and patiently, but hungrily and greedily too—like he was worried there was some place on my body, some inch of my skin he might miss. He kissed me deeply, and I could taste the whiskey on his tongue. He spoke low in my ear, his fingers inside me, telling me how hard his cock was as he rubbed it against my ass, how much he loved that I was so wet for him, how deep and hard he was going to fuck me, how many times he wanted to make me come tonight.

I was trembling, aching with need by the time he tipped me onto my back and stretched out above me. Anticipation built with every sensation. The weight of his thick, muscular chest. The thrust of his tongue in my mouth. The slick heat of our skin. The sound of our ragged breathing. The motion of his hips as he rocked between my thighs, his cock sliding against my clit, the friction enough to have me clawing his back.

I nearly wept with relief when he knelt between my legs, rolling on the condom. I held my breath as he eased inside me with a few slow, shallow thrusts, glad he was a gentleman again, at least for a moment. I'd never been with anyone so big, and my body needed time to adjust.

"Are you okay?" he asked.

I nodded, clutching his shoulders.

"Breathe," he told me.

I laughed, inhaling and exhaling a couple times. "You're just a lot bigger than anyone I've ever been with."

"Good."

"Also, it's been a while."

"For me too." He groaned, sliding in deeper. "Which is why it's a challenge right now not to tear you apart."

"Just give me a minute," I whispered, running my hands down his back, drawing my knees up. "And then you can be as rough as you want."

With one final stroke, he buried himself, making me gasp. "You sure about that?"

I squeezed my eyes shut against the deep, painful twinge—had he knocked some internal organ out of the way? "Maybe two minutes," I said, breathing in and out, relaxing my pelvic muscles, latching on to the lovely hum that was building inside me again as he began to move.

In truth, it was probably only about thirty seconds before I had my hands full of his gloriously firm ass, pulling him in deeper, lifting my hips to meet every thrust, my body begging for more even though my mind wasn't sure I could take it.

As promised, Zach nearly tore me apart. Despite the slow and gentle start, things escalated quickly—at least I think they did, but I'd lost all sense of time, I'd lost all sense of anything except his body on mine, his driving cock, his furious need to go deeper, harder, faster until his body stiffened and I felt him throbbing inside me, a strangled groan in my ear. I hooked my legs around his thighs and dug my nails into his skin, relishing every last pulse.

When he'd caught his breath, he braced himself above me. "I was too fast."

"You were perfect. That was amazing."

"You didn't come with me."

"I came twice *before* you!" I laughed. "You've already doubled the number of orgasms I've ever had with anyone else, and I don't even know your last name."

"It's Barrett."

"Mine's MacAllister."

"Millie MacAllister." He smiled, his eyes crinkling at the corners. "Cute."

I smiled too. I'd messed up his hair, and he was all rumpled and sexy. The butterflies were back. "I wish I didn't have to go, but—"

He shook his head. "You're not going anywhere."

"Huh?"

"Listen, Millie MacAllister. Down in the bar, I told you if you said yes, you'd be up all fucking night. And I meant it."

I laughed, glancing over at the nightstand clock. "But it's—"

"It's barely after midnight. What time is your flight?"

"Nine."

His grin widened. "Baby, we're just getting started."

I opened my eyes in a panic—shit! What time was it?

I bolted upright in Zach's bed, relieved when I saw the clock numbers glowing in the dark. It wasn't quite five. I still had time to sneak back to my room, pack up, and make it to the airport on time. What the hell had I been thinking to fall asleep?

Actually, I hadn't been capable of thinking at that point, I thought, swinging my feet to the floor. My mind still wasn't working right. Zach had literally fucked my brains out.

I glanced behind me at the sleeping figure of the man who'd made me see stars *five times*. His breathing was slow and even, surprisingly quiet. Gingerly, I got to my feet, suppressing a groan at the stiffness in my muscles. I was going to be sore all week.

The carpet was soft under my feet as I moved around the room, hunting for the various pieces of my clothing from last night—bustier, dress, shoes . . . but where the heck had my panties landed? Frowning, I got down on my hands and knees near the foot of the bed and felt around. At some point, Zach had turned off the lamp, so I couldn't see a thing.

Aha! My fingers encountered some lace, and I stood to step into them. Panties in place, I was struggling to manage the closures of my bustier when the lamp came on.

"Hey." Zach's voice was rusty.

"Oh. Hey." I laughed nervously. "Didn't mean to wake you."

"It's okay. Can I help you?"

"If you don't mind."

He threw the sheets aside and got out of bed, and my pulse picked up at the sight of his nakedness. I loved that he wasn't self-conscious about it. Even so, I tried not to stare, turning around and presenting him with my back, where I held the bustier closed with both hands.

He managed to work the hooks into the eyes, then bracketed my hips with his hands and pressed his lips to my shoulder.

I closed my eyes and swallowed. "I have to go."

"I know." But he didn't move.

"I had a really good time last night," I told him.

"Me too." He went over to the dresser while I pulled my dress over my head and tugged it over my breasts and hips. Deciding against strapping myself into the heels, I scooped them up in one hand and raked the other through my hair. But anyone who saw me tiptoeing down the hall in my bare feet in this dress and last night's mascara beneath my eyes would immediately know the truth—I'd had a one-night stand with a stranger in his hotel room.

A hot, mysterious stranger fifteen years older than me, who'd spanked me, ravaged my body, and made me come all night long.

My heart pumped hard as I looked at his naked backside. I wished I had more time . . . I wanted to explore the tattoos on his body, ask about them. Trace them with my fingers. My tongue.

"Here." Zach turned around and handed me a business card. "If you ever need protection in a hotel bar, call me."

I glanced down at the card. "Zachary Barrett, Cole

Security. San Diego, California." There was a telephone number listed. I looked up at him and smiled. "San Diego, huh?"

He nodded.

My eyes traveled over his shoulders, chest, arms. "You have a lot of tattoos."

He glanced down. "Yeah."

I noticed one with an anchor and rope that said US NAVY. "Were you in the military?"

"I was a Navy SEAL."

I smiled. "Of course you were."

He took me by the shoulders and kissed my forehead. "Be safe, Millie MacAllister."

"I will." I picked up my clutch from the dresser and tucked it under one arm. Zach walked to the door and pulled it open, staying behind it.

As I walked out, I blew him a silent kiss and left the room without a single regret.

I owed Winnie a nice bottle of wine.

Four

Zach

October

I WOKE UP SLOWLY, RELUCTANTLY.

I fought back at consciousness, clinging to the softness of a dream. To long hair caressing my chest. To a sweet, feminine sigh in the dark of a Manhattan hotel room. To her hands sweeping over my skin. To my lips skimming her throat. To my body moving inside her.

But the dream faded, and I was left with the reality of an empty bed in my San Diego apartment and a massive hard-on. Groaning, I reached down and stroked myself, my eyes closed tight, as if opening them might allow some visual detail to escape. I pictured her for the hours she'd been mine—walking across the bar turning every guy's head, leaning toward me with her hand on my leg, perched on the edge of my bed with her leg over my shoulder, holding onto the headboard while I spanked her, writhing beneath me as she came on my cock, the wonder in her big brown eyes when she confessed she'd never had so much sex in her life.

I couldn't remember the last time I'd been so insatiable either. There was just something about her I couldn't get enough of. I'd spent hours trying to get my fill, but when she'd walked out the door the next morning, I had the crazy urge to pull her back in because I wanted more. I'd been fantasizing about her every night for a month.

I did it now as I fucked my fist, the way her pussy tightened around me as she cried out, her hands on my ass pulling me deeper. Fuck, fuck, fuck—I grunted through my release, leaving a warm, sticky puddle on my stomach.

I opened my eyes and frowned at it, wondering if this was how it would be for the rest of my life. Waking up hard, getting myself off, showering up, going on about the business of being close to fifty, divorced, the father of an adult son I'd never even met, and worried that somewhere along the line I'd peaked, only I couldn't tell you exactly when or where that was.

During my years as a SEAL probably. That was when I'd felt the most alive, had the most purpose, done the most good. The work I did for Cole Security paid well, appealed to my protective nature, and occasionally allowed me to flex my muscles, but it didn't feed my appetite for punishing bad guys the way a raid did.

But I wasn't an idiot. Bodies aged, even if minds didn't. They got injured. They got fucking tired. You could still want the same things you always wanted, you could still crave the rush, but you start moving a fraction of a second slower every time, and eventually you become a liability to your team.

I'd never once been afraid of dying. But I was always afraid of someone dying on my watch.

My cell phone vibrated with a call on the nightstand where it was plugged in, and I let it go to voicemail while I jumped in the shower. My flight east was leaving at eleven-thirty a.m., and it was already going on eight. I was packed, but I still had some shit to do before I left.

Ten minutes later, I came out of the bathroom, threw on some jeans, and checked to see who'd called.

Mason Holt.

My son.

It was still odd for me to think of him that way—it caused a brain glitch every single time. My immediate thought was always, *I don't have a son. I don't have any kids at all.* At least, I hadn't right up until a couple months ago, when I got the email that said differently.

It was three months ago—a Tuesday in early July. Sitting in the conference room at Cole Security, waiting for a meeting to start, I'd pulled out my phone to check my email. At the top of my inbox was a message from a name I didn't recognize, but the subject line said *possible family connection please read.* I thought maybe some distant cousins on one side or the other had found me through one of those ancestry sites. Since the meeting wouldn't start for another five minutes, I opened it up.

Hello,

This will probably come as a shock to you, but I think I might be your son.

My brow furrowed, my head pulling back. Was this a joke? I glanced around the room, half expecting to see Jackson or one of the other jackasses I worked with pointing and laughing—I could see them trying to pull this kind of prank.

But the room was empty, the hum of the air conditioner the only sound. As the hair on the back of my neck stood up, I looked at the email again.

My name is Mason Holt and I'm twenty-eight years old. My mother's maiden name was Andrea Weber. She passed away a couple years ago, but she would be forty-six now.

Two sentences in, I was pretty confident that there had been some kind of mistake, and this Mason Holt had me confused with someone else. I didn't know anyone by that name, nor by the name of Andrea Weber, and twenty-eight years ago I was nineteen, stationed on a ship in the Persian Gulf.

And then I read the next sentence.

She grew up in Frankenmuth, Michigan.

My stomach lurched—

Frankenmuth.

Michigan.

Ten days' leave after "A school" graduation.

Andi—the pretty girl with the blond braids.

Memories filled in like ink spreading on paper.

My dad and stepmom lived in Frankenmuth back then, which is this tourist town that looks like someone plucked it off out of Bavaria and stuck it in the middle of Michigan. It's got German-themed *everything*—architecture, food, beer, clothing—as well as a gigantic Christmas store that's open year-round in case you need tinsel in June. It made no sense to me.

I'd gone up to visit for a few days before I had to report to Norfolk. I hadn't really wanted to go—my dad and I didn't get along great, and my stepmom thought I had "anger issues." She wasn't wrong, I *was* still angry about the way my father had left my mom—I was angry about a lot of things—but my mother said visiting him was the right thing to do, since I'd only seen him once in the last year and wouldn't be back for a while. So I made the drive from Cleveland and stayed for five days.

But I spent most of my time chasing after Andi, who I'd seen at her waitressing job at a brewpub dressed in one of those sexy Oktoberfest sort of outfits, like the chick on the St. Pauli Girl beer labels.

Later she told me it was called a dirndl, but I can't remember if that was before or after we had sex in the pub's bathroom when she got off work, or the back seat of my car, or maybe against the side of a barn on her parents' farm just outside town. She was eighteen and had graduated from high school earlier that year, just like me. But she still lived at home with strict religious parents, and if I remembered right, she was working to save up for beauty school and her own apartment. She also had a possessive ex-boyfriend who heard about me, showed up at my dad's house, and took a swing at my face.

That stupid motherfucker was on the ground begging for mercy inside a minute while I beat the shit out of him on the front lawn, my dad yelling at me to knock it off, my step-mom screaming that this was why she hadn't wanted me here in the first place.

They kicked me out, so I threw my shit in the car and left that night without even saying goodbye to Andi, and we never spoke again. A week later, I shipped out. For a while, I wondered what happened to her—had she gone to beauty school? Gotten back together with the asshole ex?—but eventually she faded from memory.

Given the decades that had passed since I'd even thought of her, the sadness I felt learning she was gone gripped me unexpectedly hard. I hoped that she'd had a happy life.

But it wasn't possible I was the father of her child . . . was it?

The room spun, and a trickle of sweat made its way down my chest. I closed my eyes a moment, took a deep breath, and read on.

She was very young when she had me, barely nineteen, and for the early years of my life, I believed her first husband, Mick Holt, was my father. His name is on my birth certificate. But he was not around much. They split when I was four, and I haven't seen him since.

Mick Holt—the asshole I'd pummeled on my dad's lawn. She'd married that guy?

Eventually she told me Mick was not my biological father. When I asked her who my real dad was, she would not give me a name. She would only say it didn't matter anymore. When I asked if he was a good person, she said, "I thought so at the time."

It fucking stung.

Even after all this time, that arrow hit the mark. I grit my teeth and read on.

We moved to Traverse City, Michigan, and she got married again, but they also divorced. Shortly afterward, she was diagnosed with lung cancer. She lived another two years. I took care of her.

My mom was everything to me, and her death was very difficult. I could not bring myself to go through her things for a full year. When I did, I found an envelope with my name on it buried at the back of a high shelf in her closet.

It was a letter in which she told me about the circumstances of my birth, and she named as my father a Zachary Barrett from Cleveland, Ohio who was in the Navy and was hoping to be a SEAL someday. After some digging, those things led me to you.

I stood up and began to pace beside the table. I prided myself on remaining cool under pressure, but this was next-level heat. Could I actually have a grown son? The answer stopped me in my tracks.

Of course I could.

Andi and I hadn't been careful. We'd been young and reckless and full of raging hormones. It was entirely possible Mason Holt was the result.

Remaining on my feet, I forced myself to finish the email.

I don't want any money from you, if you're worried. I have a good job (I'm a high school social studies teacher and track coach), I'm getting married soon, and even though I will always miss my mom, I've made peace with her death.

It's a little harder to make peace with the fact that she chose to hide my father's identity from me, but she must have had her reasons. I would like to know you, if you are really my father. Probably we should take a paternity test to determine if that's the case. I think we would have results in about a week.

I hope to hear from you soon.
Sincerely,
Mason Holt

Beneath his name, he'd written a phone number with a 231 area code. I was still staring at it, wondering what the fuck I was going to do, when Jackson poked his head in the door. "Hey. Meeting postponed, I have a—" He stopped mid-thought when I looked up at him. My expression must have set off an alarm. "What's wrong?"

I swallowed. "I just got a really weird email."

"Don't send *any* money to Nigeria."

"It's not that." My throat was dry and scratchy, and my vision was a little gray at the edges. I glanced down at my phone again, and the words were all still there.

"What is it?" Jackson came into the conference room, his forehead wrinkled with concern. "Did you get bad news?"

"I'm not sure what kind of news it is."

"Barrett, quit fucking with me." He folded his arms over his chest. "Are you okay?"

"I'm fine, but . . ." I met his eyes again. "I think I might have a son."

The voicemail was brief. "Hey Zach, just wanted to confirm that we're all set for lunch tomorrow. I made a reservation at noon, and I'll text you the restaurant name and location. Hope Italian is okay. Lori and I are really looking forward to meeting you. Safe travels."

I wrote a quick reply, saying I heard the message and lunch sounded good. I'd see him at noon tomorrow.

Setting my phone aside, I packed up the charger and added it to my carry-on bag. Sure, Italian is okay, I thought.

What better occasion was there to enjoy spaghetti and meat-balls than when meeting your grown son for the first time?

My stomach muscles clenched up the way they always did when I thought about sitting across the table from him. Having to make conversation. Having to make an *excuse* for myself. Did I owe him an apology if I'd never known of his existence?

As I pulled the pieces of my suit from the closet and packed them in a garment bag, I thought about the day the results of the paternity test came back indicating Mason Holt *was* my son.

Although I'd had a gut feeling that was the case, I still felt panicked. That wasn't a feeling I was used to. Years of having to keep calm and stay focused in situations that could derail in a hurry meant I was equipped to deal with surprise. I always knew what to do—put myself aside and protect others.

But who needed protecting here?

Mason Holt was a complication I didn't need in my life. I'd never wanted children, and now I'd have to feel guilty about having one I'd never known about. I'd have to feel shitty for abandoning Andi without even a goodbye. I'd have to grapple with the knowledge that her life had been forever altered by what we'd done—her dreams abandoned—while my life had gone on as planned.

I'd spent my entire life wanting to fight bad guys. Was I one of them?

After one sleepless night, I called Mason the next day. That initial conversation was awkward as hell, mostly just me giving stiff, automatic answers to his questions, which were pretty basic.

Where'd you grow up? Cleveland.

What was your family like? Parents divorced when I was ten. I lived with my mom.

Did you like being a SEAL? Yes.

Why'd you quit? Got wounded.

Where do you live now? San Diego.

Are you married? I was. Didn't last long.

Do you have kids? No.

What do you do? Work private security.

My only hesitation came when he asked if I had brothers or sisters. After a second of silence, I said no.

Then I glanced out the window of my apartment, and for a moment, I saw her standing there, a little girl with pigtails and chubby cheeks, a butterfly T-shirt and huge, trusting eyes.

I blinked and she was gone.

"Me neither," he said. "I was an only child too. We have that in common."

I'm not sure what was said after that, but we began emailing back and forth a couple times a week and talking by phone every Sunday.

In the beginning, I was doing it out of obligation, but after our first few talks, I found myself genuinely interested in him. I relaxed enough to ask him about his childhood, his hobbies, his job, the girl he was going to marry. He said he'd always been close to his mom, who had always worked two jobs and made sure he didn't lack for things. He'd put himself through college. I liked that.

He didn't press me for details about my relationship with Andi, and I wasn't sure if that was because he didn't want to scare me off or he didn't want the answers. Mostly he seemed interested in talking about the present.

During our third or fourth conversation, he told me more about his fiancée, Lori. How outgoing and smart she was, how much she knew about wine, how she was always volunteering for things, what a good mom she would be. "She's really amazing," he said. "I'm just glad I had my shit together when I met her. If I'd met her sooner, I wouldn't have been ready. I had so much baggage to work through."

"Sounds like you have a good therapist." Mason had mentioned therapy a few times, and it seemed like it had helped him. I'd had the opposite experience, but then again, I'd never liked talking about my feelings. My parents got tired of paying for me to sit in silence for an hour.

"I do have a good therapist, but the girl I dated right before Lori also helped me out a lot. She was really there for me when I needed someone to pick up the pieces. The relationship just didn't work out." Then he laughed. "Funny enough, she's a wedding planner, and she actually planned our wedding."

"So there were no hard feelings, huh?"

"None. We're friends. In fact, she introduced me to Lori last Christmas—after she and I'd broken up, of course."

"When's the wedding?"

"First weekend in October." He paused. "Would you like to come?"

I opened my mouth to say no, but he went on before I could think of a way to do it without being a dick.

"No pressure, but I'd love to have some family there. My mom's family isn't coming, not that I ever knew any of them that well. They weren't supportive of her after she got pregnant, and she never really forgave them."

I felt even worse. Was that why she'd married Mick Holt? She'd been turned out by her family and had nowhere else to go?

"Sure," I heard myself saying. "I could come to the wedding."

"Oh my God, this is so great. I can't wait to tell Lori. And you know what?" He sounded so excited. "Could you maybe come in a couple days early so we can spend a little time together before the wedding? The weekend will be so busy."

"Uh, I might be able to do that. I'll check my work schedule."

"Awesome. That would be great. I—I have a lot of questions that I think would be better asked in person."

After we hung up, I groaned aloud and rubbed my face with my hands. I didn't like weddings to begin with, and now I'd have to go to one by myself, and Mason would probably be eager to introduce me to everyone he knew as his father. The poor guy was obviously desperate for family. And his questions . . . I had a pretty good idea what they would be, and I didn't really want to face them. I didn't have any good answers.

But I didn't have it in me to refuse. He'd spent twenty-eight years wondering about me. His mother had worked two jobs to provide for him. He grew up not knowing if his dad was a total deadbeat or a decent human being.

Still, last night while I was packing, I started to panic about what I was going to say once we were face to face. I'd called Jackson and begged him to meet me for a beer so I could get his advice.

"I mean, what the fuck do I even say? Sorry I wasn't there your whole life?"

Jackson considered the question. "I think you take your cues from him."

"How so?"

"Well, you can't change the past. It's not like anything that happens from here on out will give him a childhood with a father. But maybe he's just curious. Maybe he doesn't want an apology. It's not like it was your fault."

"No, but you can still feel guilty about something that wasn't your fault." I was an expert at that. I had been since I was seven years old.

Jackson stared at his beer bottle and thought for a moment. "You can, but you don't have to let it drag you under."

I glanced at him. He'd lost team members as a SEAL and still carried the burden, even though he hadn't been at fault. I knew he didn't say those words lightly.

"And maybe you can alleviate some of the guilt by giving this kid what he wants, which is just to know you. Right?"

"Right."

"So I think you say you're sorry about the loss of his mom, and you wish things had gone down differently, but then maybe just let him talk. Answer his questions."

"Yeah." I tipped up my beer, wondering what exactly Mason would ask. What else Andi had told him.

"Anyway, once he gets to know what a dick you are, he'll probably change his mind and leave you alone." Jackson laughed as he lifted his beer for a swig.

I told him to fuck off, but I was grateful for his advice. He had two teenage daughters with his wife, Catherine, and he was much better than I was at relationships in general. He was a good husband and father and friend—loyal to a fault, one of those guys who actually deserved all the good things he had in life. But he'd never hesitate to tell you when you were fucking something up, or just mess with you in general if he could.

For example.

"Hey, did that girl ever call you?" he poked.

"What girl?" I knew exactly what girl.

"The one you banged in Manhattan when you were supposed to be on the job."

I rolled my eyes. "I wasn't on the job anymore, asshole. I was supposed to be on a plane, but my flight was canceled."

"Sure." He signaled to the bartender to bring us another round.

"I seriously regret telling you about her." I didn't often share personal details, but Jackson had called me out for being distracted after returning from New York, and I'd confessed that I'd met a woman I couldn't stop thinking about. "Anyway, no, she never called."

"Huh. Maybe you lost your touch."

"I didn't lose my touch." I rolled my shoulders. "It was just a one-night thing."

"I thought you said you gave her your business card."

"I did."

"So you must have wanted to see her again," he prodded.

"I wouldn't mind seeing her again." I tried to sound casual, as if she hadn't been starring in my dreams for a month. "But I've got other things to worry about."

"True," agreed Jackson.

"I don't really want to make this trip," I admitted, running a hand over my jaw.

"I know you don't." He clapped me on the shoulder. "But I also know what kind of man you are, so you'll make it anyway."

Then I'd gone home and lain awake for hours, recalling again how Mason had asked Andi if I was a good person.

And I thought about her response too.

I thought so at the time.

Five

Millie

"Earth to Millie." Winnie snapped her fingers in front of my face.

"Sorry, what?" I refocused on my sister and our surroundings—the lobby of the strength training studio where we'd just taken our usual Thursday morning class.

"Have you heard anything I've said?" Exasperated, my sister opened the locker where we'd stashed our keys and phones.

I bit my lip. Had I?

In truth, my mind was a bit fuzzy. The strength training coach's muscular arms had reminded me of Zach's, and I'd spent the entire hourlong class lost in the memories of his body above mine. I'd barely registered anything else—the exercises, the music, the other people in the room.

But it wasn't just today.

I'd been having trouble concentrating for a month—ever since I got back from New York. No matter what I was doing or who I was talking to, my mind had an uncanny ability to circle back to a night spent in Zach Barrett's hotel room. I could read entire pages of a book and not register one word. I had to ask people to repeat questions. I'd catch myself staring into space at my desk or kitchen table and realize five minutes had gone by while I replayed portions of our time together.

My vibrator had gotten more use the past few weeks than it had the past year.

"Can you repeat the last thing?" I took her puffy vest off the hanger and handed it to her.

She shoved her arms through the holes and freed her long ponytail from the collar. "I asked how the fashion show plans were coming along."

I pulled on my jacket and zipped it up. "Good. Really good, actually."

"Did you hear back from the one designer you were waiting on?"

"Yes—and she's in." I grinned. "So I've got six designers, each committed to five looks. Date set—first Saturday in March, models are hired, DJ is booked. So far, it's all going smoothly."

"Of course it is, with you at the helm."

"I need to start promoting it soon. Tickets will go on sale in early December."

Winnie clapped her hands. "I bet it sells out. I'm so excited for you!"

I was excited too—elated, actually. I couldn't believe I hadn't done this before. I'd studied fashion design at school, and my degree was in Visual Arts. I'd just never done anything with fashion except make my own clothes, because I'd gone to work for Cloverleigh Farms right away.

Which was fabulous. I loved the work, I still got to use my eye for design and be creative, and I adored Cloverleigh Farms—it was like home to me. I'd practically grown up there since my dad was the CFO and it was Frannie's family that owned it. But I still liked fashion, and wedding gowns were the perfect intersection of my profession and my interest.

"Well, sales might be slow at first, but given how many

people get engaged over the holidays, I bet interest will spike in early January, and then again after Valentine's Day. And they'll still have two weeks to purchase tickets."

"Let me know if I can help with anything." Winnie pushed the door open for me and we walked out into the crisp autumn morning. It was cloudy and cool, and smelled like rain might be coming.

"Hey, did you ever reach out to Mr. Tall, Dark, and Handsome with the tattoos and magic dick?"

"Winnie!" I glanced around us to make sure no one was within earshot. "No. I haven't." Although I kept his card in my nightstand, and just about every night, I took it out and looked at it.

"Why not?"

"Because I've been busy."

"Busy? You said it was the hottest night of your life! What's busy compared to that?"

"He lives in San Diego and I live here," I pointed out.

"Maybe you've heard of airplanes?"

I elbowed her as we approached my car. "I can't call him and suggest he get on a plane. We only spent a few hours together. I barely know anything about him." Just that he was never off my mind.

"Plan a trip to San Diego," Winnie suggested.

"I can't do that! I'll look like a crazy stalker." I pulled my keys from my pocket and unlocked my car.

"Maybe you could pretend like you need private security for something." Winnie's wheels were still spinning, her head tilted, her devious eyes looking off into space.

"Why on earth would I need private security?"

"Because there's a . . ." She snapped her fingers as she thought. "A serial killer prowling around Cloverleigh Farms!"

Laughing, I shook my head. "Face it, Win. It was a fun

night, and I'm really glad I took your advice, but I'll probably never see Zachary Barrett again."

She stuck her tongue out at me. "You're no fun. If I were you, I wouldn't just give up."

"There's nothing to *give up* on! We had a hot one-night stand, not a serious relationship." Two women gave me strange looks as they passed us by, and I lowered my voice. "Look, if he lived even remotely close to here, I might reach out. Chicago, or New York even. But San Diego is ridiculously far."

"But what if—"

"No what ifs. I'll talk to you later," I said, ending the conversation.

"Okay. Hey, Felicity and I are meeting downtown around five o'clock for drinks and dinner tonight. Want to come?"

"That sounds good." I opened the driver's side door of my car. "I'll check my work schedule and get back to you."

Ten minutes later, I let myself into my house and made myself a quick cup of coffee. While it brewed, I pulled one of my mason jars of overnight oats from the fridge and topped it with some maple syrup and cinnamon. Grabbing a spoon, I ate breakfast while scrolling through my inbox on my laptop. I checked my calendar for the day and saw nothing on it after a two o'clock appointment with a potential bride, so I sent a quick text to Win and Felicity that I could meet up with them.

After giving my cats, Molasses and Muffin, some attention, I took my coffee upstairs to get ready for work. My house wasn't big—just a kitchen with a dining area, tiny half bath, and living room downstairs, plus two bedrooms and a full bathroom up—but I'd fallen in love with it at first sight and cried happy tears the day I was handed the keys. Maybe it was

the white picket fence or the pink and yellow tulips bloom-
ing in the front yard. Maybe it was the front porch swing or
the arched front door. Maybe it was the cozy warmth of the
interior woodwork, stained a deep brown.

Sure, I'd had to rip up awful carpeting and tear off hideous
wallpaper and repaint all the walls in soft, neutral shades, but
I hadn't minded the work. It had kept me busy the last couple years, and I'd had help—my dad and Frannie had not only
helped me secure the loan but had also helped me renovate.
Felicity had been living in Chicago when I bought the house,
but she'd come up for a long weekend to help me move in.
Winnie had a fantastic eye for good finds at estate sales and
antique shops, and she helped me reupholster dining chairs,
shop for rugs, and find the perfect sapphire blue velvet sofa
for my living room. Even Mason pitched in, helping me stain
the wood floors last summer.

He and Lori were redoing their own home now.

And Brendan, the guy I'd dated before Mason, had just
moved to Denver with his new wife, Sasha. I'd introduced
them too—she used to cut my hair. Daniel, the boyfriend before that, was expecting twins with his wife, Amy. An invitation to the baby shower was on my fridge.

Reaching the top of the stairs, I took a sip of my coffee
and sighed. I was happy for them all, I really was. They were
good people and deserved to find love. My sisters too. I had a
feeling Dex was going to pop the question to Winnie over the
holidays, and then there would be another wedding to plan.
The thought of it made me smile.

Moving into my bedroom, I set the mug on my dresser
and started pulling off my workout clothes, tossing them in
a laundry basket. I glanced at the bed, and for a moment, I
imagined Zach sleeping there, just like he had been in the
hotel room when I'd tried to sneak out.

After my shower, as I combed through my wet hair, I

fantasized what it might be like if he saw me standing there at the mirror. He might give me one of those low, growly sounds and reach for the towel wrapped around me, yanking it off. I'd laugh and say *no, I have to go to work*, but he wouldn't let me refuse him. He'd grab my arm and pull me back into bed with him. His body would be warm and firm as he stretched out above me, his hips and chest heavy and masculine over my curves. He'd bury his face in my neck and tell me how good I smelled—I remembered how he'd liked the scent of my perfume—and his mouth would travel down from there, over my breasts and stomach and hips. He'd push my thighs apart with enough force to tell me he'd brook no resistance, and his tongue would sweep up my center with those long, languid strokes that made me arch and moan and beg for more.

Suddenly I realized my eyes were closed, my nipples were hard, and I was frozen in place with the hairbrush halfway through my damp locks. Between my legs I felt the tingle of arousal.

Setting my brush down, I went over to the edge of my bed and sat down. Opened the nightstand drawer. Took out his card. I stared at it for a full minute, wondering if Winnie was right and I should reach out. Was there something there worth pursuing?

Yeah, said my lady parts. *Orgasms.*

I stuffed the card back into my drawer and closed it.

My two o'clock bride, whose name was Taylor, came with her mom to look at Cloverleigh Farms as a potential venue for her wedding. She apologized that her fiancé wasn't available, but he traveled a lot for work, so she was doing some of the initial research on her own.

"My mother sort of invites herself along," Taylor

whispered to me as we walked from the inn toward the wedding barn, where we hosted indoor ceremonies and receptions. "But she's so critical, she stresses me out."

I eyed her mother, who'd hurried through the glass doors into the barn ahead of us. "Some mothers are like that," I said. "But it's your day, not hers."

Later, Taylor and her mom sat across from me at my desk as I listed Cloverleigh's available dates for a Saturday wedding next summer and fall. "There aren't too many," I said apologetically. "We tend to book up fast for summer. Have you considered a Friday night wedding? I have some Sunday afternoons available this spring too."

"Maybe we could do that," Taylor said. "I just have to—"

"I think that's too soon," said her mother. "Taylor needs more time to lose the weight."

Taylor's chin dropped, color rising in her cheeks. "Mom."

"Not one of the dresses you've tried on fit," her mother said, lips pursed. "And we've gone to three different bridal salons."

Taylor, who was plus-sized and short, met my eyes. "I'm having some trouble finding a dress."

My heart went out to her. "I understand."

"Everything is either billowy like sheets or all covered up." Taylor shook her head. "That's not what I want."

"What kind of dress do you want?" I asked, thinking I might be able to point her in the right direction.

"I'd like a dress that shows off my curves," Taylor said, her eyes flicking toward her mother. "Something glamorous and elegant but also sexy. My fiancé loves my curves."

"That's all well and good, but they don't make dresses like that for bodies like yours," snapped her mother, who was short like her daughter but several sizes smaller. "I've been telling you for years to lose the weight."

I bit my tongue, although the conversation was triggering

terrible memories. My real mother, Carla, had been hard on me about my size too. After she'd abandoned us and moved back to Georgia, we only saw her a couple times a year, and those visits always involved comments about my appearance.

You look just like me at fourteen, Millie. If you weren't so heavy, you could try on my prom dress.

What on earth is your dad feeding you? He must not want you to have boyfriends.

You're never going to be a professional dancer if you don't control your weight.

For years, I took what she said to heart. I cut gluten and dairy and sugar and fat. I deprived myself of what the rest of my family and friends ate in the misguided attempt to look like the slender, small-boned girls in my ballet classes (pink tights are so fucking brutal), even though it was never going to happen.

And I was miserable and hungry and exhausted all the time. I hated my body, I hated myself, and I started to hate dance. I spent most of my spare time crying in my bedroom. Finally, I went to my dad and Frannie and I admitted I didn't want to study ballet anymore—I was tired of the way it made me feel about myself. They understood and told me the choice was mine, and they encouraged me to do what would make me happy. They made me feel loved and appreciated and gave me the reassurance I needed to *be* myself and *love* myself.

But Taylor didn't have that kind of parent.

"You know what," I said, focusing on the teary-eyed bride-to-be in front of me, "I know a few designers with size-inclusive lines. And they make beautiful, sexy, stunning dresses. I'll email you their names."

"Really?" Taylor perked up.

"Yes. Also, I'm hosting a fashion show for curvy brides in early March if you'd like to come. Depending on the wedding date you choose, you might see something there you could get in time for a summer wedding."

"That sounds amazing." She smiled. "Thank you so much."

Just after five that evening, my sisters and I ducked into Southpaw Brewing Co, a downtown microbrewery with great food, spacious leather booths, and fantastic service. It was owned by Tyler Shaw, a former MLB pitcher who'd married our Aunt April. When he saw us come in, he came over to greet us and led us to a booth in a quieter area toward the back.

"How's everything going?" he asked. "Did you make it in before the rain?"

"Yes, and I hope we make it out too, because I forgot an umbrella," I said, sliding in across from Winnie and Felicity.

"Me too." Winnie unzipped her coat and shivered. "I need a hot toddy. I'm chilled to the bone."

"Coming right up." Tyler smiled. He was in his early fifties, broad-chested and handsome in a mature way that reminded me of Zach—dark hair with a hint of gray, brown eyes with tiny lines at the corners, chiseled jaw—although Tyler was clean-shaven where Zach had a beard. The memory of that beard on my cheek, belly, and thighs sent a little shiver up my spine.

"And some menus would be good." Felicity wriggled out of her jacket. "I'm starving."

"I'll send something over right away," he said.

A few minutes later, we had drinks and an order of onion rings on the table, crispy and hot, coated with batter made from one of Southpaw's hand-crafted ales. While we sipped and munched and looked over the food menu, I told my sisters about the appointment that afternoon. "I felt so bad for this girl. Her mother was so mean."

"That's awful," said Felicity.

"She said they'd been to three salons and not one of them had a dress she liked in a size that fit," I said, getting worked up all over again. "Shopping for your wedding dress should be a joyful experience. It shouldn't make you feel bad about yourself."

"I've heard similar things from brides at Abelard," Winnie remarked. "This is why your event is going to be such a hit, Mills. Curvy brides will get to see what's out there."

"But is that enough? One show won't change the shopping experience for brides. And shopping in general when you're plus-sized is not terribly fun." My sisters had been shopping with me enough times in our lives to know this already, and they nodded sympathetically as I went on. "It sucks to see something cute and be told it doesn't come in your size or be directed to the back of the store where the clothes are all drab and unshapely. That's why I end up sewing things I really want. I totally understood where Taylor was coming from."

"Is she going to come to your show?" asked Felicity.

"I think so, and I told her I'd email her a list of designers I know that do beautiful plus-sized dresses." I sipped my wine. "She mentioned that her fiancé loves her curves. That made me happy."

Our server appeared and we put in our orders—vegetarian chili for Felicity, club sandwich for me, black and blue burger for Winnie.

"That reminds me," said Felicity, "a friend of mine from culinary school who lives in Kansas literally flew to another state to shop for her wedding dress at a bridal salon that specializes in gowns for curvy women. I think she went to Georgia."

"Really?" Winnie looked at Felicity and then at me. "A

whole store that specializes in plus-sized wedding dresses? Is there one of those near us? Or even in this state?"

"If there is," I said, "I haven't heard of it."

Winnie picked up an onion ring and bit into it. "Mills, I could see *you* opening a shop like that, with your design background and all your wedding planning experience. I mean," she went on after swallowing the bite in her mouth, "if you ever wanted to do something different."

"That would be a pretty giant career change," I said. But something about the idea intrigued me.

"Not really," Felicity countered. "You'd still be helping people experience their dream wedding. I mean, what's more important to a bride than her dress?"

"The groom?"

She rolled her eyes and pushed her glasses up her nose. "Okay, besides the groom, the dress is always what the bride most wants to love, and it's probably the thing she's been thinking about since before she even liked boys or girls or whoever she's marrying."

"She's right," Winnie said. "I had an entire file folder of wedding dress photos before I even hit middle school."

"I remember. You were *obsessed* with getting married." I laughed. "Even your prom dress was white."

"Hey, you designed it." Winnie nudged my foot with hers beneath the table.

"I know. And I loved doing that—the dress was beautiful on you."

"Speaking of white dresses," Felicity said in a suggestive tone. "What are the odds of a proposal this holiday season, Winifred?"

Winnie's cheeks went pink. "I don't know."

"Oh, come on," I teased. "You've got no idea whether or not Dex has been ring shopping? He hasn't dropped any hints?"

"No." Winnie lifted her shoulders. "I think it might be too soon."

"But you've been together over a year already," Felicity pointed out. "That's a long time."

"You're just saying that because you married Hutton after dating him for a month." Winnie poked Felicity's shoulder. "But Dex has two little girls. They're only six and nine. He has to make sure they'd be okay with it."

"Hallie and Luna *adore* you," I said. "They're probably pressuring Dex to get a move on."

"Maybe," Winnie said, laughing. "They do keep asking me if my cat and I can move in with them and their cat."

I laughed. "If I were you, I'd dig out that old file folder."

"Okay, enough. Don't jinx me." Winnie picked up her beer and took a drink. "Let's talk about *your* love life."

"Uh, it's nonexistent."

"Is not," Felicity said, her eyes flashing with mischief. "I heard you had a hot one-night stand with a mysterious stranger in a hotel room last month. And there was spanking involved."

I glared at Winnie. "Gee. Wonder where she might have heard that."

"You know I can't keep secrets!" Winnie protested. "Especially between us three. Neither of you should tell me things you don't want the other to know."

"So it's true?" Felicity prodded. "It really happened?"

"It's true. It really happened. And I would have told you sooner, but I've hardly seen you since I got back. I've been so busy at work."

"So tell me now." Felicity propped her elbows on the table and her chin in her hands. "Who was he?"

"His name is Zach Barrett. He works private security out of San Diego, but he was in New York on business. He's forty-seven." I put my hands up. "That's honestly all I know."

"What did he look like?" Felicity asked.

"Tall, dark, and handsome, beard, tattoos, big hands, magic dick," Winnie answered breathlessly.

Felicity's jaw dropped. *"Really?"*

I laughed and nodded. "Really."

"And. *And* . . ." Winnie was bouncing around in the booth like a pinball. "He rescued her from some married creeper that was trying to hit on her."

"He did?"

"Yes. He was a perfect gentleman . . . right up until we got to the elevator." I giggled. "Then he went a bit rogue."

Winnie swooned. *"God, I love this story. I wish it wasn't over."*

"So wait, the spanking," said Felicity. "He just did it? Or did he ask you?"

"Actually, I sort of requested it."

My sisters exchanged a look. "Good for you," Winnie said.

"Did you like it?" asked Felicity.

"I did, but I think it's something I only liked because it was him." I'd given this some thought. "Like, if he was a different kind of guy, someone more like my usual type, I don't think it would have been as hot."

"Because you date *boys*, not men," Winnie said.

I opened my mouth to defend myself, but the server arrived with our food.

"So did you exchange numbers or anything?" Felicity stirred her chili. "Will you see him again?"

"He gave me his card, which has a phone number on it, but I don't really see the point in calling him." I picked up a quarter of my sandwich. "He lives so far away."

"I disagree and think she should reach out," said Winnie, squirting ketchup onto her fries.

"We've been over this, Win." I gave her my bossiest big-sister look. "I'm not calling him."

"Give me one good reason why not."

"It's been a month. He probably doesn't even remember me."

My sisters exchanged an exasperated look. "He remembers you," said Felicity dryly.

"Because I'm busy at work."

Winnie blew a raspberry.

"Because I don't want to start something that doesn't have the kind of ending I'm looking for," I said firmly. "Not at this point in my life."

Winnie's posture deflated a bit. "Yeah. I guess I get that."

"Good." I took a bite of my sandwich.

But he was on my mind all night.

We left the restaurant just after seven, squealing as we hurried through the pouring rain without umbrellas. I waved good-bye to my sisters and jumped into my car.

Back at home, I was in my jammies by nine, just the way I liked.

After I slipped between the sheets, I lay there for a moment. Then I opened the drawer and pulled out Zach's card again. I ran my fingertip over his name. With my pulse quickening, I picked up my phone and tapped his number into the keypad. Then I started a message.

Hi, it's Millie MacAllister from . . .

Wait, from what? From last month? From New York? From hotel room sexcapades?

Delete.

Hello, this is Millie MacAllister. I don't know if you remember me, but . . .

But what? But you spanked my ass and I liked it? But you

gave me five orgasms in one night and thank you sir, may I have another?

Delete.

Hey, it's Millie. What are you wearing?

DELETE.

This wasn't me. It felt too awkward. What if he wasn't the sexting type? What if *I* wasn't the sexting type? I'd never done it before.

Sighing, I set my phone on the charger and tucked his card back into the top drawer. Then I reached into the second drawer and pulled out my Lelo.

Switching off the lamp, I let memory and fantasy take me away.

Six

Zach

I KNEW WHO MASON WAS THE MOMENT I SPOTTED HIM.

I'd handed my coat to the hostess and glanced into the restaurant's dining room, my eye immediately going to a dark-haired young man with a slender, athletic build. He sat at a table for four with only one other person, a woman with curly brown hair. When he saw me, he stood up.

I began walking in his direction and nearly stumbled. Not because the resemblance to me was so strong—although it was there, in the height, in the coloring, in the way his hands unconsciously clenched and unclenched at his sides—but because I knew in my gut I was about to meet my *son*.

My insides were churning, and I felt tension mounting throughout my shoulders, neck, and back. I swallowed hard as I approached, prepared to extend my hand. Instead, Mason threw his arms around me.

"It's true," he said, his voice catching. "I wasn't sure if it would be, but it is. You *are* my dad."

I was so stunned by his embrace, it took me a moment to recover. Awkwardly, I put my hands lightly on his back. Patted it a few times. I didn't know what to say.

Mason let go of me and stood back, laughing sheepishly.

"Sorry." He pushed his hair off his face in a gesture I recognized as one I'd made a thousand times in my youth. "I get a little emotional sometimes."

"But it's one of his best qualities." The woman at the table rose to her feet and held out her hand. "Hi. I'm Lori Campion, Mason's fiancée."

I shook her hand. "I'm Zach Barrett."

"It's nice to meet you." She had a pretty smile. "Please sit down."

I took the seat across from Mason, who lowered himself into his chair and stared at me with awe. "I can't believe I'm really meeting you. I looked for a photo of you online, so I'd recognize you, but couldn't find one. You don't have social media or anything."

"No." I loosened my tie a little. "I've never had any of that." And Kimberly, my ex-wife, had wiped her social media profiles clean of our relationship, so it didn't surprise me that he hadn't been able to find any pictures.

"I thought maybe my mom would have kept one," Mason said, "but I searched everywhere in her house without any luck."

"I'm not sure we took any pictures. We didn't know each other very long." *And we were too busy having unprotected sex.*

The server appeared and asked me if I'd like a drink, and I looked up at him with extreme gratitude. "Whiskey. On the rocks, please."

"Sure. We've got a couple options from Michigan distilleries. Journeyman—"

"Sounds good."

He laughed. "Okay. Coming right up."

"So how did it happen?" Mason asked earnestly.

"Sorry?" I tugged at my collar.

"Like, how did you meet my mom? What happened with you guys? Why didn't she ever want me to know about you?"

"Honey." Lori put a hand over Mason's. "Maybe let him get his drink first."

"Okay." Mason closed his eyes and took a breath. When he opened them, I realized they were blue, and I saw the resemblance to Andi. He had the shape of her face, her high forehead. "I'm sorry, Zach. I promised myself I wouldn't overwhelm you with questions about the past. I just . . . have a lot of them, I guess. And you're a connection to my mom, a part of her life she never shared with me. I just want to understand her better—understand the decision she made to keep you from me. And it never seemed right to ask you this stuff over the phone, or by email."

I needed a breath too. "I get it. And I'll answer your questions as well as I can, but I'm not sure anything I have to say will give you what you're looking for."

"Mostly, I'm looking for honesty."

"I can do that."

He smiled. "Thanks. I'd like to gain perspective on my past, as I take steps toward my future." He glanced at Lori. "We're looking forward to having our own family, but I feel like it's important that I know where I came from too. It never felt right that I couldn't say who my real dad was or why I didn't know him."

"It wasn't right," I said, glad as fuck when the server returned with my whiskey. I barely even let him put the glass on the table before I picked it up and took a few swallows.

"Let's put in our orders now," suggested Lori.

I quickly scanned the menu and ordered the first thing that caught my eye. As soon as the server retreated, I picked up my whiskey again. We made small talk for a couple more minutes before Mason leaned his elbows on the table and met my eyes. "So is it okay to ask now?"

After one more generous swallow, I set the glass down. "I should probably start by saying that even though I had no idea you were, uh, conceived or born, I'm really sorry that you grew up without a father. If I had known, things would have been different."

"Would you have married her?"

"If that's what she wanted." For a second I wondered about that . . . what *had* Andi wanted? When she first discovered she was pregnant, did she try to find me? Or was she so mad about the way I'd left, she kept the baby a secret as a way to punish me?

"It's hard to know for sure what she wanted," Mason said. "I know that she married her high school boyfriend before I was born, and I'm guessing that was because her parents shamed her into it."

"I remember they were pretty strict," I said. "She told me they hated that she worked in a bar."

"I barely remember them." Mason shrugged, his eyes growing a little cold. "And they were never that interested in me."

"I'm sorry," I said again.

"So did you meet her where she worked?" Lori asked.

I took another sip of whiskey. "Yes, in the pub where she waitressed. I was eighteen, same as she was. I'd joined the Navy right after high school graduation, gone to boot camp and then A School, and I had a few days before I had to report for duty in Norfolk. My mom guilted me into going up to Frankenmuth to visit my dad."

"Your parents were divorced?" asked Lori.

I nodded. "They split when I was nine. It was—they had—" Swirling the whiskey in my glass, I debated how much to reveal. "Things were tough at home."

"And you had no brothers or sisters?" she asked.

I hesitated. Took a sip. "Actually, I had a sister."

"You did?" Mason was surprised, since I'd hidden the truth when he asked about siblings before.

"Yes. Her name was Penelope, but we called her Poppy. She was four years younger than me." I swallowed hard. "We lost her when she was three."

Lori gasped. "I'm so sorry. Was she sick?"

I shook my head and drained the last of my whiskey. "It was an accident."

Immediately, Lori put her hands over her cheeks. "Oh, how awful. I'm really sorry, Zach."

"Me too," said Mason quietly.

I shoved the image of the little girl in the butterfly shirt from my mind. "Anyway, the marriage never recovered. My dad left and eventually remarried. My mom and I stayed in Cleveland." I looked Mason in the eye. "I'm sorry I wasn't honest when you asked me on the phone about siblings. It's not something I talk about."

"I understand," he said. "It's okay. Thank you for telling me now."

It struck me that Andi had managed to raise a sensitive, empathetic son despite how hard it must have been for her, and how easy it would be for Mason to be accusatory or bitter. It made me want to be as forthcoming as possible with him. "Truth be told, Mason, I wasn't all that mature or responsible in those days. I had a lot of anger, I was hot-headed and reckless. I wanted to settle things by yelling or fighting. The Navy was doing its best to whip me into shape, but I wasn't there yet."

"Eighteen is young," Lori said.

"Yeah. Didn't feel that way, of course. I thought I knew everything. Anyway, I saw Andi at the bar where she worked and thought she was cute. We spent a few days having a good time, but being careless about it."

"A few days? That's it?" Mason questioned.

"That's it. Her ex-boyfriend—Mick, the one she

married—got wind of me and showed up at my dad's ready to fight." I shrugged. "So I fought him."

"He was a jerk. I hope you kicked his ass." Mason set his jaw, and I saw my younger self in his pugnacious expression.

"I did, but my dad and stepmother were furious and tossed me out. I was so mad I left without saying goodbye to Andi."

"And she never tried to get in touch with you?" Lori asked.

I shook my head. "Not that I know of. I always figured she was so angry that she just deleted my number and decided, *to hell with that guy.*"

Mason exhaled. "That sounds like her. Mom had a hot temper too. And man, could she hold a grudge. I could see her realizing that you'd left without saying anything and swearing she'd never utter your name again."

"But even after she found out she was pregnant?" Lori was incredulous. "That's a heck of a grudge."

Guilt slammed my chest like a wrecking ball. "I swear, if she'd tried to contact me, Mason, I would have responded. I can't say I would have been thrilled, but I would not have ignored her."

Mason picked up his beer glass and drank. After setting it down, he nodded slowly. "I believe you. If my mother never even wanted me to have your name, it must have been because she never wanted you to know."

I wanted to apologize again, but the words were starting to sound hollow.

"At least you know now, right?" Lori said, her tone brighter. "And even though we'll probably never know why Andrea made the choice she did, maybe it doesn't matter. We can't change it. But we can move forward as a family."

Mason smiled at her, patting her hand on the table. "Yes. Exactly."

The server arrived with salads a moment later, and I dug in as if I were starving, grateful for the distraction.

"How was your flight in yesterday, Zach?" Lori asked.

"Fine."

"Did you have a chance to see any of the area today? Autumn is a really beautiful season around here."

"I took a run this morning. It is a pretty area."

"I think we're going to get some rain tonight," said Mason, "but hopefully it clears up quickly."

"Rain on your wedding day is supposed to be lucky, right?" Lori smiled and shrugged. "Maybe rain during your rehearsal is lucky too."

"You should come to the rehearsal dinner, Zach," Mason said. "I mean, if you want to. It's tomorrow night."

I picked up my water again and took a few cold swallows.

"Mason and I were thinking it would be a less hectic time for you to meet my family than at the actual wedding," Lori explained. "But we don't want to put pressure on you."

I cleared my throat. "I'll give it some thought."

Just after two o'clock, I went back to my hotel room and crashed on the bed. I wasn't sure if it was the change in time zone, the six-mile run I'd taken that morning, the big meal, or the emotionally exhausting conversation I'd just had, but I was wiped out. I fell asleep within minutes.

When I woke up, the room was dark. I checked my phone—it was after five. There were several messages from Jackson regarding an upcoming job and one from Mason.

Thank you so much for meeting us for lunch. Lori and I had a great time. It was so good to finally meet you in person, and I feel like the pieces of my past and myself I was missing are all falling into place. We'd love for you to come to the rehearsal tomorrow. If you want to. It's

**at Cloverleigh Farms, and we're all meeting in
the lobby at 4:45.**

Setting my phone aside, I lay on my back and tossed an
arm over my head. I knew what the right thing to do would
be—go to the fucking rehearsal and play whatever role Mason
asked me to. Would it make up for the past? For my immature
hasty departure from Andi's life? For his going essentially fa-
therless for almost thirty years? No.

But no matter how much I told myself this wasn't
my fault, I couldn't quite bring myself to fully believe it.
Somewhere in the timeline, I'd fucked up, whether it was
having unprotected sex or beating up her ex or taking off
without a goodbye. My hands were not clean.

After texting back that I'd be there, I turned on the TV
and flipped through the channels. I watched a few Seinfeld re-
runs, then I turned it off and wandered over to the window,
pulling the curtains aside. It was just starting to rain, but I
needed some air. I grabbed the keys to my rental SUV and
left the hotel, not sure where I was headed—maybe I'd grab
a drink and dinner somewhere. It was almost seven and I was
starting to get hungry.

Heading in the direction of downtown, I spied a place
called Southpaw Brewing Co. that looked good. There were
no parking spots on the street, so I pulled past it to circle the
block. At the corner, I waited for a trio of women to cross
the street before I made my turn, and for a second, I thought
I saw Millie among them. I stared at their backs through my
blurry windshield, but it was dark and they were moving fast,
hurrying through the rain. But there was something about
that long hair, and the way this woman carried herself, that
struck me as familiar.

The car behind me honked, and I pulled forward, tossing
one last glance at the women over my shoulder.

Seven

Millie

FRIDAY MORNING WAS GRAY AND DRIZZLY, AND WINNIE TEXTED that she didn't feel like going to HIIT class. I grabbed an umbrella and went by myself, and afterward I walked up the street to Frannie's bakery, Plum & Honey. Her coffee was always the best, and I wanted to run Winnie's idea about the plus-sized bridal salon by her.

Frannie was someone whose judgment I trusted, and she'd started her own business too. Plus, she'd grown up at Cloverleigh Farms—that's where she'd met our dad—and I knew if *she* said leaving the security of my job there wasn't bananas, it would be the truth.

Beneath the striped awning, I shook off my umbrella, then went inside. Frannie looked up from where she stood pouring coffee behind the counter. "Well, good morning. What a nice surprise."

"Hi." Leaving my dripping umbrella by the door, I approached the marble counter and pointed at the pot in her hands. "Got some of that for me?"

"Always. To go? Or can you sit for a minute?"

"I can sit for a minute. I want to get your take on something, if you have time."

Frannie looked pleased. "I always have time for my girls. Want breakfast? I just took scones out of the oven—blueberry lemon thyme, your favorite."

"Mmm. Okay." The bakery wasn't as crowded as usual—probably because of the weather—and I grabbed a stool at the white marble counter. After shrugging out of my coat, I pulled some hand sanitizer from my bag and gave my hands a quick rub.

"So what's up?" Frannie asked, placing a cup of steaming black coffee and a small plate with a scone on it in front of me.

I gave her a brief rundown of my meeting yesterday and the conversation with Winnie and Felicity over dinner last night. "Felicity mentioned this friend of hers that had to go out of state to find a shop that carried dresses in her size. It's just not right."

"No, it isn't," Frannie agreed. "That's why you're doing the fashion show, right?"

"Yes, but that's a one-time thing. It will be done in a day. And brides will still have to special-order any dress they see that they like."

A crease appeared between her brows. "I see what you're saying. It's not a long-term solution."

"Exactly." I fidgeted on my stool. "I mean, the story of finding your wedding dress is one a woman will tell her children and grandchildren. No one wants that story to be, 'Well, I was treated like crap and nothing fit, and in the end, I settled for a gown I didn't really love because my options were so limited.' Shopping for the dress should make a bride feel celebrated, it should be part of the love story, not an exercise in frustration and shame."

"You sound really passionate about this," Frannie said.

"I *feel* passionate about it. If curvy brides aren't free to

69

choose a dress style that makes them feel beautiful because the industry thinks they need to cover up, what are we saying? That only certain bodies are worthy of telling a love story? I *reject that*!" I banged a fist on the counter twice.

Frannie smiled at my fervor and nodded. "Good. Everyone should."

"I feel this spark of—of inspiration. Of wanting to be part of the change. I know the fashion industry is making strides toward body positivity, but the progress might not be quick enough for a bride around here who needs a dress in four months." My mind was going a hundred miles per hour now. "If and when *I'm* ready to look for a wedding dress, if I don't find something I like around here, I know designers I could call. Or I could always design my own gown. But that's not the case for most women, you know? I want to help."

"Millie, I think you know the answer to whatever question you came in here to ask me," Frannie said wryly.

"But I love what I do now," I fretted, "and *where* I do it, so is it nuts to consider leaving that job to start my own business? To upend my life? I just bought a house! I can't afford to go broke."

Frannie shrugged. "It's a bold move, and a risk, but I've never known you to shy away from a bold move. Do some research. Crunch some numbers. Reach out to those plus-sized salon owners in other states and maybe to some designers. Then see how you feel."

The bell rang as a customer came in off the street, and I picked up my coffee again. "You better get back to work. Thanks for listening."

"I'm always here for you." She blew me a kiss and moved over to the display case to greet the couple who'd come in, and I picked up my phone to scroll through my messages.

That's when I noticed I had a voicemail from Mason.

It struck me as a little odd, since we didn't normally call

each other, and I hoped everything was okay with him and Lori. Mason had come a long way, but he could still be emotional and sensitive. I crossed my fingers there hadn't been any drama, and the wedding was still on.

Breaking off a corner of the scone, I popped it into my mouth as I listened to his message.

"Hey, Millie." Mason sounded excited, almost out of breath. "Just wanted to let you know there will be one extra person at the rehearsal today. Believe it or not, I found my biological dad—I discovered his name in a letter my mom wrote to me before she died, a letter I only came across last summer when I was going through her things. Anyway, after some hunting and a paternity test to make sure he was really the guy, we started talking. He's really cool—a Navy SEAL!—and he was shocked to learn of my existence.

"We don't really know why my mom never told him, but anyway, that's a longer story I'll have to tell you later. The important thing is, I found some real family and he'll be there for me at my wedding. We met in person for the first time at lunch yesterday, and it was amazing. Lori and I invited him to the rehearsal, and he said yes! I don't think he'd be comfortable with anything too official—he's sort of reserved—but maybe we can find some way to seat him in a special place or something?

"I'm just really pumped that I actually have a dad, and that he wants to be part of my life. I can't wait for you to meet him." His voice lowered a little. "I know it might be strange to say this, since we're exes and all, and we can't be *too* close of friends out of respect for Lori, but I really appreciate how good you were to me when I was struggling, and I know I wouldn't be in this awesome place in my life without your help. Thanks for everything. See you tonight."

Wow. That was not what I expected. I stared at my phone

in awe for a moment, then set it down and picked up my coffee.

"Everything okay?" Frannie asked, coming over to top off my coffee. "You look like you've seen a ghost."

"Yeah, fine. I just had this crazy voicemail from Mason. He found his biological dad."

Frannie's eyebrows shot up, her blue eyes going wide. "Really?"

"Yes." I outlined what Mason had told me in the voicemail.

"So they've established contact?"

"Yes. Apparently he's coming to the wedding." I shrugged. "Coming from *where*, I don't know, but I didn't get the impression he's local."

With the coffee pot still in her hand, Frannie looked off into the distance. "I can't imagine being told I had an adult son after so many years. That has to be strange. I wonder if he has other kids—like if there are brothers and sisters to be met."

"Mason didn't say." I broke off another piece of my scone and ate it. "But I kind of hope so. Mason only ever had his mom, and he always used to say how much he envied our family, how big it was and how close we all were. Discovering relatives he never knew about would be like Christmas morning for him."

"I wonder if they look alike. Maybe I'll be able to pick him out." Frannie and my dad were attending the wedding, since Lori worked for Cloverleigh Farms. In fact, I'd have several family members there—Lori's boss in the winery was my Uncle Henry, married to Frannie's sister Sylvia. And my Aunt Chloe, another of Frannie's sisters, was CEO of the entire operation. She'd be there with her husband, Oliver.

"I guess the dad is coming to the rehearsal tonight as well," I told Frannie. "It sounds like Mason wants him to have some kind of role in the ceremony." I took another bite. "I wonder if he's married and bringing his spouse. Maybe they could be seated before Lori's grandparents or something. I can't imagine he'll want *too* much attention. 'Reserved' was the word Mason used to describe him." I picked up my coffee for a sip. "This is so crazy—it's like soap opera stuff!"

"What's his name?" Frannie asked.

"You know what? Mason didn't say. Just that he's a Navy SEAL." Which made me think of Zach again. Kind of an odd coincidence. But then, Dex was a former SEAL too. There must be thousands of them.

Frannie smiled at me. "Should be an interesting night."

After a hot shower, I blew out my hair and put on a black sleeveless dress with a mock turtleneck and a hem that hit my knees. Over it I wore a camel-colored blazer, and I slipped a pair of leopard-print heels into my work bag. Once my makeup was done, I stepped into my flats, snatched my umbrella, and headed out.

On my way to Cloverleigh Farms, I stopped at an office supply store to grab some file folders—I wanted a place to put all my research about bridal salons. As I was hurrying back to my car, I saw a man across the parking lot get out of an SUV and hustle toward a huge gym at the far end of the strip mall. Something about him reminded me of Zach—the beard? The broad shoulders?—and I squinted, trying to see him more clearly. But before I could get a good look, he'd disappeared into the building.

I stood there for a moment at the side of my car, wondering if I'd lost my mind. A chill moved through me.

Then I laughed at myself and shook it off, tossing my umbrella in the back seat before sliding in behind the wheel. Clearly, the number of orgasms I'd given myself while thinking about him were getting to me.

Still, the image of the man's broad back and long strides stayed with me all day.

I was meeting the Holt and Campion wedding party in the main lobby of Cloverleigh Farms at quarter to five, so at four-fifteen, I shut down my laptop, slipped into my blazer, traded my flats for the heels, and reapplied my lipstick. Not Red Carpet, of course—being the wedding planner meant doing your best to blend into the background, so I chose a more neutral beige gloss.

When I was ready, I walked over from the wedding barn to the inn's lobby. No one had arrived yet, so I snuck past the front desk into the back hall where the admin offices were.

My dad's door was open, and I poked my head in. *"Hey."*

He looked up from his computer, his face easing into a smile that creased his cheeks and wrinkled his forehead, but I still thought he was the most handsome dad in the world. The gray in his hair brought out the sharp silvery-blue of his eyes, and nothing lit them up like a surprise visit from his wife or his girls. *"Hey, Mills. You look nice."*

"Thanks."

He closed his laptop. *"Are your ears burning? I was just talking about you."*

"You were?"

"Yes. Frannie called and told me she saw you this morning and you were all fired up about maybe starting your own business."

"Oh. Yeah." I leaned against the doorframe. *"It's just a crazy idea right now."*

"Frannie didn't think you sounded crazy." He sat back in his chair and folded his arms over his chest. *"Want to talk about it?"*

"I do," I said, glancing over my shoulder in the direction of the lobby. "But I don't have time right now. Mason's rehearsal is starting in a few minutes."

"Oh, right." My dad nodded slowly. "You feel okay about that?"

"Sure." I looked at him quizzically. "Why wouldn't I?"

"I don't know. Winnie mentioned something about you feeling sort of down that the last few guys you've dated went on to get married pretty quickly."

"Jesus." I shook my head. "I don't know why I tell her anything in confidence. It was no big deal—I was just in a mood."

"Good. He didn't deserve you. None of them did."

I rolled my eyes. "Okay, Dad."

"I'm serious. I know you're the oldest and used to doing things first, but don't you dare settle for someone less than worthy." He pointed at me. "You are Millie fucking MacAllister, and you deserve the best."

I laughed. "Spoken like a truly unbiased father. Anyway, I did a little research today, but I definitely need advice."

"I'm always here for you."

I blew him a kiss and left his office, heading back up the hallway toward the lobby. As I came through the door behind the reception desk, I noticed several people had gathered in front of the lobby's large stone fireplace. Smoothing my blazer, I smiled at the employee working check-in, slipped around the desk, and approached the group.

I saw Lori standing with a couple I presumed to be her parents, a group of three young women that were likely bridesmaids, a couple guys that I recognized as friends of Mason's, a little boy and girl darting behind the towering Christmas tree, and Mason himself, talking excitedly to a tall, broad-shouldered man who had his back to me. His father?

As I got closer, I felt a strange crackle in the air—almost an electrical current. The same shiver I'd felt earlier in the parking lot crept up my spine. Something about the man's stance was familiar. The big shoulders. The salt-and-pepper hair. The back of his neck.

But there was no way.

Touching a hand to my jittery stomach, I kept walking, one heel in front of the other. Mason smiled when he saw me. "There she is. I was just talking about you. Mills, this is—"

At that moment, the man turned to face me.

I stopped dead in my tracks, my legs threatening to buckle. "Zach," I said, before I could stop myself.

From the look on his face, I could tell he was just as shocked as I was. "Millie?"

"My father, Zach Barrett," Mason finished, his voice trailing off. He looked back and forth between us. "Wait, you two know each other?"

The look that passed between Zach and me was quick and desperate. But just like in the hotel bar, somehow we agreed on the plan without a word. "This is a surprise," he said, offering his hand.

I couldn't believe how controlled his voice was. "It sure is," I said, hearing the waver in mine.

"We met in New York about a month ago," Zach explained to Mason while I numbly put my hand in his. No one saw how hard he squeezed it. "We were both stranded at the same hotel during the hurricane. We ended up talking at the bar."

"Really?" Mason looked dumbfounded.

Lori came over, looking curious, and slipped her arm around Mason's waist. "What's going on?"

"Uh, Zach and Millie . . . know each other, I guess." Mason cocked his head. "So you met in a hotel bar?"

"Yes," I replied, gaining some equilibrium back. "In New York City, while I was there for the wedding planner expo. Actually, it's a funny story." I laughed nervously, putting my hands behind my back as if everyone might see that one was flaming hot because Zach had just touched it. "There was this terrible jerk who wouldn't leave me alone, and Zach was kind enough to come to my rescue."

"Wow, really?" Lori smiled at us. "What a coincidence."

"So then you introduced yourselves?" Mason still appeared off-balance.

"Yes," I said, moving slightly away from Zach. I could sense his nearness as if his body was radiating heat. "I offered to buy him a drink to say thank you, but he wouldn't let me."

"No thanks were necessary," Zach said with a shrug of those shoulders I'd seen naked. "I was just glad she wasn't offended that I stepped in."

"You probably couldn't help it," said Lori. "Being a Navy SEAL and a bodyguard and all. If you see someone that needs protection, you just jump in and do it. Gut reaction."

"Right." Zach glanced at me. "It was a gut reaction."

"And then what?" asked Mason.

"We chatted for a moment and that was it," I said, wishing I was a better liar. I wasn't as awful as Winnie, but I wasn't an expert either. "I had an early flight the next morning, so I went off to bed."

Zach nodded shortly, as if he'd done the same.

"When was this again?" Mason's eyes moved back and forth between us.

"Uh, early September?" I tried to play it off like I wasn't sure, when I knew for a fact it had been four weeks and two days.

"And you never put it together? The connection?" Mason almost sounded suspicious. Or maybe that was my nerves.

"Nope," I said, risking a glance at Zach. "I actually don't even think we told each other where we lived."

"It was a short conversation," agreed Zach. "Just the one drink."

"Wait, I thought you turned down the drink." Mason looked at Zach. "Because no thanks were necessary."

Zach and I exchanged another look. "He turned down my offer to *pay* for it," I clarified. "He insisted on paying."

"So you did have a drink together," Mason said.

"Yes. Just one." I felt heat in my cheeks and knew I looked like a kid who'd been caught stealing. "And then we said goodnight."

"Too funny," Lori said, her delighted grin in stark contrast to Mason's uncertain expression. "Well, I think this is great. Zach thought he wouldn't know anyone here, and now he already has a friend. Millie, you should join us for dinner."

"Oh no, I really can't," I protested. "But thank you for asking. Is everyone here? Should we go over to the barn and walk through the ceremony?"

"Everyone's here," she confirmed. "But are you sure you can't make it to dinner? Mason, tell her to come."

"You should come," Mason said, and maybe this was only in my head, but his tone lacked its usual warmth.

"Thanks, but I can't tonight. I'm—I'm having dinner with my dad." I gestured over my shoulder. "He's already here waiting for me. I mean, he works here. He's the CFO. He's—he's my dad." My babbling made no sense whatsoever, but Zach's eyes on me were too much to handle and Mason's weirdness was making me sweat. "Okay, then, should we go?"

Without waiting for an answer, I turned and walked for the back door that led to the path toward the barn. As soon as my back was to them, I closed my eyes and concentrated on staying upright.

Knowing Zach was watching me from behind made my legs tremble.

Eight

Zach

GODDAMN, SHE WAS BEAUTIFUL.

What was it about her that took all the oxygen from a room? Not to mention the way she sent blood rushing to my crotch. The sight of her brought back memories that caused my cock to surge.

But I couldn't let on.

Immediately I'd seen how flustered Millie was, how uneasy Mason appeared, and my instinct to protect kicked in. I thought I'd done a good enough job smoothing things over—just the one error about the drink, and Millie had corrected course there.

Now, as I walked behind her, admiring those curves I'd been dreaming about since the night we'd met, I thought how fucked-up this situation was. She was Mason's ex-girlfriend? What were the chances?

It was easy to see how we didn't put it together—I didn't even know she was from Michigan, let alone that she was a wedding planner. And she'd had no idea I had a newly found adult son getting married. A guy that she'd dated. A guy that she'd slept with.

Jesus.

I'd wanted to see her again. But not like this.

Even as my gut turned over, I hurried past her to get the door, and she murmured her thanks without making eye contact as she moved through it. Remaining in place, I held the door for everyone else. Mason and Lori were last, and we walked together toward the barn.

"Thank goodness the rain stopped, but it's chilly, isn't it?" Lori rubbed her arms and hurried ahead. "I'll meet you guys in there!"

Mason and I walked shoulder to shoulder. I sensed his discomfort but didn't know what to make of it.

"So it's weird that you met Millie before," he said.

"Small world, I guess." I tried to sound casual.

"And you had a drink."

"Yes."

"And that's it? Nothing happened?"

I glanced sharply at him. "Happened?"

"You know. Between you and Millie." He shrugged, stuffing his hands in his pockets. "Sorry if this is weird to ask, I just got a strange feeling in there that there was more to the story."

"There wasn't. There isn't."

"I guess it's not my business anyway," he said. "You're both adults, and it's not like you knew that she was my ex-girlfriend, or she knew that you're my father. I just . . . I guess I just like things to be out in the open. I've spent so many years of my life feeling like things were hidden from me. Wanting to know the truth and never getting answers. I hate that feeling."

"I understand."

We reached the door and he put a hand on it but didn't pull it open. He looked me in the eye. "It means a lot to me, your honesty. We can't change the past, but we can set the tone for the future. So if you give me your word, I'll believe you."

If I was going to tell the truth, I had to do it now—but

there was no way I'd do it without Millie knowing. I had to keep up the lie. "You have my word. Nothing happened."

He smiled, looking younger than twenty-eight, giving me a glimpse of the boy he'd been. "Okay. Thanks."

For the next forty minutes or so, Millie and I successfully avoided eye contact. The room was all set up for the ceremony tomorrow, rows of white chairs set up on what was probably a dance floor at the far end of the room with a gold runner between them. A large arch made of greenery and decorated with white flowers stood at the head of the aisle in front of massive windows, and beyond it the autumn landscape of the farm was visible, trees aflame with scarlet and gold and burnt orange. It reminded me of seasons many years past, making me a little nostalgic for my early childhood in Ohio.

I mostly stayed out of the way as Millie went over the order of who'd be seated when, how the wedding party procession would go, and the timing of it all. She answered tons of questions from Lori and her mother in a reassuring and professional manner. Obviously excellent at her job, she impressed me even more because I knew that her mind must be reeling.

"So it goes groom and groomsmen in position, Lori's grandparents seated, Lori's mom seated, bridesmaids, maid of honor, flower girl and ring bearer, and then Lori and her dad," Millie said. "Should we walk through it?"

"What about Zach?" Mason asked. "When does he get seated?"

"Oh." Millie checked a clipboard, like the answer might be there somewhere. "Um, he could be seated . . . after the grandparents, before Lori's mom?"

"I really don't need to be recognized." I put up my hands,

inwardly hoping Mason would reconsider. "I don't feel right about it, honestly."

"But it's important to me," said Mason. "And you should sit in the front row."

"I know," said Lori's mom, a well-dressed woman in a burgundy suit. "Why doesn't he escort me to my seat? That way my husband can stay with Lori."

"That's perfect." Lori nodded enthusiastically. "Great idea, Mom."

Mrs. Campion walked over to me and smiled. "Okay with you, Zach?"

"Of course."

Laughing, she offered me her arm. "Should we practice?"

"Yes," said Millie, moving with efficiency to line everyone else up. "Lori and Mr. Campion, you'll be out of sight over there. Gentlemen, you'll line up with best man and groom last and head up the aisle to your place to the right of the arch. Ladies, flower girl, and ring bearer, you'll be with the bride— line up with maid of honor and kids last."

I did my part, walking Mrs. Campion up the aisle, leading her to her seat in the front row on the left, and then taking a seat in the first row, as Mason had requested.

The rest of the rehearsal went quickly, and then everyone headed back to the main lobby of the inn. I tried to linger behind in the hopes of catching a minute with Millie alone, but she stayed with the group, leading the way back across the path. It was dark now, and a few flurries were drifting down from the sky.

In the lobby, the group reassembled and made plans for driving over to the restaurant where dinner was being held. "Want to ride with us?" Mason asked me.

"No, thanks. I'll meet you there." I gave him a stiff smile. "I'm just going to use the men's room before I leave."

"Okay," he said, helping Lori with her coat. "No rush—our

reservation isn't for another half hour, so we'll probably hang out in the bar first. You've got the address?"

I nodded. "All good."

Millie was still talking to Mrs. Campion, so I wandered out of the lobby toward the bar at the back of the inn. It was dark and intimate, and I wished more than anything Millie and I could spend the evening sitting at a corner table getting to know each other better . . . and then getting naked back in my hotel room.

But that was impossible.

She was Mason's ex-girlfriend.

Grimacing at the thought, I ducked into the men's room off the hallway. When I came out, I stopped short at the sight of Millie sitting at the bar by herself. That long wavy hair cascading down her back sent a pang of longing through me.

I glanced toward the front door, where I should've been heading, and back at her, where I wanted to be. In a split second, I made my decision and crossed the room in her direction.

I touched her shoulder. "Hey."

She turned, surprised. "Oh! Zach, hi." Glancing around me, she said, "I thought everyone left."

"They did. I stayed back a minute. I was hoping to talk to you." I looked down at the empty stool next to her. "Can I sit?"

"Of course." She already had a martini in front of her, and she lifted it for a sip.

"Are you waiting for your dad?"

"Ah, that was a bit of a fib. I thought it best if I didn't go to dinner, given the, um . . ." Her eyes dropped to my crotch for a half-second. "Circumstances."

"You're probably right." The bartender approached, and I ordered an Old-Fashioned, figuring I had enough time for one quick drink.

"So this is a weird coincidence, huh?" She stirred her drink with the olives on the pick.

"To say the least."

"I mean, I had no idea you were—" She shook her head and didn't finish the sentence. "Not in a million years."

I fought the urge to stand closer to her. "You know, I thought I saw you downtown last night, crossing a street. Then I was like, nah . . . couldn't be."

"Oh my God, same!" Her eyes went wide. "I thought I saw you this morning in a parking lot, going into a gym."

"That was me," I confirmed.

"It was probably me on the street too. I was downtown last night with my sisters."

I nodded. "I had a feeling. But I told myself I was seeing things. What are the odds?"

"Speaking of numbers." She looked at me curiously. "How is the math even possible? Not that it's my business, but—"

"I was only eighteen. And I never knew about him," I said, feeling like I owed her an explanation. The last thing I wanted her to think was that I'd abandoned a young pregnant girl. "Mason's mom was only eighteen too, and we had a reckless thing that only lasted a few days. I had no idea she got pregnant, and she never told me about him. Or told him about me."

"It's such an odd choice to make—to keep a child from his father." Millie's expression was distressed. "I don't understand it."

"The circumstances were less than ideal," I said. "Believe me, if I could go back knowing what I know now, I'd do things differently. But as it is, I can't bring myself to judge Andi— Mason's mom—for the decision she made. We were kids ourselves, barely out of high school. And I didn't exactly leave her with the best impression of me." I gave Millie the quick version of what had gone down in Frankenmuth that fall.

She nodded slowly. "So you think she kept your son from you as punishment?"

"I don't want to make any assumptions, but I think it's possible."

"Wow."

My drink arrived and I took a swallow. "Anyway, when Mason reached out a couple months ago, I was shocked. But even before the paternity test came back, I just had a gut feeling it was true. All the facts lined up."

"Mason left me a voicemail telling me he'd found his real dad, and that he'd be at the wedding," she said, shaking her head, "but he never said your name."

"He's mentioned you to me before too—just not by name."

She looked surprised. "He has?"

"Yes. He spoke about a former girlfriend who helped him through a hard time, and he said she was planning his wedding."

A quick laugh escaped her. "And I thought *that* would be the oddest thing about this weekend."

"I'm sorry, Millie."

"It's not your fault." She sat up a little taller. "But I definitely think it's best if Mason *never* knows the truth."

"I thought we covered well enough." I ran a hand over my hair. "But he suspected something."

Millie set her martini glass down with a clink and seemed to choke a little. "What?"

"As we walked over to the barn, he asked me if anything had happened between us."

"He *did*? But—but what gave him that idea?"

"I don't know for sure. He just sensed the tension, I guess. I don't know Mason that well, but maybe he's really perceptive."

"He is." She twisted her hands together. "What did you *say*?"

"I said the only thing I could say—nothing happened."

Millie looked relieved, her shoulders loosening. "Okay. Good."

"He told me that he's spent much of his life searching for truth and feeling like things were being hidden from him." I took another drink.

"His mom," said Millie quietly. "It must be so hard for him that his mother kept you a secret. They were close."

"In one of our first conversations, he mentioned something about working toward forgiveness." For a moment, I wondered if I was betraying Mason's confidence by sharing this information with Millie, but I wanted her to understand that if the stakes were anything less than earning my son's trust and respect, I would have loved to spend time with her again. "I think reaching out to me, establishing a connection, is part of that."

"Of course."

"He said how much honesty means to him, how glad he is that I've been open with him." I closed my eyes. "I just couldn't bring myself to take that away from him. I don't want him to think I'm—I'm—just some asshole who doesn't care about honor or responsibility or blood ties."

Millie put a hand on my arm. "I get it, Zach."

"It probably sounds fucking stupid, but one of the things he initially told me was that when he was growing up, he asked his mother if his father had been a good guy. And her answer was, *I thought so at the time*." I shook my head. "I don't know if it was true then. But I'd like it to be true now."

"It *is* true now. And it doesn't sound stupid at all." She rubbed my bicep before taking her hand off me. "I think we both need to put Mason's feelings first, and that means keeping what happened between us to ourselves."

"Not that we did anything wrong," I said quickly.

"No, but I don't need to prove that point by telling people

I slept with my ex-boyfriend's dad before I knew who he was." She laughed a little. "God. It sounds so ridiculous."

"It does." The memories heated my blood even now. "But it sure was fun."

Her eyes met mine, and she blushed. "It was."

"And if the circumstances were anything other than what they are," I said quietly, "I'd want to do it all over again tonight."

The pink in her cheeks deepened. "How long are you in town?"

"I leave Monday." I focused on my drink for a moment, turning the glass in my hand. "I've thought about you a lot."

"I've done the same," she whispered, as if it were an awful secret. "I almost called you a couple times."

I tossed back the rest of my cocktail, refusing to let my brain imagine what those phone calls might have entailed. "I guess it's good that you didn't."

"Yes."

Setting the glass on the bar, I turned to her, determined to do the right thing. "Well, Millie MacAllister, it was nice to see you again."

"You too." She offered me her hand, and I took it, holding it a little longer than was polite.

I kept my voice low. "You're as beautiful as I remembered. Maybe even more so."

The color in her face deepened and her long, thick lashes swept down. "Thank you."

I couldn't resist kissing her cheek. After pressing my lips to her soft, warm skin, I put my mouth near her ear and whispered, "I know it's wrong, but I can't leave without kissing you."

She inhaled sharply.

I straightened up and let go of her hand. "I'll see you tomorrow."

Nine

A S SOON AS I WAS SURE ZACH WAS OFF THE PREMISES, I texted Winnie and Felicity.

Emergency! Emergency!

Who is available for wine at my house?

Winnie replied first. **Shoot! I'm helping with a wine tasting at Abelard until 8. Can I come then? I'll bring a bottle.**

While I was typing a response to her, Felicity chimed in. **I am! Hutton left for a business trip this afternoon and my catering gig was an afternoon thing. I'll bring some snacks.**

Perfect, I responded. **I'll see you guys there in 20.**

Winnie sent another text. **What's the emergency?**

Felicity sent a row of arrows pointing up at Winnie's question.

It's too much to explain over text, I told them. **But have either of you ever accidentally slept with someone's dad?**

Felicity answered first. **Um . . . no.**

Then Winnie. **I slept with Hallie and Luna's dad. But that was on purpose. Whose dad did you sleep with????**

Another row of arrows from Felicity.

I'll tell you when you get here, I said. **But remember that thing I said about being cursed? IT. IS. TRUE.**

Winnie ended up getting off work a little earlier than expected, picked up Felicity at her house, and they arrived together. Felicity had catering bags filled with food she'd made testing out recipes over the last couple days, and Winnie carried two bottles of wine from Abelard Vineyards, where she worked.

"Talk," she said, as she grabbed a corkscrew from a kitchen drawer and opened a pinot noir. "What's this emergency and whose dad did you bang?"

"You have to promise not to judge," I said, taking three glasses down from a shelf and placing them on the counter by Winnie. "And Winifred, so help me God, you cannot breathe a word of this to *anyone.*"

"I won't," she said, offering me her pinkie. "Pinkie swear."

I hooked my little finger to hers and looked her right in the eye. "Thank you. This cannot get out."

Felicity switched my oven on and spun to face me. "I'm dying, Mills! What did you do?"

I backed up to the kitchen table and flattened my palms on its edge, bracing myself. "Okay. The guy I slept with in New York last month? The hot mysterious stranger who spanked me?"

"Yes?" Felicity and Winnie chorused, looking at me intently.

"Turns out, he's Mason's biological dad."

Winnie's jaw fell open.

Felicity's eyes blinked behind her glasses. "What?"

"Wait a minute. Wait a minute." Winnie waved her hands in the air, as if she was erasing the words I'd just spoken. "Hot spanking stranger is *Mason's . . . dad*?"

"Yes! Remember how I told you he never knew who his biological father was? Evidently—and I just found this out *today*—his mom wrote down the guy's name in a letter that Mason discovered last summer while finally going through her things. He reached out."

"Holy balls!" Winnie shrieked. "Talk about a plot twist!"

"How does he have a son that old?" Felicity asked.

I told them what I knew about the fateful few days Zach had spent in Frankenmuth.

"Frankenmuth," Winnie tittered. "Who knew it was such a hotbed of sexual scandal?"

I glared at her. "Anyway, the girl—Mason's mom, Andi— never told Zach she got pregnant. But it's true."

"Paternity test confirmed it?" Felicity asked.

I nodded. "Yep."

"So when did you finally put it together?" Winnie wondered.

"Today at Mason and Lori's rehearsal, when I walked into the lobby and Mason introduced me to him. I almost passed out."

Both of them were silent a moment, and then Winnie turned around and poured three glasses of wine. Handing one to me, she said, "Here. You've earned this."

"Thanks." I took a hefty swallow. "It was so weird, you guys."

"What happened next? Did you let on?" Felicity asked as she pulled a baguette from her bag and took out a cutting board.

"No. We covered." I recounted the G-rated version of the story we'd told about how we met. "And I thought we did a good enough job, but later, after everyone else had gone on to dinner, Zach came into the bar—where I was applying vodka to the wound—and told me that Mason asked him if anything had happened between us."

Winnie gasped. "How did he answer?"

"He said no! What could he say?" I tapped my chin in jest. "'Hmm, actually, now that I think of it, I *did* bone your ex-girlfriend a few times at that hotel.'" I squeezed my eyes shut and shook my head. "It's just so weird."

"But you didn't know," Felicity pointed out, slicing the baguette. "So it's not like you did anything to be ashamed of."

"I guess not." I looked into my wine. "You guys, I need to get something out, but you can't judge me."

"No judging," Winnie promised.

"He's so hot," I moaned, stretching out the word *hot* like melting mozzarella. "Like, so unbelievably hot. I don't care whose dad he is, that man is *smoking*. Seeing him today was just like—" I searched for words to describe the feeling. "A punch in the gut. Or maybe in the lady bits. I have such a huge crush on him."

"Why not invite him over?" Winnie asked.

I gaped at her. "I can't do that!"

"Why not? You're two single, consenting adults." She paused. "Wait, he's single, right?"

"As far as I know."

"There, see?" She lifted her shoulders. "And what Mason doesn't know won't hurt him. Call him up."

"*No*," I said again, even though my body was begging for *yes*. "Zach doesn't want to start building their relationship with a lie, and I don't blame him. We had the one night together, and that's all it will ever be."

"But Millie," Winnie pressed. "For once, you found a guy who's not a lost puppy! What if this is it?"

My neck stretched forward. "Are you listening to yourself, Winifred? Are you picturing me sitting at the Thanksgiving table with two men I've slept with, and they're father and son? Are you imagining the way everyone will be staring at me, wondering what happened to my sense of decency? Does Mason say, 'Hey *Mom*, can you pass the turkey?'"

Both my sisters burst out laughing. "Yeah, I guess that won't work," Winnie admitted.

Felicity took a sip of her wine, then began brushing the slices of baguette with olive oil. "It's just a bummer you had so much fun with him, and he's here for the weekend and probably wishing he could see you again too."

He was. I knew he was. But it didn't matter.

"Well, it's no use wishing for what we can't have," I said, doing my best to push Zach out of my mind. "How about we watch a movie?"

Later that night, long after my sisters had gone, the lights were out and I was lying in bed with my vibrator beside me.

But instead of using it, I lay awake, wondering what Zach was doing. Was he still out with the wedding party? Was he in his hotel room alone? Was he thinking about me? Or had he been more successful than I had at filing our chemistry in a box labeled UNSAVORY and moving on with his thoughts?

I flopped onto my side and stared at my nightstand. I tapped my phone to see what time it was—just after eleven. He was probably still out, right? So I shouldn't text him. Someone might see it.

Then again, it's not like my name would show up on his phone, I reasoned. He didn't have me saved in his contacts or anything.

Biting my lip, I slowly pulled the drawer where I kept his card open. Reached inside. Took it out.

Then I rolled onto my back and stared at it in the dark. Slid my finger over its edges. Remembered the sound of his deep, rough-hewn voice in my ear. *I know it's wrong, but I can't leave without kissing you.*

I reached for my phone.

He probably won't reply anyway, I told myself. He's probably still out having fun or asleep already.

I typed his number into my phone and hit message.

Still thinking about you, I typed. **I hope you're having a good night.** Then before I lost my nerve, I hit send.

I was still holding my breath when three dots appeared. I let it out in a whoosh when his reply came through.

> **Thinking about you too. The night would be better if you were here.**

Oh my God. Oh my God. What did that mean? Was he still out? Was he saying he wished I'd come to dinner?

Where are you? I asked.

> **My hotel room. Call me?**

I gasped. Heart pounding, I did what he asked.

"Hey." That voice. Just one word from him caused my nipples to tingle.

"Hi," I said softly. "How did it go tonight?"

"Fine. A little weird, but fine."

"Weird how?"

"Weird to hear myself introduced as someone's *dad* all night long."

"Oh."

"I cut out pretty quickly after dinner. Grabbed a bottle of whiskey from a liquor store on my way back here. I was hoping a drink would help me fall asleep."

"But it didn't?"

"Nope."

"Maybe it's jet lag keeping you up."

"It's not jet lag."

"What is it?"

He didn't answer right away. "I'm glad you reached out."

"You are?"

"Yes."

I closed my eyes. "Even though it's wrong?"

"It's just a phone call. What could be wrong about that?"

"I don't know."

"I guess it might be considered wrong if I asked what you were wearing."

My lower lip fell open. Heat bloomed in my nether regions.

"But tell me anyway," he said. "And then take it all off."

I sucked in my breath again. Then I sat up, whipped off my cotton top, and lay back again before wriggling out of my flannel bottoms and panties. "I was wearing very cute red and white pajamas," I told him. "But now I'm naked."

"Good girl."

I shivered and pulled the covers up again. "What about you? What are you wearing?"

"Black pants with a drawstring waist."

I pictured him lying there in a dark room, chest bare, pants low on his hips. "Untie the string."

"I'm way ahead of you."

I flattened a palm on my stomach. "How far ahead?"

"Far enough that I've got my cock in my hand, and every word you say is making it harder."

Oh, fuck. I glanced at the toy next to me. "What are you thinking about?" I asked breathlessly.

"Your body. Your mouth. Your eyes. The taste of your pussy on my tongue."

"God, I love your tongue," I whimpered, sliding my hand between my legs.

"I wish I was fucking you with it right now." His breathing was louder. Faster.

"Let's pretend," I whispered, moving my fingertips over my clit.

"I forgot what a bad girl you are," he said, like it delighted him. "Are you touching yourself?"

"Yes."

"Are you wet from the stroke of my tongue?"

"*Yes*."

"Good. Now suck your fingers."

I brought my fingers to my mouth, brushed them over my lips, then sucked them, being sure to make a little noise about it.

He groaned. "God, I wish that mouth was on my cock."

"Me too," I whispered. "I didn't get to do it that night."

"Put your fingers between your legs again," he ordered. "Put them inside you, as deep as you can reach, then rub your clit."

I did what he asked, eyes closed, thighs open. "Zach. It feels so good."

"I want you to come for me," he said in that tone I'd been fantasizing about all week, the one that said *there will be no refusal.* "Don't stop until it happens."

Oh God, oh God . . . I willed myself not to think as I worked my body into a frenzy. I focused on everything outside my head—the tension building between my legs, his breathing growing ragged in my ear, the silvery darkness behind my eyelids. I let the memory of his tongue and his hands and his body on mine work as hard as my fingers, and in no time at all, I was gasping and sighing and lifting my hips as the waves crashed through me.

"Such a good girl," he rasped. "Listening to you come made my cock even bigger."

"I wish you were here to fuck me instead of your hand," I breathed. "I've wished you were here so many times."

He laughed suddenly, low and sexy. "Have you done this before, you wicked thing?"

"Yes," I confessed. "I have a toy. It's not nearly as good as the real thing, but it was better than nothing."

"Do you have it now?"

"Yes."

"Turn it on."

I reached for the Lelo, my pulse hammering wildly. "Okay."

"Now put the tip inside your sweet, wet pussy. Just an inch."

I did what he requested, moaning in agonized pleasure. "I want more."

"Do you like my cock inside you?"

"Yes," I hissed.

"I'm giving you more. Can you feel it?"

I slid the toy in a little deeper. "Yes."

"Now take it out again. Hold it against your clit."

The hum against my swollen, sensitive bud was almost too much. "Oh, God . . . I can't take it . . ."

His breath was labored, his words a struggle. "I want you to ride me."

"Huh?"

"Do as I say."

"But—"

"Listen to me," he demanded. "Get on your knees. Put the toy on the bed."

I obeyed, flipping onto my knees, centering the toy between my thighs, and sinking down onto it. I moaned as it thrummed inside me, the short arm vibrating against my clit, the long arm pressing against that spot that made my entire lower body begin to clench. "You're so deep," I whispered, grabbing onto the headboard with my free hand, just like I had in his hotel room. "You're so hard. And I'm so wet. So tight."

"Yes," he growled. *"Fuck yes. You're amazing. You're so fucking hot. And you're such a good girl."*

His praise was like gasoline on the flames. "You're going to make me come again," I whispered, widening my knees to take the toy even deeper. My insides tightened like a vise. "So close."

"Fuck yes. Come again for me. Come on my cock. Just like that. Just like—" And his words devolved into a long, sensual moan that sent me over the edge and I circled my hips as the climax hit, remembering the hot, pulsing throb of him inside me, yearning to feel it again.

A moment later, I opened my eyes. On the other end of the line, I could still hear him breathing. Quickly, I maneuvered the toy out from under me and switched it off. Tossing it to the floor, I sat with my legs pressed together, feeling self-conscious. Now what?

"Hey," he said. *"Give me a minute?"*

"Of course." I waited, my heart decelerating from an end-stretch gallop to a more gentle canter. But I was still nervous—what was there to say to each other?

"Okay, I'm back."

"Hi," I said. My voice cracked.

He laughed. *"You okay?"*

"I think so."

"But you're not sure?"

I exhaled. "I'm trying to decide how terrible I should feel about this."

"Like on a scale of one to ten?"

"Sure."

"One," he said.

"No way. It's got to be more than that. I'm the one who texted you."

"But I told you to call."

"And then I *did.*"

"I told you to take your clothes off."

"True." I had to laugh. "That *was* pretty early in the conversation. If we even had a conversation."

"There was some talking. I'm almost sure of it." He paused. "Although I had a hand in my pants the whole time. So I'm thinking I'm definitely a ten, and you're maybe a three."

"The whole time, huh?"

"I was thinking about you even before you texted. Which is probably why things escalated so quickly. The whiskey also played a role."

"So did the wine I consumed tonight." I leaned back against the headboard. "I was trying to drown my shame."

"I don't want you to be ashamed, Millie."

"Aren't you?"

"Not for what happened in New York. We didn't know about the connection. It was not an informed decision."

"And tonight?" I asked quietly.

"Tonight." He exhaled. "Yeah, tonight's a little different."

"I could say I only texted you to say goodnight, but I'd be lying," I told him. "Deep down, I wanted what happened to happen."

"I did too. Actually, I wanted it in person, but this was a close second."

I laughed, but it was tinged with regret. Then I forced myself to say the truth. "But I think we'd better draw the line right here and now, and we need to mean it this time. This can't happen again, not even over the phone."

"I agree."

"So I'm—I'm going to delete your number, okay? And you delete mine. That way we won't even be tempted."

"Okay."

"Okay." I hesitated. "So I guess I'll say goodnight for real. And I'll see you at the wedding."

"The wedding. Right."

"And I'm going to be cool and professional tomorrow, even though that's not how I'll feel on the inside. Don't take it the wrong way."

"I understand." He paused. "You're not going to wear that black dress you had on in New York, are you?"

"No."

"Good. Then there's a chance I can keep my hands to myself."

I smiled. "Goodnight, Zach."

"Night."

Ten

Zach

I WAS MORE NERVOUS GETTING READY FOR MASON'S WEDDING than I had been for my own.

In fact, I hardly remembered my own wedding. My ex had made every decision, and her wealthy father had paid all the bills. I showed up in a tux, repeated some words, watched her slide a ring on my finger, put one on hers, and mostly stayed out of the way after that. Honestly, I didn't feel much of anything, probably because I was doing my best to ignore the gut feeling telling me marrying Kimberly was a mistake.

She was a local television news reporter in San Diego, but she was hoping to move into broadcast journalism on a national level at one of the giant news networks. I figured she'd probably achieve it, since she was smart and articulate, beautiful in that TV personality sort of way with the shiny hair and the super white teeth, but beyond that, she was the most ambitious person I'd ever known, and when she wanted something, she went after it with everything she had. Including me. I had no idea why she'd wanted to get married so badly, but we'd only been dating for about six months when she started dropping hints.

I told her I'd never planned to get married. She liked that—a challenge.

I told her I didn't want kids. She said she didn't either—in fact, she said I should get a vasectomy before the wedding.

I reminded her how often I traveled for work, that I was only home about half the time. She said she was fine with that—it would make the nights I was home more special.

And she asked me if I really wanted to spend the rest of my life alone, an empty bed every night, a silent house. I had to admit there was something off-putting about that. The guys I'd known in the Navy were all married with families now. My co-workers all had wives and kids. Being the odd man out as I got older wasn't all that appealing. At least if I got hitched, I'd have a plus-one. And honestly, her need to be the center of attention suited me. It kept conversations and eyes focused on her.

So I said okay. Bought the ring she'd picked out. Popped the question at the restaurant where she'd made a reservation. Tried not to grimace when the photographer she'd obviously hired approached and asked to take some photos, which showed up later on Kimberly's social media, filtered to death and accompanied by hashtags like #DiamondsAreAGirlsBestFriend and #Blessed.

And I had the vasectomy.

The wedding was a monster affair that took her longer to plan than our actual marriage lasted. Which was mostly because she hit her thirty-fifth birthday and realized a few things, not the least of which was that she *did* want to be a mom, she hated how often I was gone, and when I was home, she said I neglected her emotional needs—I was too closed off.

Within months, she fell in love with a producer at the station, announced she was leaving me, and moved in with him. They were married now, and last I heard, she was pregnant.

And I was preparing to attend my grown son's wedding,

the memory of hot phone sex with his ex-girlfriend fresh on my mind. The woman I'd sworn to myself I wouldn't touch. The one I'd promised Mason I hadn't touched. The one I couldn't stop thinking about touching again.

But I wouldn't.

Last night had been a good time but a bad decision, a whiskey-influenced reaction to jumbled-up feelings—anger, guilt, loneliness. When my phone lit up with Millie's message, I'd jumped at the chance to escape my reality and indulge in fantasy instead.

At least we hadn't done anything in person. Was phone sex even technically sex? Generally, I was someone who saw things in black and white, but I felt there might be some room for interpretation there.

Still. It couldn't happen again. No matter that she made me feel younger and more alive than I'd felt in years—she was off limits.

I frowned at myself in the bathroom mirror and straightened my tie. Readjusted the knot. Smoothed my lapels. Checked my zipper. I ran a hand over my beard, dismayed that there seemed to be more gray in it than I'd noticed yesterday. Picking up my hairbrush, I smoothed the hair back above my ears. After setting it down again, I studied my reflection and noticed the two furrows between my brows. They made me look old and tense. I tried to relax my facial muscles, but the lines remained.

I turned off the light.

There. Much better.

Millie hadn't lied about keeping things professional. She was cool and businesslike as she reminded everyone where to go and what to do, dealt with everyone from musician to photographer to florist to officiant with courtesy and efficiency, and got the ceremony going on time.

We only made eye contact once, when greeting each other, but stayed a good five feet apart. I think she nodded in my direction. I shoved my hands in my pockets.

After waiting in a back room, I played my part dutifully, escorting Lori's mother to her seat and taking a chair opposite her in the front row. Mason and his groomsmen were already in place, and he smiled nervously at me and pushed his hair off his face with that familiar gesture. I returned the smile, hoping it was reassuring, although I knew all eyes were on me, wondering who I was and why I'd walked Mrs. Campion up the aisle but sat on the groom's side. The only other guests in the front row with me were a gay couple Mason was close to through his running club and his mentor teacher, plus her husband.

Lori's side was much fuller, and I was glad I'd shown up for Mason, even though I wasn't comfortable and already wondered how long I had to stay at the reception.

When the ceremony was over, I walked back down the aisle solo and went straight for the bar at the far end of the room. I was standing off to one side sipping a cocktail and trying to be invisible when Mason found me. "Hey, Zach."

"Hey, Mason." I shook his hand. "Congratulations."

"Thanks." He grinned. "We're taking some photos now. Would you please be in some of them?"

I swallowed the *no* that my mouth wanted to form and tossed back the rest of my drink. "Sure."

"Great. Follow me." He led the way back to the front of the room, where the wedding party and Lori's family had gathered in front of the massive windows. The arch had been removed, and the photographer's assistant was lining everyone up. She noticed Mason and smiled.

"You found him?"

"Yes." He gestured to me and said proudly, "This is my dad."

I felt woozy and off balance, but I stood where the woman directed me to stand, between Mason and his groomsmen. My gut was tight, imagining myself in these wedding photos—I felt like I was ruining them somehow. I didn't deserve this place of honor in his photos or in his life. But I stood there and tried to look at ease, if not happy. I hoped those damn lines between my brows weren't showing.

Mason asked for me to be in a photo with him and Lori and her parents, and I did that too. Then I posed for one with just him. All the while, I could feel everyone's inquisitive stares and hear their curious whispers. Anyone who'd been at the rehearsal dinner knew the story, so it was bound to be making the rounds by now.

I took a moment to mop my forehead with a handkerchief. Mason looked at me and said, "You okay?"

"Yeah. Just a little uncomfortable." I tucked the white cotton square back into my pocket. "Photo sessions aren't really my thing."

"I understand. We're done now. Thank you so much for this." And he threw his arms around me, just like he had at the restaurant two days earlier. "It means so much to me. And somehow I feel like my mom is watching, and it means a lot to her too."

That caught me off guard. "Huh?"

"After all, she sent you, didn't she?" Mason released me and smiled. "I decided the letter was always meant to be found. She had a plan for us all along. And I'll tell you another secret."

I wasn't sure I wanted to hear another secret. "Okay."

He leaned closer and whispered, "Lori is pregnant. You're going to be a grandpa. Isn't that great?"

My left eyelid twitched. Had he said grandpa? Fucking *grandpa?*

Lori approached and hooked her arm through Mason's. "Ready for some champagne, Mr. Holt?"

"I am, Mrs. Holt. But none for you," he added softly. They grinned at each other, and I continued feeling like I was having an out-of-body experience.

"Thanks for being here, Zach, and for the role you played." Lori smiled at me. "I know this can't be easy."

"It's fine. I'm fine." Stiffly, I leaned forward and kissed her cheek. Forced some nice words. "Congratulations."

Back at the bar, I ordered a double shot of whiskey and made a beeline for the room I'd been in before the ceremony began. I needed a moment alone to pull myself together.

What the fuck was happening to my life?

I was so agitated, I didn't realize I'd chosen the wrong door off the back hallway until I'd shut it behind me and found myself in an office.

Millie was standing at the window, and she spun around fast. "Oh!"

"Sorry," I said, backing out of the room. "My mistake."

"Zach, wait! Is everything okay?"

I exhaled. "I don't know. This whole fucking weekend is insane. I feel like I've entered some kind of alternate reality."

"I know. I feel it too."

"I just had to get away for a minute—I didn't realize this was your office."

"I snuck away for a moment as well." She saw my drink. "That looks good."

"I can share." I crossed to the window and offered her the glass. Our eyes locked as she lifted it to her lips and took a sip.

"Thanks," she said, taking one more drink before handing it back to me.

She wore navy tonight, and although there was nothing overtly sexy about her outfit—the dress hit her at the knees, had a high neck and sleeves that came to her elbows—somehow it still hugged her curves in a way that made it hard for me to take my eyes off her. My mind started to wander into dangerous territory, imagining what she'd looked like last night as she straddled her vibrator, pretending it was me.

I started to get hard.

"I saw you taking photos with the family," said Millie, breaking the silence. "That was nice."

I swallowed more whiskey. "Could you tell how miserable I was?"

"No. You looked perfect. You *look* perfect." Her cheeks grew pink as her eyes traveled over my clothing, face, hair.

"I should go," I said, because I knew if we remained in here alone, things would happen we'd both regret.

"And I should get back to work."

"Want the rest?" I held up what was left of my drink.

She hesitated, then shrugged. "Sure." She took it from me and tipped it up, while I drank in her throat and neck and pale, pretty hands. I could smell her perfume.

When the whiskey was gone, she lowered the glass and stared into it. Then slowly, she raised her eyes to mine.

In half a second, our bodies and mouths slammed together, the glass shattering at our feet. Our tongues were hot and demanding, our arms clinging tight. I moved her away from the window and backed her up to the edge of her desk, dragging my lips down her throat and her dress up her thighs.

Her hands groped at my crotch, and she moaned when she found me already hard. I fumbled with my belt. She tugged off her underwear. In no time at all I was positioning my cock between her legs.

"Wait," she said between loud, panting breaths. "Do you have a condom?"

"No. But I've had a vasectomy."

"You've had a vasectomy?" Shock was evident in her voice.

"Yeah." I spoke with my lips against her neck. "My ex-wife requested it."

"You had a *wife*?"

"Briefly." I picked up my head and looked her in the eye. "Do you want to talk about this now?"

She shook her head.

"Good." I eased inside her, and we both groaned. Her legs wrapped around me, and she grabbed the back of my neck as I drove inside her hard and fast and deep. I fucked her with a passion bordering on fury, as if I was punishing her for my rapidly unraveling life, as if I was trying to prove I was still in control by ravaging her body.

Needless to say, it was over fast. I realized too late I wasn't even sure she'd finished. Jesus, now I was *that* guy.

"I'm sorry, Millie." I rested my forehead on hers, my heart still pounding.

"For what?" Her chest rose and fell quickly.

"The adolescent speed. Being so rough."

"It's fine."

"Did you even . . ."

"This wasn't about that," she said quickly.

"This should always be about that." I reached between us, placing my thumb on her clit. "Let me—"

"No." She grabbed my wrist. "Really, Zach. It's okay. Listen, there's a roll of paper towels on the file cabinet in the corner. Could you maybe bring it to me? I don't have any other clothes here, and—"

"Of course." I carefully disengaged from her body as she tried to protect her clothing by sliding off the desk and keeping her dress at her hips. After I brought her the paper towel, I turned around to pull myself together and give her some privacy.

"There's a mirror on the inside of that closet door," she said.

"Thanks." I went over to the closet, opened the door, and checked my reflection in the mirror. My suit looked okay, and my tie was still knotted, but my face was sweaty and flushed. Beneath my clothing, my back was hot and damp. I smoothed my hair where Millie's fingers had tousled it.

She walked toward me, and I backed away from the mirror so she could use it.

I watched as she pulled out her ponytail and redid it, smoothed her dress over her curves, turned around and checked out her back by looking over her shoulder.

"You look perfect," I told her.

She smiled and faced the mirror again. "My face is so pink. I look like I just got off the treadmill."

I came up behind her and wrapped my arms around her waist. Kissed her temple and met her eyes in the mirror. "You're beautiful."

She placed her arms on top of mine and tipped her head back against my chest. "Thank you."

"There's probably no chance we can skip the rest of this wedding, is there?"

"Nope."

Exhaling, I dropped my arms. "I didn't think so. Should I go out first?"

"Sure." She fanned her face. "I need a minute anyway."

"Okay." Adjusting my cuffs, I walked to the door and grabbed the handle. Then I looked over at her. "Can we talk later?"

"Do you think that's a good idea?"

"Maybe not in person. On the phone?"

"Do you think *that's* a good idea?"

"Can we at least be trusted to text?"

"Honestly, Zach, I'm not sure. And we were supposed to delete each other's numbers last night."

"Did you do it?" I asked.

She hesitated, then shook her head.

"I didn't either."

Her cheeks grew even more pink. "We are not good people."

"I wouldn't go that far." I pulled the door open, listened for a moment, then glanced into the hall. All clear. I looked back at her. "I'm not going to stay too long, so why don't you text me when you get home? I'd like to talk."

"You're not leaving because of me, are you?" She looked adorably concerned. "Mason is so happy you're here, and I'd hate to—"

"It's not because of you," I said firmly.

She didn't appear fully convinced, but she nodded. "Okay."

I left the room and pulled the door shut behind me.

Eleven

Millie

A S SOON AS THE DOOR CLOSED, I LET OUT MY BREATH. Closed my eyes. Listened to the rapid fire of my pulse.

What the actual fuck was I *doing*?

I'd just banged the father of the groom—at a wedding I'd planned—on my *desk* while I was on the *job*!

While my *parents* were seated at the reception!

All that was bad enough without adding in the fact that the groom was my ex-boyfriend.

I opened my eyes and studied my face in the mirror, taking deep, slow breaths until my complexion returned to its normal color. "It's fine," I told the person in the mirror. "It's all good. You're going to go out there and act like you're not a harlot with no moral compass who can't keep her hands to herself or her panties in place."

I mashed my lips together to make sure the face didn't argue, then I gathered my courage and left the room.

Normally, I didn't stay until the very end of a wedding, but tonight I did. Maybe it was guilt, maybe it was that I wanted to make sure every single detail at the reception was taken care of for Mason and Lori, maybe it was that the sooner I was alone with my conscience, the sooner I'd have to think about what I'd done.

Zach and I didn't speak again after he left my office, and I was careful to avoid even looking in his direction for fear of establishing accidental eye contact and bursting into flames.

But peripherally, I noticed that he avoided the dance floor, stuck to the side of the room, and conversed with very few people. Around nine-thirty, I realized I hadn't seen him in a while and figured he'd gone back to his hotel.

I'd probably never see him again, and the thought left a pit in my stomach.

The wedding wrapped up around eleven, and the bride and groom were among the last to leave. Mason and Lori both hugged me, saying over and over again that this had been the best night of their lives and they could not have been happier.

"It was my dream wedding in every way," said Lori with misty eyes. "Thank you so much, Millie. I know this could have been awkward, but you never made it feel that way."

I smiled. "I'm glad."

"You're the best, Mills," said Mason, putting his arm around his wife. "In so many ways, this could never have happened without you."

"I'm happy for you guys," I said, and I meant it. "So you're off to Aruba, right?"

"Yes," said Lori. "We leave Monday."

"I'm jealous! Have a great time." For a moment, I fantasized what it would be like to take a trip like that with Zach. No one around who knew us, nothing to hide, just sun and sand and tropical drinks with little umbrellas floating on top. His hands rubbing sunscreen onto my skin. Crazy hot sex between cool hotel room sheets.

What was *wrong* with me?

When everyone was gone and the staff was tearing down

the room, I retreated to my office, ditched my heels, and fell back onto the small couch. Stretching out my legs, I stared at my toes, refusing to look at my desk, where Zach had taken me so roughly. It was intoxicating to be wanted that way by a man so self-possessed and restrained at all other times. I remembered how he referred to himself when telling me about the affair with Mason's mom. *I was a daredevil with a lot of anger issues and a short fuse.*

It seemed like the ghost of old Zach was making an appearance. And speaking of the old Zach . . . he'd been *married*? I recalled what he said about having a vasectomy—because his ex-wife had wanted him to. I wondered when that was, how long he'd been married—for God's sake, did he have other children? Was he even for sure divorced? What did I really know about him?

Someone knocked on my office door, and I pulled myself together. "Yes?" I called. "Come in."

It was Nelson, the manager, with a question about final count for a luncheon we were hosting tomorrow afternoon. I got up to find my phone and check my email, and Nelson noticed the broken glass.

"Shit. Accident? Or did you get mad and throw it?" he teased.

"Accident." I avoided his eyes. "The count for tomorrow is one-thirty-five."

"Got it. Want me to bring you a broom?"

"Nah. I know where it is." I shooed him out. "Go on and finish up so you can get home. It's been a long day."

"Thanks. Let me know when you're ready to leave and I'll walk you out."

I nodded, and he shut the door behind him.

Reclining on the couch, I glanced at my three new text messages. One was from Winnie, one was from Frannie, and one was from a number I recognized as Zach's.

My breath caught in my throat. Should I read it? I decided to defer the decision by dealing with the family messages first.

Winnie wanted to know how everything had gone today. Frannie complimented me on the wedding tonight and invited me to Sunday dinner tomorrow night. I thanked her, replied yes to dinner, and sent Win a note that it had gone fine and I'd call her tomorrow.

Then I stared at the final unread message with trepidation.

I didn't have to read it. I could just delete it. Then I could delete his number like I was supposed to last night. Forget about him and move on. Did I really need to know more about him or rehash what we'd done? What would be the point?

Nothing could ever come of this. We couldn't *date*, for God's sake. He was Mason's dad. I had no desire for a secret relationship—I was too old to sneak around. Nor did I want a long-distance relationship. And we were not on the same page in terms of life goals. I wanted a family. He'd had a vasectomy.

We were not meant to be. Every single sign pointed to no.

But . . . I could at least read the message, right? I didn't have to respond. I could read it and *then* delete his number.

I opened his text.

> **Hey. I know I said I'd wait for you to reach out, but I can't stop thinking about you. I feel like I owe you so many apologies. But as soon as I start typing them, I realize it's bullshit. Because I'm not sorry. Being with you feels so good, I can't regret a single thing we've done. In my head, I know it's wrong and can't go on. But I hope you know that every other part of me wishes it could. I'd still like to talk to you tonight, there are things I'd like to explain, but I understand if you'd rather not.**

I read it several times, completely torn. I knew what I *should* do. And yet, just like Zach couldn't bring himself to apologize, I couldn't make myself delete his message or his number. Not yet, anyway. I wanted a few answers first—at the very least, I wanted to know that he was the man I'd thought he was.

Instead of texting, I called him.

"Hello?" His voice made my belly quiver.

"Hi," I said hesitantly.

"Are you home now?"

"No, I'm still at work. But the guests are all gone."

"You're there alone? Is that safe?"

I smiled. Maybe he *was* the guy I thought he was. "It's fine."

"But you're not going to walk out to the parking lot alone, are you?"

"There are still employees here, and I will walk out with someone," I assured him.

"Okay. Good."

"You're back at the hotel?"

"Yeah. I just packed up. I'm leaving early in the morning."

"Oh, I thought you were here until Monday."

"I changed my ticket and got on a six a.m. flight tomorrow. I'll call Mason and explain that something came up at work."

"Did it?" I asked hesitantly.

"No. I just feel like I should leave."

"Because of what happened tonight with me?" I sank deeper into the couch, as if under the weight of additional guilt.

"It's not your fault," he said quickly. "I think it's a combination of intense attraction for you combined with a fear of—of . . . I don't know."

"I think you do."

He exhaled. "You're right. I do. I'm just ashamed to say it."

"Listen, I think you and I are past the point where we need to feel shame about anything we say to each other. As long as you don't tell me you're married."

"I am *definitely* not married."

"Good." I breathed a sigh of relief.

"Did you really think I might be?"

"Not in my gut. But there were some surprises tonight."

"There were," he agreed.

"So what are you scared of?" I played with the hem of my dress.

"Same thing every guy my age is scared of—getting older. That's why it's so stupid and fucking cliché."

"It's not stupid," I argued. "And it's not just guys. Women are afraid of getting older too. I'm afraid of it."

"But you're young."

"That's relative. I'm sure an eighty-two-year-old woman would consider thirty-two young. But I always assumed I'd be married with a family at this age. I'm not even close."

"You want kids?"

"Yes." I paused. "You mentioned you had a vasectomy."

"Yeah. About four years ago. Right before I got married."

"Was it a difficult decision?"

"Not really."

I chewed one side of my bottom lip. "It's none of my business, but . . ."

"You can ask."

"You never wanted kids?"

"No."

"Why not?"

"Just never did."

"And your ex-wife didn't want kids either?"

"She said she didn't, which was why she asked me to get the vasectomy. At the time, she was very focused on her career. But that changed, and we split up." He paused. "She's pregnant now."

I gasped. "Wait a minute. She made you get a vasectomy, then left you for someone who could father children?"

"She didn't make me," he said. "It was ultimately my choice. And she didn't leave me because of that—she left me because she fell in love with someone else, a producer at the TV station where she worked as a reporter."

"Oh. I'm sorry."

"Don't be. It was for the best. Honestly, I was not a good husband."

"I'm not sure I believe that."

He laughed, and the sound warmed me. "No?"

"No. I mean, I don't know you very well, but from what I *do* know, it's hard to imagine you were not a good husband— unless you were unfaithful or something."

"I was never unfaithful," he said firmly. "I was just gone a lot for work, and she's someone who needs constant attention. She got lonely."

"Oh."

"And I knew she would," he went on. "I think that's what bothers me the most—I knew the marriage was a bad idea. Any time I ignore those gut feelings, things go wrong. I should have trusted them."

"I trust my gut too," I told him. "In fact, that's why I called you."

"Oh yeah?"

"Yes. I was starting to doubt you were the man I thought you were, and I wanted to know for certain that I hadn't been wrong about you. My gut told me you were a good man, but I had some questions."

"I'm not sure if my answers are confirming your gut feeling about me or contradicting them."

"Confirming them," I said, a smile creeping onto my lips.

"I still believe you're a good man, Zach, even if you have some impulse control problems."

"When you're around, I do."

"Just me?"

"Just you." His voice grew deeper. "I haven't felt like this in a long time."

I hesitated, then confessed. "Me either."

"I wish we could—that we weren't—" He stopped. "I wish a lot of things right now. But since I'm a grown man who's seen enough in his lifetime to know wishes don't come true, I'll just say goodnight."

My heart sank. "That's probably best. But I wish things were different too. In fact, I almost wish you weren't such a good man."

Silence. "Millie."

"Yes?" I could barely breathe.

"I should go."

Closing my eyes, I swallowed hard. "Okay. Goodbye, Zach."

"Bye."

I ended the call, set my phone down, and rested my forehead on my fingertips. Took a few deep breaths.

Well, that was that.

Needing a distraction, I slipped my shoes back on and crossed the hall to the utility closet to get the broom and dustpan. Back in my office, I swept up the splintered glass, trying not to remember how good it had felt to give in to that overwhelming urge to grab him and kiss him and feel his hands on me. I carried the dustpan over to the trash and carefully dumped the broken pieces into the bin, refusing to look at the edge of my desk where he'd taken me so passionately and possessively—he'd apologized for the pace, but it thrilled me to imagine I was so irresistible to him, he couldn't hold back.

And I had no doubt that if I'd let him, he would not have left my office without making me come.

But the truth was, the more orgasms he gave me, the more generous he proved himself to be, the more alive and beautiful he made me feel, the more I wanted him. Taking his hand off me had been the right call.

I returned the broom and dustpan to the closet, swapped my heels for my boots, and put on my coat. After turning off the lights, I poked my head into the kitchen and asked Nelson if he had a minute to walk me out. He said of course, and accompanied me out to the parking lot. The rain had started up again, and I opened up my umbrella.

"I'm right over there," I said, gesturing at my SUV. "You get back inside before you're soaked to the bone."

"I'll make sure it starts," he said.

I gave him a grateful look, then hurried to my car, hopped in, and started the engine. After it revved up, I waved to Nelson and watched him hustle back toward the barn. Flipping on the wipers, I buckled my seatbelt and let the car warm up for a minute. The radio was off, so when my phone began to vibrate on the passenger seat, I heard it.

I picked it up and looked at the screen. The number was Zach's.

I paused for half a second, then answered. "Hello?"

"I changed my mind."

My heart skipped a beat. "About what?"

"I don't want to be a good man tonight. I just want to be the one in your bed."

I closed my eyes. Then I gave him my address.

I made it back to my house first, and I had just enough time to take a quick shower and throw on a robe before I heard his knock. I gave my throat a quick spritz of the perfume he liked, hurried down the stairs, and threw open the door.

"Hi," I said, breathless at the sight of him. He'd changed out of his suit and wore dark jeans beneath his black wool coat. His hair was tousled from the wind and rain. "Come in, it's cold out there."

He stepped over the threshold and I pushed the door shut behind him. As soon as I turned around, he caged me against the door, his arms bracketing my shoulders. He leaned in close enough for me to feel his breath on my lips. "I shouldn't be here."

I shook my head. "No."

"Tell me to leave."

"No."

"Then tell me you want me as badly as I want you."

"I could." I unbuttoned his coat and pushed it off his shoulders. "But I'd rather show you."

Twelve

Zach

"Y OU TOOK OFF YOUR SUIT." SHE POUTED, MAKING ME want to bite that plump bottom lip.

"You liked the suit?"

"I liked the idea of taking it off you." She pulled my shirt from my pants and ran her palm over my crotch, her lips curving into a smile when she found me hard.

"You thought about taking it off me?"

"Mmhm." She rose up on tiptoe, putting her lips at my ear, and whispered, "You know what a bad girl I am around you."

"What else did you think about?"

"This." She unbuttoned my shirt and opened it, spreading her hands on my chest over the tight white cotton of my T-shirt. "This," she went on, unbuckling my belt. "Thisssss," she sighed, dragging my zipper down slowly. "And this." She slipped her hand inside my boxer briefs, wrapping her fingers around my thickening erection.

"You didn't get enough of my cock tonight?"

She shook her head. "I can't ever seem to get enough of you."

I braced an arm against the door behind her. "What a co-incidence. That's exactly how I feel about you." Lowering my lips to hers, I stroked her tongue with mine. "I want the taste of your pussy in my mouth again."

"You can have it—eventually."

"Eventually?"

"Yes." She knelt and shoved my jeans down so that my cock sprung free. Then she took it in her hand and brought the tip toward her mouth, softly brushing her lips over the sensitive crown. "But there's something else I've been thinking about."

"Yeah?" I wished there was a fucking light switch nearby. I was dying to watch my cock slide into that mouth. There was a light on upstairs, spilling down into the hallway, but Millie was in my shadow.

"Yeah." She licked my shaft bottom to top, sweet and slow, as if she wanted to catch every drip. "I had no regrets when I left your hotel room that night," she said, her breath a caress on my skin, "but I did wish I had more time."

"To do what?" I wanted to hear her say the words.

She looked up at me, and even in shadow I saw the playful expression. "To get on my knees for you."

I groaned as she swept her tongue in a circle around the tip, making every muscle in my lower body tighten with anticipation.

"To take you in my mouth." She took the first couple inches of my dick between her lips and sucked, working her fist up and down my length in deliciously slow, firm strokes. "To make you come and taste it on my tongue."

"That's what you want?"

"That's what I want." She flicked her eyes to mine. "So give it to me."

Instinctively, I began to move—careful thrusts that wouldn't scare her or choke her, coaxing her to take me deeper. She moaned and obeyed my wordless command, sliding her mouth down my shaft and back up again. Her fingers moved to my balls, teasing, fondling, closing gently around them and tugging slightly and softly. Her other hand slid up my abdomen, her fingers wide and palm flat against my flexing muscles.

My free hand threaded into her hair, and my breath came faster. I was torn between giving in to the savage beast inside me that just wanted to fuck her mouth until I came and the man who wanted to take his time, savor this moment, commit every detail to memory.

I wanted her to know how fucking good this felt, but I couldn't even speak. I tried some words, but what came out was a garbled snarl that sounded more angry than anything else. But it must have turned her on, because she moaned and took me deeper, sliding a finger along the sensitive place between my balls and my ass that nearly made my legs give out. My vision went dark—or maybe I just closed my eyes, I couldn't fucking tell—and I leaned into my palm against the door, my hips driving faster, deeper, harder.

Millie's sounds went from slow, sweet sighs to quick, panicked pants, and I knew she had to be struggling to breathe. But she didn't let up—instead she gripped my ass with both hands and let me fuck her glorious mouth like I'd been fantasizing about doing since the moment I saw her. And if that made me a jerk, fuck it—I didn't care. The only thing that mattered was how deep she took me and my fist in her hair and the ache in my balls and the tension in my thighs and the *fuck, fuck, fuck, yes* of the climax surging through me and pouring into her. She took every drop and sat back on her heels, swallowing and breathing hard.

I loosened my grip in her hair. "Christ. That was—are you okay?"

She wiped her mouth with the back of her hand and looked up at me. "Yes."

"I thought maybe I choked you."

"It was a close call. But I asked for it, didn't I?"

I smiled. "I like that about you."

She reached for my hand, and I helped her up, noticing for the first time the hard tile floor in front of the door.

"Your poor knees. That had to hurt."

She shrugged, her smile coy. "Clearly, I didn't mind."

"I'll make it up to you," I said, hitching up my jeans. "Like a proper gentleman should."

"I know you will." She laughed and put her arms around me, pressing close. "I like that about you."

Up in her bedroom, she walked over to the nightstand and switched on a lamp. She wore a pink silk robe that set off the gorgeous creamy color of her skin and the gold in her hair. Her curves tantalized me, and I could see the pert tips of her breasts through the thin material, begging for my lips.

"So this is my room," she said, and she almost sounded a little nervous.

As hard as it was to take my eyes off her, I glanced around, curious. Her bed was neatly made, and my eyes lingered on the white wooden headboard. I pictured her hanging onto it, fucking her vibrator while I spoke in her ear. The vision sent a jolt of lust through me, and even though I'd just had an orgasm, my dick responded as though it was gearing up for another. I looked at the nightstand next to her—was that where she kept her toy? Would she let me use it on her tonight?

My eyes returned to her, but she was focused on removing pillows from the bed, tossing them onto the floor, which was covered by a thick white rug. She kept her back to me, and I got the feeling she was avoiding eye contact.

I moved around the bed and took her by the shoulders, turning her to face me. "Hey."

She stared at my chest. "Hey."

I tipped her chin up. "What's going on in there?"

Reluctantly she met my eyes. "I suddenly felt weird."

"Why?"

She pressed her lips together and glanced toward the windows. I followed her gaze, thinking maybe she was worried about neighbors watching, but the blinds were closed. "Because—because Mason."

Instantly, I understood. "He's been here."

She nodded. "It didn't occur to me when I invited you over."

"Me either."

"Not that our relationship was very sexual," she went on quickly. "It wasn't. We spent a lot of time together, but our chemistry was definitely more friendly than physical."

"It's okay." I brushed her hair back from her face. "If you want me to leave, I will."

"I don't want you to leave."

"Good."

"I guess I just wish things were different." Then she shook her head and laughed. "How many times are we going to say that?"

"Tell you what." I pressed my lips to her forehead. Her cheek. Her throat. I inhaled the scent of her perfume. "Let's *make* them different."

"What do you mean?" Her voice was already slightly breathless.

I untied her robe and it fell open. I slid it down her arms and kissed her shoulder. "I mean," I said, slipping one hand up the back of her neck and the other around her lower back, "let me do something to take your mind off anything or anyone else."

"What you're doing is a damn good start," she said, tilting her head while my lips devoured her throat and my hand moved over her ass, curved around her hip, slipped between her thighs.

"And it will be a damn good finish," I promised, easing her onto the bed. "But I plan on taking my time."

She propped herself up on her elbows and watched me undress with her bottom lip caught between her teeth. "I want to know about all your tattoos," she said, her eyes wandering over my skin.

"Later." I stood naked before her and pushed her knees apart. Then I glanced at the nightstand before letting my gaze travel up her thighs to her pussy to her breasts to her eyes. "You know what I want?"

"What?"

I reached over and hooked my fingers through the handle of the top drawer. Paused.

She gasped. "Bottom drawer."

I pulled it open and spotted the vibrator—and my business card. A stroke of my ego. Smiling like a cocky bastard, I reached in and pulled it out. "Look what I found."

Her cheeks flushed. "That's where I keep it."

"I like that." I took the card and dragged the width of it along her inner thigh, from her knee to the apex of her body. Then I did the same on her other leg, up her outer thigh this time, and over her hip, across her stomach—she shivered—between her breasts. I teased one nipple with it, then the other, licking my lips as I watched them grow hard. Leaning over her body, I took one perfect peak in my mouth, circling it with my tongue before sucking hungrily.

Her hands moved to my hair and stayed there while I feasted on her delectable curves. Abandoning the card, I eased a hand between her thighs again, finding her warm and wet. I slipped a finger inside her, then rubbed it over her clit in slow, deliberate strokes. Her legs hooked around the backs of my thighs, pulling me closer. "Zach," she pleaded. "I want you."

"I want you too." I straightened up and reached into the

drawer for her toy. "But first, I want to play a little." I turned it on and positioned the tip at her entrance. "Is this okay?"

Propped up on her elbows again, she looked adorably nervous, but she nodded.

"Have you ever let anyone do this to you before?"

"No," she whispered, her eyes wide.

"Good." I eased the humming toy in slowly, gratified by her throaty moan, the way her head fell back. My cock grew hard again as I moved the vibrator in and out of her pussy, a little deeper each time. When it was buried inside her, a smaller piece of it thrummed against her clit and she cried out with pleasure, her hips lifting off the bed.

"Fuck," I growled. "Fuck, you're so hot." My eyes grew even wider as her hands moved to her breasts and she plucked at her taut pink nipples. Need began building in me, greedy and demanding, ferocious and hot. I clenched my jaw and breathed hard as I enviously watched the toy disappear into her tight, wet heat again and again. As I listened to her moan when I held it in place and angled it just right. As I imagined the way her body was growing tighter around the vibrator, the way her pussy would throb against it.

It was more than I could take. I pulled the toy out and set it aside, climbing onto the mattress and pulling her on top of me so we lay lengthwise on the bed. Frustrated, she tried to roll onto her back again and take me with her, but I kept her where I wanted her, covering her mouth with mine, thrusting my tongue between her lips.

She gave up struggling and straddled me, grinding against my cock. I knew she was close, but I wanted something else. I slid down the mattress on my back, hooking my hands under her legs and easing her up toward the headboard.

She grabbed onto it, lifting her hips. "What are you doing?"

I grabbed her thighs, pulling her down again, so her pussy

hovered right above my mouth. "What does it feel like I'm doing?" I swept my tongue up her center.

"I'm not sure—"

"You don't want me to fuck you with my tongue?"

"I do, but I'm just worried that you won't—"

I lifted my head off the pillow and sucked her clit, making her moan with indecent delight. "I won't what?"

"I don't know," she said desperately. "Breathe?"

"Baby, you took my breath away the night we met." Playfully, I bit her inner thigh. "Now fucking sit on my face before I lose my mind."

With a sound that was half-laugh, half-moan, she carefully lowered herself over me again and began to rock her hips above my mouth. It was heaven on earth, if you asked me. Who needed oxygen when you had this kind of heat?

I eased two fingers inside her and instantly felt her muscles clench around them. I pressed deep, twisting my wrist to find exactly the right angle and pressure, never letting up with my mouth. I knew I'd found the spot when her insides clamped even tighter, she cried my name and stopped moving except for the flutter of her clit against my tongue and the rhythmic spasms of her core on my fingers. The moment the tremors dissipated, I flipped her onto her back and thrust inside her, my cock aching for another release.

She was hot and soaking wet, and I drove my hips above hers with a hard, pounding motion while she grabbed my ass and bucked up beneath me. I came fast, and so did she, my body going plank stiff above hers as we shared the simultaneous, pulsing joy of release.

"Oh my God," she whispered. "Oh. My. God."

"Sorry." I knew my weight must be crushing her and tried to lift my chest, but she pulled me to her again.

"Don't go." She buried her face in my neck and kissed my throat. "Don't go yet."

"I'm not going anywhere." I adjusted our position, rolling to my side and taking her with me. "There. Now I won't smother you."

She kept one leg slung over my hip, and curled one arm beneath her head. Her other hand slid over my shoulder. "Smothered by the Navy SEAL. I'm pretty sure I read that book. It was hot."

I laughed, propping my head in my hand. "You read books about Navy SEALs?"

"I read all kinds of books. But I admit, I have a thing for military heroes."

"Oh yeah? Was your dad in the military or something?"

She frowned at me. "You just ruined it."

I grinned. "Navy?"

"Marines."

I nodded slowly. "Hmph. I guess they're okay."

She laughed. "You'd like him."

"I doubt he'd like me."

"Why not?"

"How old is your dad?"

"Fifty-six."

Fuck. Her dad was less than ten years older than I was. And she was closer to *my son's* age than mine. "There you go."

"Listen, my stepmom is ten years younger than my dad, so he would not have room to judge us."

"There's more than just our age difference to judge," I pointed out.

She sighed, her smile disappearing. "True."

I tipped up her chin. "I didn't mean to make you feel bad."

"I think if I didn't feel bad, something would be wrong with me. Don't *you* feel bad?"

"Let's talk about something else," I said.

"Okay." She focused her attention on my tattoos. "Can I ask about them now?"

"Sure."

"Which one did you get first?"

"The one on my chest with the skull."

Her hand moved over it, like she was smoothing its rough edges.

"And which one is your most recent?"

"The bone frog."

She traced the bones inked on my shoulder with one fingertip. "What does it mean?"

"It's a way to honor a SEAL lost in the line of duty."

"Oh," she said softly. "A friend?"

"Yes. Someone on my team. A mission didn't go as planned."

"I'm sorry." Her eyes met mine. "Was it hard? The things you did?"

"I guess so. But we were trained well."

"Did you like it?"

"Yeah."

She ran her fingertips down my arm, following them with her eyes. "What made you leave?"

"I was wounded on that same mission. Took some machine gun fire to my right arm." I rotated my shoulder so she could see the scar, although it was camouflaged pretty well by tattoos.

She gasped and hugged my right forearm to her chest, as if it had just happened.

"It's fine. I had a few surgeries and it healed better than expected. I lost some range of motion, that's all. It could have been a lot worse."

She kissed my knuckles. "I'm glad you're okay."

"Thanks."

"So which tattoo is your favorite?" she asked.

I thought for a moment, then decided to be honest, even if it meant opening a wound. "This one." I rolled to my back so she could see the angel wings on my left ribcage and the words *little sister* beneath them.

She studied the ink for a moment, then touched it gingerly. "You have a little sister?"

"I did," I said quietly. "We lost her when she was three."

"Oh, Zach. I'm so sorry." Her voice caught. "What happened?"

"She drowned in a lake near our house. It was an accident."

"How old were you?"

"Seven."

"God, that's so tragic. It must have been terrible for you. And for your parents."

"It was."

She kissed my chest. "I'm sorry. I didn't mean to get into sad things. And I know you don't like talking about yourself."

"It's okay." I put a hand behind my head and changed the subject. "Have you ever wanted a tattoo?"

"I've thought about it. I just never made up my mind about what I wanted. Now it's probably too late."

"What makes you say that?"

"I don't know. I'm kind of old to get my first tattoo, aren't I?"

"Not at all. In fact, I think the older you are, the more likely you are to choose something meaningful. And you only live once, you know?"

"That's true. My sisters and I sometimes talk about getting matching tattoos. I think when the twins are old enough, we'll probably do it."

"The twins?"

"I'm the oldest of five sisters. The two youngest are twins."

"*Five sisters*?"

"Yes." She giggled. "There are three MacAllister girls from our dad's first marriage. Me—I'm the oldest. Felicity—she's twenty-eight and runs a catering company, and she just got married this past summer. And Winnie—she's twenty-four, and she's in charge of events at Abelard Vineyards, which isn't far from here. And her boyfriend Dex was a SEAL."

"I like him already."

She smiled. "The final two MacAllister sisters are Audrey and Emmeline. My dad remarried when I was twelve, so they're a little younger. Seniors in high school."

"I cannot imagine being the father of teenage daughters, let alone five of them." I shook my head. "That's insane."

"He's a good dad. And Frannie, my stepmom, is amazing. My biological mom . . . not so much."

"Do you have a relationship with her?"

Millie was silent for a moment. "That's complicated."

"You don't have to talk about it. I was just curious."

"I don't mind, really. My real mom's name is Carla, and she left my dad when I was ten. I mean, she left all of us—my sisters and me too."

"Fuck. Really?"

"Yeah. Just . . . changed her mind about having a family and left. She blamed my dad, of course. Said he didn't love her enough. But it was bullshit—I knew it even then."

"I was about that age when my dad left too. But he left my mom for someone else."

"There might have been someone else for my mother, I'm not sure. She moved back down to Georgia and in with her parents, and she never came back."

"Not even to visit?"

"Not really. She'd make a lot of promises about visits, but rarely followed through. I learned pretty fast not to believe anything she said." Millie was silent a moment. "She was hard on me."

"What do you mean?"

"She used to get on me about my weight all the time. I was a serious dancer growing up, and she'd always point out how thin ballerinas were. She obsessed over her own size too. She was just very focused on appearances, and she had a way of making me feel bad about mine."

"That's shitty."

"I used to get these horrible stomachaches whenever she would visit, and then I started getting them whenever she tried to contact me. After a while, I started wishing she'd just stay out of my life." She sighed. "But then I'd feel so guilty. She's my mom, and you're supposed to love your mom."

"Parents can really fuck you up." *Like what I'm doing right this second*, I thought. If my son knew what I was doing, he'd lose all respect for me. He'd think I was a liar and a dick.

"Yeah, but she taught me some valuable lessons too," said Millie.

"Like what?"

"I have a pretty good bullshit detector, honed by years of listening to her lies. I don't automatically trust that everything anyone tells me is true. And I've learned not to look outside myself for validation—you can't base your self-worth on someone else's feelings," she said vehemently.

I nodded slowly. "So you don't trust easily?"

"Not really." She raised her eyes from my chest. Her lips curved into a shy smile. "Although I suppose I trusted you pretty easily, going up to your hotel room like that."

"That's right. I could have had nefarious intentions. In fact, I'm pretty sure I did." I rolled on top of her and pinned her wrists to the mattress. "And still do."

She laughed. "Clearly, I did not mind."

I kissed her deeply, slowly, as our bodies came alive again. My cock started to swell, and I groaned. "I have to go."

"Right now?"

I looked down at her beautiful face, felt her warm, soft skin against mine, caught the lingering scent of her perfume. My heart was ballooning in my chest and beating much too loud. Too fast. "Yes," I told her. "My flight leaves at six. I need to leave for the airport in just a couple hours."

"You could change your flight," she said softly. "Leave later in the day?"

"What good would that do? Even if I stayed for a week— or two weeks—what are we going to do, sneak around in the dark like teenagers breaking curfew? Hiding from people we care about? Hoping no one sees us and starts to talk?"

"I know," she said again, her eyes closing. "I know everything you're saying is true. I know it isn't right to hide what we're doing, and I know we can't see each other again once you leave. This could never work—on so many levels. It's just . . . wrong." But even as she spoke the words, she twined her legs around mine, digging her heels into the backs of my thighs, pulling me closer.

"So wrong," I said as I set a rhythm over her, fully hard once again.

"But it just feels so right," she whispered. Her eyes opened, locking with mine. "Stay, Zach. Stay a while longer. Just because it feels so good."

"God, you're tempting," I growled. "If you were anyone else, I'd have been gone already."

"Give me tonight," she whispered. "We can have tonight and make it last."

I should have said no. I should have gotten out of her bed, put my clothes on, kissed her cheek, and said goodbye. That would have been the right thing to do, and doing the right thing mattered to me.

But in that moment, she mattered more.

Thirteen

Millie

I WOKE UP WITH HIS ARM AROUND ME, MY BODY TUCKED INSIDE the curve of his chest and hips and legs.

For five full minutes, I didn't move—I didn't shift, I didn't stretch, I didn't blink. I barely allowed myself to breathe, afraid of breaking the spell.

But I did smile. I couldn't help it.

Last night had been incredible. I'd never had so much fun with anyone. I'd never trusted anyone so deeply. I'd never been with anyone as generous as he was demanding, as tender as he was strong, as playful as he was aggressive. I'd never let anyone do the things to me Zach did, and I'd never wanted to please someone the way I wanted to please him. From the blowjob at the front door to the vibrator game to sitting on his face—all of it was brand new. With anyone else, I'd have been scared and self-conscious. But Zach had a way of putting me at ease, making me feel confident and sexy, even when he made it seem like I had no choice but to do what he said.

Was it his tone of voice? His maturity? His age? I'd grown up the oldest sister, so setting the tone and being in charge came easily to me. It was a role I was used to playing in relationships too, and because I tended to date guys my sisters called "lost puppies," the dynamic never varied. I'd grown comfortable with it. I felt safe with it. Having the upper hand—physically and emotionally—meant I was rarely insecure or worried about being abandoned.

When someone needed you more than you needed them, it gave you power.

With Zach, I didn't feel that sense of power, but I also didn't feel like I needed it. This wasn't a relationship. It couldn't be.

It was a fling.

Secret. Forbidden. A little dangerous. *So* unlike me.

Maybe that was the key—I was finally off the hamster wheel, like Winnie said. Granted, jumping off blind the way that I did came with an unexpected hitch (I'd jumped right into the arms of my ex's dad), but not on purpose. And was it so wrong to let myself have this *one thing* for fun? As long as no one got hurt?

Zach stirred behind me, his breathing becoming louder and more irregular. Light was filtering through my bedroom blinds, hazy and soft.

"What time is it?" he asked sleepily.

"I'm not sure, but I think you missed your flight."

His arm tightened around me. "Oops."

I laughed and snuggled back against him. "What will you do?"

"Guess I'll have to rebook."

"Will you still leave today?"

He exhaled. "I don't know. Originally, I told Mason I was available for some kind of wedding brunch. What about you? Are you working?"

"Nope. I have today off. What time is the brunch?"

"Eleven, I think. What time is it now?"

I reached for my phone and checked the time. "It's just

before eight." Then I saw Mason's name pop up on the screen. "Oh my God."

"What?"

I looked back at him over my shoulder. "I just got a text from Mason. I'm scared to read it."

Zach fell onto his back and closed his eyes.

"Maybe it's nothing." I opened it up and read it out loud. "Hey Millie, just wanted to thank you again for last night. Everything was perfect. Lori and I also wanted to invite you to brunch this morning if you're not busy. It's at eleven at Marmalade, just immediate family and a few close friends. We'd really like to treat you for going above and beyond for us—plus we have a special announcement. Hope you can make it." I looked at Zach, but his eyes were still closed. "I'll tell him I can't come."

He exhaled and brought his hands behind his head. "You can go if you want."

"No, I don't belong there." I quickly replied to Mason, thanking him for the invitation but saying I was meeting my sisters for breakfast at our mom's bakery. "Done." I set my phone back on the charger and snuggled close to Zach again. "That's just awkwardness we don't need."

"No." He put an arm around me.

"I wonder what their special announcement is."

Zach exhaled heavily. "I think I know."

"You do? Can you say? Or is it a secret?"

He didn't say anything right away. And then, "Lori is pregnant."

"Oh! Well, that's nice. Mason has always wanted a family."

"Yeah."

Then it hit me. I gasped and sat up, looking down at him. "Holy shit. You'll be a—"

"Don't say it." He clapped a hand over my mouth and shook his head. "Just don't say it."

I pushed his hand down and tried to suppress a grin. "When did you find out?"

"Last night at the reception. Right before I found you in the office."

"Oh." I recalled his addled mental state when he'd wandered in, whiskey in his hand. "Guess that explains why you seemed so distraught. I thought it was just the photos."

"I'm sorry I wasn't honest with you. Mason had just told me, and I was still processing it. It's not that I didn't trust you. I was just . . . shocked. And embarrassed, I guess."

"Embarrassed?"

"Yeah." He laughed bitterly. "I don't want to be a—you know. I'm not ready. I wasn't even ready to hear I had a son, let alone a . . ." His brow furrowed. "I don't like feeling like I'm not in control, and it just seems like all these unpredictable, uncontrollable things are piling up."

"I get it. You've been hit with a lot all at once." I tried to find a bright side as I studied him lying there naked in my bed, but I got distracted by his body. The muscles, the ink, the chiseled jaw. He was so damn hot. Suddenly I started to laugh.

He looked over at me, his scowl deepening. "What's so funny?"

"I'm sorry," I said, collapsing into giggles. "But it's just so ridiculous. You do not look like any grandpa I've ever known."

He rocketed off the mattress and tipped me onto my back, my head at the foot of the bed. "Hey!" he barked. "I told you not to say that word."

"Uh oh. Are you going to punish me?"

His dark eyes narrowed. "I think you know the answer to that."

An hour later, we said goodbye at my front door.

He squeezed my hand. "I had a really good time last night. I know it wasn't right, but I'd do it all over again."

"Me too." I hesitated. "I'm trying not to ask if you can come back later tonight."

"I need to look at flights and see when I can rebook, but I'll let you know. Don't worry, I won't leave without saying goodbye."

"You don't owe me anything," I said.

He smiled. "Enjoy your day off. I'll talk to you later." After one more quick kiss, he carefully looked up and down the street before hurrying out to his car.

I watched him drive off and breathed a sigh of relief when he made it out of sight without anyone coming out to grab their Sunday paper or walk their dog. Granted, I was a grown woman who was free to have a man sleep over, and it's not like my neighbors would know who Zach was, but still . . . the guilt was there.

Shutting the door behind him, I went into the kitchen to make coffee, wincing a little at my sore muscles. As I waited for the cup to fill, I rubbed my butt, which still stung from this morning's spanking.

Molasses and Muffin sat on the kitchen floor, eyeballing me with their critical-cat faces.

"Don't judge me," I told them. "I never misbehave like that, and you know it. Just let me have this."

Anxious for a distraction, I decided I'd spend my day doing some research about plus-sized bridal boutiques in the Midwest. When the coffee was ready, I looked at my hard wooden kitchen chairs and thought better of it. Instead, I grabbed my shoulder bag, which held my laptop and new file folders, and went into the living room. Gingerly lowering myself onto the plush velvet sofa, I managed to find a comfortable position and settled in.

My third cup of coffee had long grown cold when I

realized I'd been working for over three hours. I sat up straighter and stretched before picking up my phone. My mom had texted reminding me about dinner this evening, and I also had a message from Winnie's boyfriend, Dex.

> **Hey Millie. Could you call me? I have a question about Winnie. I'm at the station today so anytime works.**

I called him back right away.

"Hello?"

"Hey, it's Millie. How's it going?"

"Good. Thanks for calling me."

"Sure. Is this an okay time? I'm not preventing you from fighting a fire, am I?"

He laughed. "No fires yet today. Slow morning."

"What can I do for you?"

"Uh, first, can you keep a secret?"

I smiled. "Yes. Your girlfriend is the only MacAllister sister who can't."

"Right. She definitely doesn't know about this. But it involves her."

My pulse picked up. "Oh?"

"I'm going to ask her to marry me this Christmas."

"Oh my goodness! Oh Dex, that's wonderful! I'm so happy for you!" My throat grew tight, and my eyes blurred with tears.

"Thanks. So listen, I had the girls help me pick out some possible rings, but I could really use a grown-up's opinion, preferably someone who knows Winnie like you do."

"I'd be happy to help," I said, even more excited. "What works best?"

"Would it be possible for you to meet me at the jeweler's tomorrow? It's my day off, so any time works."

"Of course. I'm off on Mondays too, so why don't we say eleven? Just text me the name of the store and I'll be there."

"Great. Thanks, Millie. And if Felicity wants to come too, that's okay with me. I just didn't have her number."

"I'll let her know, and don't worry—she can keep a secret too."

"I appreciate it. It's hard enough to make sure the girls don't let it slip."

I smiled. "They must be so excited."

"They are. They've been begging me to marry Winnie since practically the day we moved in next door to her."

"That was quite a day," I teased, recalling the story Winnie had told later that evening—the steam from her shower had set off the smoke detector in her bedroom. She was standing on a suitcase in her birthday suit attempting to disconnect it when Dex burst in, worried that there was an actual emergency, his daughters right behind him. "I'm sure they'll never forget it."

"I won't either." He laughed. "I'll see you tomorrow."

"Bye, Dex." I ended the call and leaned back, the smile still lingering on my lips. Winnie was going to be so happy. I wondered when they'd get married, if Win would choose Cloverleigh Farms where she'd grown up, or Abelard Vineyards where she worked, or somewhere totally different.

I glanced at my laptop on the coffee table, still open to the website of a shop in Maryland that boasted sample sizes up to 32W and gowns to fit almost any budget. Testimonials from happy brides were moving tributes to the owner and staff, who made full-figured women feel welcome and beautiful, women who'd been "laughed at" in other salons when they requested a size 16 dress.

And those stories were not unique—I came across many such personal narratives, reviews and blog posts and quotes full of praise for shops that treated plus-sized brides like queens after they'd been disappointed and stressed out by traditional salons that made them feel unwelcome and unworthy.

There were photos of gorgeous, curvy brides on their wedding days glowing with happiness, stunning in their gowns. Brides of all skin colors and body types. Brides with pink hair, blue hair, rainbow hair. Brides wearing their glasses, showing off their tattoos, lifting their dresses to reveal sneakers or cowboy boots or bare feet on the sand. Brides marrying other brides, also dressed in beautiful gowns—or sometimes dressed in suits. Grooms who gazed at the women they'd just married with looks of pure joy and thrilling disbelief, as if they couldn't believe their good fortune.

More than once, I'd teared up scanning the pictures and reading about their experiences, which often included details about how far they'd traveled just to have the kind of luxurious, personalized service they'd dreamed of since they were small.

There was only one such shop in Michigan, and it was down near Detroit. I'd left a voicemail message for the owner, Alison, explaining who I was and asking if I might chat with her about her business.

More and more, I was feeling in my gut that a career change was the right thing to do.

Closing my laptop, I went upstairs and took a shower, loath to wash away the night before, but reluctant to show up at my parents' house for Sunday dinner with the scent of sex on my skin. It was going to be hard enough hiding the truth from my sisters—I didn't often keep secrets from them.

But this felt like one I might tuck away for myself.

When I arrived at my parents' house, Winnie, Felicity and Hutton were already there. After offering to help Frannie and

Felicity in the kitchen and being shooed away, I poured a glass of wine and went into the family room, where my dad and Hutton sat on the couch discussing the hockey game on TV, the twins were lying on the floor looking at their phones, and Winnie was curled up in an easy chair, glancing at a photo album.

"What's that?" I asked, taking a seat on the ottoman in front of her.

"Dad and Frannie's wedding pictures," she said wistfully, turning another page.

I sipped my wine to hide my smile. "Seems like yesterday."

"It does." Then she giggled. "Those stupid shoes hurt so bad, remember?"

"Yes." I leaned over to peek at the photos and saw Winnie, Felicity and me grinning at the camera in our matching pink dresses and gold sequined shoes. "But we insisted on them."

"They were fancy!" Winnie laughed and flipped the page. "We wanted to be fancy. Oh, look at them."

We studied the photo of our dad and Frannie, dressed in their wedding day attire, standing on the edge of the vineyard at Cloverleigh Farms. They were chest to chest, but Frannie was smiling at the camera and our dad was looking down at her, an expression of wonder and love and protectiveness on his face. Gooseflesh blanketed my arms. "That was such a happy day."

"I hope my wedding is as beautiful as theirs," said Winnie with a sigh.

"I'm sure it will be." Hoping I sounded casual, I asked, "Think you'll get married at Cloverleigh Farms?"

"Honestly, I don't even care where it takes place. I just want it to be Dex at the end of the aisle." She actually looked concerned that it might not play out that way.

I took another sip of wine. "Why wouldn't it be? I thought everything was going well."

"It is," she said. "But we used to talk about the future more than we have been lately. It was more of an abstract thing, though . . . maybe the literal thing, the actually getting married, is too scary."

"I don't think you need to worry, Win," I said, being careful not to give anything away. "Everyone can see the way he looks at you."

"How does he look at me?"

"Like that," I said, pointing to the photo of our dad and Frannie. "Exactly like that."

Winnie's face lit up, and I felt the slightest twinge of envy. Would anyone ever look at me that way? I took another swallow of my wine.

"So everything went well last night?" Winnie asked, closing the book and hugging it to her chest.

"Yes," I said, dropping my eyes into my wine glass.

"Was Zach there?"

"Um, yeah. He was there." Another hurried sip.

Winnie cocked her head. "And?"

"And what?"

"Did you talk to him?"

I could feel my face heat up. "A little. Not much."

"Well, was it—" She stopped and gasped. "Oh my God."

"What?" I looked at her and watched her eyes light up with mischief, her jaw fall open.

"You guys did it again," she whispered.

My cheeks were on fire. "We did not."

"You did too!" she practically yelled, causing Audrey to look over at us.

"Come here." Setting my wine glass aside, I stood up and gestured for her to follow me. Leaving the photo album on the chair, she trailed me up the stairs to the second-floor landing. Peeking around her to make sure we hadn't been followed, I grabbed her sleeve and pulled her into my old bedroom, which was now the guest room. I shut the door and spun around to face her.

She was grinning ear to ear.

"Shhhhhh!" I admonished, as if she'd spoken.

"I didn't say anything!"

"You were thinking it."

"Am I wrong? Did you and Zach not hook up last night?"

I hesitated too long.

"*You so did*," she said, clapping her hands with each word. "I can tell just by looking at you. So how was it? As good as the first time?"

My mouth opened to argue with her, but I gave up. "It was even better."

She squealed, covering her mouth with her hands.

"Be quiet!" I glanced at the closed door. "I don't want anyone to hear you."

But just then, the door opened, and Felicity appeared. "What are you guys doing up here? Dinner is ready."

"Millie slept with her ex's dad again," Winnie said breathlessly.

"Winnie!" I glared at her. "This is why I didn't want anyone to know!"

"What, it's not like you were going to keep it from us," she pointed out. "You tell us everything."

"You *can't* tell anyone else," I told her. "I mean it."

She zipped her lips.

"So it happened?" Felicity leaned back against the door and blinked at me.

"Yes. Last night."

"After the wedding?"

"Yes. And . . ." I hesitated to reveal more, but I was dying to confess.

"And what?" Winnie squeaked.

"And during."

"During!" both my sisters shouted at once.

"I need more." Winnie made *come here* motions with both hands. "Give me everything."

"I was taking a break in my office during the reception, and he wandered in there by mistake—he needed a break too. It was a lot for him, being introduced as the father of the groom all night. He was overwhelmed."

"Does he know about the baby?" Felicity asked.

Winnie stared at her. "What baby?"

"Lori is pregnant," Felicity said. "I saw it on social media this afternoon."

I nodded. "Yes. He knows. And he's feeling sensitive about it."

"I don't blame him." Winnie started to laugh. "He's going to be a—"

"Don't say it," I warned her, raising one finger.

"But Mills, it's too good," she said, the giggle fit overtaking her. "You're banging a—"

"*Don't say it!*" I yelled, putting my hand over her mouth like Zach had done to me this morning.

Swatting my arm away, Winnie flopped back onto the bed and kicked her feet with glee, her eyes watering. "Why? Because you guys never made any jokes about me having a crush on *Dad* when you found out Dex was a single father who'd been in the military?"

"Okay, listen." Felicity put her palms in the air. "It doesn't really make any difference whether he's a—a—" She glanced at me. "A certain age. It's more the issue of who he is."

"I know that. Believe me. We both know it." I sank down on the bed beside Winnie. "And we feel terrible."

Winnie, sobering up, put an arm around me. "I'm sorry for laughing. But we don't get to choose who we fall for, and—"

145

I jumped off the bed. "I didn't fall. No one fell. There's no falling."

My sisters glanced at each other and then at me. "Okay," said Felicity, her tone cool and easy. "That's good."

"We're just having fun," I clarified. "That's all."

"So it's ongoing?" Winnie asked.

I twisted my hands together. "I don't know. When he left this morning, he—"

"He slept over?" Her voice rose dramatically.

"Well, yes." I shifted my weight from one foot to the other. "We thought we only had the one night, because he had an early flight back to San Diego, but he missed it. He was going to brunch with Mason and Lori, that's all I really know. I haven't heard from him since he left my house around nine."

"Someone could have seen him," Winnie said seriously.

"I know." I looked back and forth between my sisters. "Look, we have to go downstairs to dinner, but first you *have* to promise me you won't let anything slip about this—ever."

"Promise," said Winnie.

"Promise," Felicity echoed.

I relaxed slightly. "Okay. Let's go."

At dinner, Frannie asked if I'd given any more thought to opening a bridal salon.

"I have, actually," I said, taking another bite of Felicity's roasted acorn squash with rosemary and garlic. "In fact, I spent the entire day today doing research."

"Like a wedding dress shop?" asked Emmeline.

"Yes, one that caters to plus-sized women," I said. "It can be really difficult and not fun at all to find a dream gown in larger sizes. I hear it from brides all the time."

"It's the same with homecoming and prom dresses," said

Audrey. "I can never find anything to fit me on top, and if I do, it's too big on the bottom. It's like they don't make dresses for people with boobs."

"Audrey." Frannie gave her a stern look. "We have company."

"I'm just saying, it's a good idea," Audrey pushed back. "I bet it would be a really popular place."

"What about your job at Cloverleigh Farms?" asked Emmeline. "Would you keep it?"

"No, I wouldn't be able to do both," I said. "And that's one huge reservation I have."

"Maybe Winnie could take over for you at Cloverleigh," suggested Frannie.

"I wouldn't ask her to leave Abelard," I said quickly.

"Well, hang on." Winnie picked up her wine glass. "I do love working at Abelard, but I wouldn't necessarily turn down the opportunity to take over events at Cloverleigh Farms."

"Would you be able to leave on good terms?" our dad asked. Abelard Vineyards was owned by Winnie's best friend Ellie's family. Ellie worked there too, as manager of their tasting room, although she'd just had a baby, so she was taking some time off.

"Definitely," said Winnie. "With Ellie out, her mom has been working a lot more—she was the original event planner there, remember, and she only left that job because they were going to spend time in France. But they're back full-time now that the baby is here. I could easily talk to her if you decide to leave, Mills."

"I'll keep you posted," I said. "Right now, I'm really just gathering intel. I *think* the demand is there, and there's no other shop like it within four hours in any direction, but it's not a decision I'd take lightly. I'd have to get a loan, find a space, remodel, contact designers . . . it's a lot."

"You know you'd have help," said my dad. "I know plenty

of people at the bank that could help you secure a loan as long as you had a solid business plan."

"Oh, I would." I set down my fork, suddenly too excited to eat. "I'm going to work on that."

"I'd be glad to help you out with a loan, Millie," said Hutton.

I looked over at my handsome brother-in-law. He was so unassuming and quiet, it was easy to forget he was a billionaire—he'd made a fortune thanks to some sort of mathematical algorithm he'd created for a cryptocurrency exchange. "You would?"

"Sure. I think you're on to something. A good business idea starts with a solution to a problem—you've identified a problem, a solution, and a hole in the geographical market. I could help you with the business plan too."

I beamed at him. "Thank you, Hutton!"

"I could help you look for a space," offered Frannie. "And I know a commercial real estate agent I could put you in touch with."

"That would be awesome," I said. "I've already started a Pinterest board with inspirational photos."

"And if we can't do the renovations ourselves, we can find good people to do it." My dad picked up his beer. "That's easy."

I looked around at my family, grateful for the millionth time. "Thanks, everyone. I'll keep you posted."

After dinner, Winnie was sitting with the twins and our parents in the family room while Felicity and I finished up the dishes. "Hey, I'm glad it's just the two of us," I said quietly, handing her a serving bowl I'd just washed.

"What's up?"

I glanced into the family room to make sure no one could hear. "Dex is going to propose at Christmas."

"Shut *up!*" she stage whispered, her eyes popping. "Are you serious?"

"Yeah. I talked to him today. He wants my opinion on the ring before he buys it. We're meeting at the jeweler's tomorrow at eleven. You're invited too."

"Shoot—I can't tomorrow," she said. "I'm catering a lunch. But call me afterward and tell me everything!"

"Okay." I handed her a small platter to dry.

"Did he say where he's doing it?" she asked. "Maybe he'll do it at the Cloverleigh Farms Christmas Eve party!"

I frowned. "I don't think Dex is the public proposal type."

"Yeah. Maybe you're right." She sighed. "Win is gonna be so happy."

"She is," I agreed, handing her another serving bowl.

Felicity was quiet as she dried it. "It will happen for you too, Mills."

"I know."

"Like when you least expect it."

"That would be nice."

"I love your new business idea," she said a minute later. "I think that's the kind of thing you have to do. Focus your attention on some other part of your life, and then bam! Love will just slam right into you."

I laughed. "I don't need anything to slam into me. It would just be nice to meet someone who wants the same things I do. He doesn't have to be perfect. He just has to, you know, need someone like me in his life."

Felicity tipped her head onto my shoulder. "Everyone needs someone like you in their life."

"At least until they meet *the one*," I muttered.

"What do you mean?"

"Mason is the third boyfriend of mine in a row to marry the woman he dated right after we broke up."

"So?"

"So you don't think it means there's something wrong with me?"

"Millie, don't be ridiculous. There is nothing wrong with you because three of your exes went on to meet their wives after dating you." She turned to face me with a barely suppressed grin. "There's something wrong with you because you're fucking one of their dads."

I gasped. And promptly soaked her with the kitchen faucet sprayer.

Fourteen

Zach

I T WAS CLOSE TO FIVE BY THE TIME I FINALLY GOT BACK TO MY hotel room.

At the foot of the bed was my suitcase, which I'd packed last night and opened back up this morning, pulling out something to wear to brunch. I'd rebooked my six a.m. flight home for tomorrow, which left me with an entire evening to fight the urge to see Millie.

Dropping back onto the bed, I tossed an arm over my eyes. All through brunch, I'd had to sit across from my son, who'd looked at me with an esteem I didn't deserve. He was curious and inquisitive, as always, especially about my time in the Navy. After boasting to the table about my being a SEAL, he asked all kinds of questions about what the training was like, whether Hell Week was really as bad as people said, what kinds of missions I'd been on, how I'd been wounded. Everyone there had been attentive and interested, but two straight hours of talking about myself had exhausted me.

It was the exact kind of situation I hated—being the center of attention—but I felt so guilty every time I looked into Mason's guileless eyes that I couldn't bring myself to shut down his questions or deflect to another topic.

So as much as I was dreading their "special announce-ment" and the reminder of what that meant for me, I found myself glad when Mason put his arm around his wife and told the table they were expecting a baby next spring. At that point, the table erupted into happy tears and well wishes. People got up to hug. Someone thumped my back and congratulated me. I think I grunted a thanks.

After brunch, Mason and Lori invited me to see their house. I followed them back to a two-story brick colonial on a picturesque, winding street. They gave me a tour, and then insisted on driving me around town so I could see the houses they'd both grown up in, the elementary schools they'd attended, the playgrounds where they'd played tag and Red Rover, the high school where Mason taught, the track he'd been running all his life, the soccer field where Lori had scored so many goals, the coffee shop where they'd had their first real date, the restaurant where Mason had proposed, and the cemetery where Andi was buried.

"Should we visit?" Mason asked.

My stomach churned, but thankfully, Lori was the one to demur.

"Oh, honey, not now," she said, patting his shoulder from the back seat. "Another time. It's so cold today."

Finally, we arrived back at their house, and although they invited me to come in for something warm to drink, I said I had some work stuff to do. "I have to go on an assignment tomorrow, so I should prepare."

Mason looked disappointed. "Oh. Okay. Well, it's been really great spending time with you."

"You too." I received long hugs from both of them.

"Thank you so much for coming," Lori said. "It meant so much to both of us."

"You're welcome," I said. "Thank you for including me. And congratulations."

"I wish we had more time," said Mason. "I feel like I've barely scratched the surface of all the conversations I'd like to have with you."

"Maybe you could come back at Christmas," suggested Lori. "I bet you haven't had a white Christmas in a while."

I could see Millie again.

The thought popped into my head immediately. No matter how hard I tried, I could not stop thinking about her and what we'd done.

What I wanted to do again.

"I'll try," I said.

"You could stay with us, if you wanted," Mason offered.

But then I couldn't spend nights with Millie.

"I'll give it some thought." Then I lifted my hand in a wave, said goodbye once more, and jumped into my rental car. On the drive back to the hotel, I'd felt like the lowest human being on earth.

Placing both hands behind my head, I stared at the ceiling in my room and wished I had the energy to go work out. A grueling session with heavy weights or a miserable ten-mile run on the treadmill would serve me right. I needed to be punished for what I'd done. For what I wanted to do. I needed someone to tell me I was being an asshole for even considering going back to her house tonight.

I grabbed my phone and called Jackson.

"Hello?"

"Hey," I said. "I think I fucked up."

"That's nothing new. What did you do?"

"I may have slept with my son's ex-girlfriend."

Jackson coughed. Or maybe choked. *"May have?"*

"Okay, I did."

"Wow. Let me go in another room. Hang on." He said something to someone—his wife, probably, which meant I was interrupting their family time on a Sunday and made me feel even worse. The background noise on his end receded, and I heard something that sounded like a door closing. "Okay," he said. "So you slept with your son's ex. Can I ask what in the hell you were thinking? Or were you thinking at all?"

"I didn't realize who she was, at least not the first time it happened."

"*The first time*? Jesus, Barrett. Have you lost your mind? Do I need to send in a team?"

"Let me explain." I sighed heavily. "Remember the woman from New York City?"

Silence, as he put it together. "No fucking way."

"She was Mason's ex."

"No. Fucking. Way." He started to laugh. "That is so messed up."

"Tell me about it. I've been thinking about her nonstop for a month and then out of nowhere she *appears* at the rehearsal, and she's introduced to me as the wedding planner. But before Mason can even tell her my name, she blurts it out. It was obvious we'd already met. And Mason had already mentioned that the wedding planner was his ex, so I put it together immediately—what we had done."

"But it's not like anyone *else* knew."

"No. Millie and I both played it casual. We said we'd had one drink together and that was that. But Mason seemed on edge about it right away. It was obvious he suspected something had happened that night."

"You guys were *that bad* at acting?"

"I didn't think so, but a few minutes later Mason asked me point blank if anything had happened with her."

"What did you say to him?"

"What the fuck could I say? I lied!"

Jackson started to laugh again.

"It's not funny," I said. "Because then he says how much it means to him that I've been so honest and open about everything—the past, my relationship with his mom. He said he's spent his entire life looking for the truth and never getting it, so honesty is important to him."

"Oh, shit. Yeah, that's complicated." Jackson grew quiet. "But technically, you didn't do anything wrong—not the first time, anyway. How'd you let it happen again?"

I exhaled. "I don't know. I swear to God, Jackson, I promised myself I wouldn't touch her, but I have no fucking control where she's concerned."

"That doesn't sound like you."

"It isn't. And it's driving me crazy." I slapped a hand on my forehead. "It's like I'm eighteen again. I'm the same impulsive, horny shithead that got a girl pregnant because he couldn't keep it in his pants."

"So get out of there. You went to the wedding, now come home. Take yourself out of the dangerous situation."

"I am. I'm leaving tomorrow."

"So what's the problem?"

I paused, knowing what I was about to say was all kinds of fucked up. "The problem is I've got twelve hours left here, and I want to spend them with her."

"Are you *nuts*?"

"Yes. She just . . . does something to me, Jackson. I know it sounds stupid and weak, but she does. I can't explain it." I closed my eyes. "I keep trying to twist the pieces around, like I'm looking for some kind of loophole that would make one last night with her okay."

"There isn't one."

I frowned. "I knew you'd say that."

"Of course you did. It's why you called. You know what you have to do—stay away from her and get on that plane."

"I haven't even told you the worst part."

"Jesus Christ. How much worse can it get, Zach?"

"Mason's wife is fucking pregnant. I'm going to be . . . I can't even say it."

Jackson burst out laughing. "Aww, you're going to be a grandpa! Or will it be Pawpaw? Grandpappy? Hmm, I think you're more of a Gramps."

"I feel like I'm in the Twilight Zone."

"Well, Pop Pop, you're not. This is your reality now— you've got family. And the Zach Barrett I know would put his family first."

"I hear you."

"Good. Because sex with a hot young thing is great, and I'm sure it's making you feel like you're drinking from the Fountain of Youth, but dude—find a hot young thing that isn't your son's ex."

After hanging up with Jackson, I went down to the hotel gym and worked out. When I got back to the room, I cleaned up, ate overpriced room service, and watched some stupid TV. The hours I had to kill were dragging.

Around nine o'clock, I called Millie.

"Hey," she said softly. Just hearing her voice made me long to be next to her.

"What are you up to?"

"I'm watching Antiques Roadshow."

"Antiques Roadshow?"

"Yes. I'm addicted. Have you ever watched it?"

"Never."

"Zach Barrett, you are missing out! People bring in their garage sale finds and stuff they inherited from long-lost aunts or shit they just have sitting around in their attics, and they find out what it's worth. I mean, sometimes it's just junk— which is terrible if the person paid a lot of money for it—but sometimes people discover they bought a ten-thousand dollar pair of French porcelain vases for five bucks at the church yard sale!"

I laughed. "Sounds . . . exciting?"

"It is! This show has drama, intrigue, suspense, mystery, emotion—whenever I need to escape the real world, Antiques Roadshow is where I go."

"I'll remember that."

"How was your day?" she asked.

"Okay, I guess." I wondered what she was wearing.

"You survived brunch?"

"Barely."

"I'm sorry. Was it hard to be around Mason?"

"Yeah." I frowned. "Harder than I thought it would be. I don't deserve the way he looks at me or speaks about me— not just because of you, but the whole situation. I wasn't there for him. I'm not Father of the Year."

"But he likes you. He's proud of you."

"Yeah." I squeezed my eyes shut.

"I heard they announced Lori's pregnancy. One of my sisters saw it on social media."

I didn't want to think about that. "How was your day?"

"Good." Her tone brightened a little. "I did a bunch of business research, and then I went to my parents' house for dinner."

"What kind of business research?"

"I'm thinking of opening a wedding gown shop," she said. "Specifically, a shop that caters to plus-sized brides."

I asked her to tell me more about it, and she talked excitedly about the fashion show she was putting on next spring, what she'd discovered about supply and demand for a shop like she envisioned, how she knew exactly who her ideal customers would be, how nervous she was to make a career change, but also how passionate she was about her ideas. Listening to her was so captivating, I didn't even realize how much time had gone by until she brought it up.

"Oh my God, I've literally just rambled for twenty minutes," she said. "You're probably bored stiff."

"Not bored at all," I told her. "And believe it or not, I'm not stiff either."

She laughed. "As soon as the word *stiff* was out of my mouth, I was like—oh crap."

"For once, I am talking to you without a hand in my pants, I promise. I told myself before I called you that I would act like a responsible adult and not a hormonal teenager."

"I like both sides of you." She paused. "I wasn't sure if you'd come over or call or . . . or what."

"I wasn't sure what to do either."

"So you're leaving tomorrow?" There was no mistaking the hope in her voice.

"Yes. On that six a.m. flight. But Millie." I steeled myself.
"Yes?"

"I can't see you tonight."

Silence. "Okay."

"It's not because I don't want to—you have to know that."

"Totally," she said, her tone more businesslike than it had been before. "I agree one hundred percent."

"If things were different," I said, hearing the note of desperation in my voice, "if the circumstances were *anything* other than what they are, I'd be on your doorstep right now. Actually, I'd probably already be in your bed."

"It's better that you're not," she said curtly. "Honestly, what's the point? This can't go anywhere. After this weekend, we probably won't see each other again."

"Yeah." It was the truth, but it still made my chest cave.

"Well, I should get to bed."

"Me too."

"Have a safe trip back."

"Thanks. Good luck with your business idea."

"Thank you." A few silent seconds ticked by. *"Goodbye, Zach."*

"Bye."

I ended the call and stared at my phone for a minute.

Then I deleted her number.

Then I lay there in the dark, telling myself I'd done the right thing, even if my room felt cold, lonely, and depressing.

Then I reminded myself that sometimes doing the right thing meant sacrifice. I'd always understood that, and I'd put myself in harm's way countless times to protect others. In this case, I didn't even have to risk bodily harm, I just had to give up one last night with her.

Then I got off the bed, grabbed my keys, and drove to her house.

Fifteen

Millie

I WAS CURLED UP ON THE COUCH, SIPPING A CUP OF TEA WHEN I heard the knock. At first, I thought I'd imagined it. I went still and listened.

Then I heard it again.

Right away, I knew who it was, and I honestly debated not answering. Only thirty minutes ago, we'd agreed that we should not see each other. *He* was the one who'd stated it first. And he was right. Not only was it wrong, but we'd risk someone catching him coming or going. Beyond that, the last thing I needed was to get hung up on Zach Barrett—my ex's dad, who lived across the country, who'd already had a vasectomy because he'd never wanted kids in the first place, and who'd be a grandfather within a year.

But it could happen. It could easily happen.

He was gorgeous and protective and kind. He might not wear his heart on his sleeve, but I'd felt it beating hard against mine. He cared enough about the son he'd never known about to come here and try to make amends. He made me laugh. He made me feel good about myself. He gave me the kinds of orgasms I'd only read about.

He knocked again. Louder this time.

Turning the TV off, I closed my eyes. Inhaled and exhaled. If I answered the door, would I have the strength to turn him away?

I'd have to find it somewhere.

Rising from the couch, I realized with dismay that I was not looking my best. I wore no makeup, my hair had not been washed today, and I had on plaid flannel pants and a T-shirt so old that its original color was lost to memory. But whatever—maybe it was better this way.

My cats, who'd cautiously wandered into the hallway to see what the excitement was, looked at me expectantly. "I'm telling him to leave," I whispered, grasping the door handle. "Now go away."

They scurried back into the kitchen, and I took one more deep breath before pulling the door open.

There he stood. Tall and bearded and brooding and hot as fuck. My resolve weakened, but I stood firm. Allowed no hint of a welcoming smile.

"I wasn't going to come," he said.

I lifted my chin. "I didn't want you to."

The standoff lasted ten full seconds.

He lunged for me at the same moment I reached for him. I stumbled backward as his body slammed into mine, vaguely hearing the door bang shut behind him. We tore at clothing, our breath coming hard and fast, our kiss becoming more like a battle with lips and tongues and teeth as weapons. We tumbled to my living room floor, groping, gasping, growling, grinding. We were naked inside a minute. My back on the Moroccan wool rug. His chest above me. My nails clawing at his back. His cock driving into me with the force of a freight train.

We were loud and rough and quick—it seemed no time at all had gone by, no chance to stop and think, no opportunity to slow down and reconsider our decision before we were crying out with the release—our bodies refusing to be denied.

Afterward, Zach braced himself above me. "I want you to know, that wasn't the plan."

Irritated, I pushed at his chest. "Let me up."

Surprised by my anger, he disengaged from my body. I scrambled to my feet, threw my T-shirt on, and hurried into the small downstairs half-bath, where I cleaned up and studied my face in the mirror. Matted hair, flushed face, puffy lips. I scowled at myself. I wasn't even sure why I was so mad, but I was. I splashed some cold water on my face, patted it dry, and brought the towel out with me.

When I came out, Zach had already gotten dressed and stood in the dark living room like he wasn't sure what to do with himself. Ignoring him, I knelt down on the rug and felt around for a mess. I didn't feel any wetness, but I scrubbed at the spot anyway. Hard. Like I was trying to erase what we'd done.

Zach let it go on for a moment, watching silently. "You're going to put a hole in that rug."

I pressed my lips together.

"Talk to me." He walked over and took me by the elbow, bringing me to my feet. "You're angry."

"You said you couldn't see me tonight. You said you couldn't come here."

"Millie," he said quietly, his eyes burning into mine. "If I could stay away from you, don't you think that I would?"

My breath caught. "I shouldn't have let you in."

"Don't be mad at yourself—this is my fault."

"I'm mad at both of us, Zach! What are we doing?" I tossed a hand in the air.

"I don't know," he said quietly.

"We keep saying this has to stop, and then we don't stop. What is our problem?"

"We like each other?" The fact that it came out as a question nearly made me smile.

"But we're not animals," I argued. "We have instincts, but we also have morals."

"Actually, some animals do have morals."

I looked at him. "You know what I mean."

He smiled—barely. "Sorry. I know what you mean."

"I just—I can't understand why it's so hard for us to do what we know is right. We are not bad people. So why are we acting like it?"

"I think it's complicated."

"But it shouldn't be," I said heatedly, shaking my head. "We're *making* it complicated. Every time we give in to this—this—whatever it is, we're making things worse." To my chagrin, my eyes filled with tears. "How can something that makes me feel so good also make me feel so bad?"

"Hey. Come here." Zach pulled me into his chest and wrapped his arms around me. I let him envelop me in his masculine warmth, pressing close to his firm, broad chest. I wasn't a child, but Zach had a way of making me feel cosseted and safe when he held me like this.

In fact, the pure bliss of it set off an alarm in my head, and I tried to pull away. Zach just held me tighter.

"There's nothing wrong with *us*," he said. "It's just everything outside that door that's the problem."

"I know. And when we're together, I get so carried away, I convince myself nothing out there matters. But it does."

"It does," he agreed.

"That's why I should tell you to go now, before someone sees your car on the street."

"And it's why I would leave if you asked."

I closed my eyes. "What if I don't ask?"

"Then I would stay."

"God. I feel like I have an angel on one shoulder and a devil on the other. The angel is telling me to say goodnight."

"And the devil?"

"The devil says all our problems would be solved if I just move my car out of the garage and you pulled yours in."

"I'm not sure that solves all our problems, but it takes care of the immediate one."

I pressed my cheek to his chest, tucking my head beneath his chin. "Since you're already here tonight, maybe you could just stay. And in the morning, we'll say goodbye and part as friends."

"I'll move both cars," he said. "Where are your keys?"

"Did you always want to be a SEAL?" I asked, tucked in the crook of his arm. I had no idea what time it was—somewhere in the middle of the night—but we were post-round two, finally cooled off enough to pull the covers up to our chests.

"I always wanted to fight bad guys," he said.

"And did you?" I ran my fingers along the scar on his right arm.

"Yes."

"What do you think gave you such a strong sense of justice? Or was it just that you wanted to be a badass in uniform?"

He didn't answer right away. "It was losing my sister."

I stopped moving my hand on his arm. "Poppy, right?"

"Right." The room seemed even more silent. "It was my fault."

My stomach dropped. "What?"

"It was my fault," he repeated, his tone matter-of-fact.

I sat up and looked at him. *"What do you mean? I thought you said it was an accident."*

"It was my negligence that caused the accident. I was supposed to be watching her."

"But you were only seven!"

"I was old enough." His voice was reedy. *"We were playing outside. I left her alone in the front yard while I went into the garage to find the pump to put air in my bike tires. She wandered. We lived near a lake."*

My throat clutched, and my eyes watered. *"You poor thing. Your parents blamed you?"*

"No. But I didn't need them to blame me. I knew it was my fault."

"Oh, Zach, it wasn't." I lay down again, wrapping my arms around him. *"Don't say that."*

"Other kids my age, friends of mine, hated having their little sisters around. They'd be so mean about it. But I never minded."

I kissed his chest, holding my lips to his skin.

"There was no one to punish for it," he said. *"It felt like a crime, but there was no bad guy—just me."*

Tears slipped from my eyes. *"You weren't the bad guy, Zach."*

"I was so angry—so fucking angry after that. I was just waiting to be able to put it somewhere. I wanted to fight. And I didn't care if I got killed or not. I didn't give a single fuck. I just wanted to fight the bad guys and protect the innocent. Like I'd failed to protect her."

I didn't know what to say, so I just held him.

My heart ached for him—for the little boy who blamed himself for his beloved sister's tragic death, for the angry teenager determined to fight bad guys because he couldn't fight himself, for the man in my bed who still carried it all with him.

"I've never said this stuff to anyone," he said.

"Thank you for telling me," I whispered, wiping my eyes.

He kissed my head. *"Do you wish you'd have told me to leave earlier?"*

"Not at all. We're going to be friends, right? Friends trust each other with their deepest secrets."

"So what's yours?"

"Well, don't tell anyone, but I banged my ex's dad."

"Very funny." He shifted onto his side and propped his head in his hand. *"I'm serious. Tell me something about you. Something no one else knows."*

"Hmmm." I tried to think of something I'd never even told my sisters. "There is *one* thing . . . but it's embarrassing."

He tapped my nose. *"Tell me."*

"Okay." I took a breath. "Over the past few months, I've been googling something kind of weird."

"Millie, we all watch porn."

I slapped his chest. "It's not porn. It's . . . sperm banks."

"Sperm banks?" He made a face. *"Like for donor sperm?"*

"Yes. Lately I've been starting to worry that if I don't find the *one*, I might miss out on my chance to have a family. I hate to say people are right about the biological clock thing, but there's truth there. Once you hit thirty-five, you're considered of *advanced maternal age*."

"I remember Kimberly—my ex-wife—saying something similar."

"Anyway, it's just something at the back of my mind. Nothing I'm obsessing over."

He stroked his hand up and down my shoulder. *"So tell me about this* one. *What are you looking for?"*

"Well, he has to be a nice person. Smart, but I don't need a genius. He should have a solid job, something stable. And

I'd like it if he could make me laugh, or at least had a good personality."

Zach stared at me. "That's it? A nice guy with a stable job, not too smart, somewhat funny?" He shook his head. "Babe, you're selling yourself short."

"I'm not," I argued. "I didn't mention money because I know it doesn't buy happiness. And I didn't mention looks because those fade. I've *seen* Beauty and the Beast. I *know* beauty lies within."

He laughed. "But you could do so much better than the average Joe you just described. That guy is beneath you. You'd be bored."

"Boring would be fine," I countered, sitting up. "Boring is at least safe. I don't want someone who thinks he could run out the door and find a better life—I want him to need me. I never want to be scared he'll leave." The words were out before I realized what I was saying. I wanted to double back and try to explain it in a way that didn't make me sound afraid and insecure, but I thought maybe it would be better if I just stopped talking.

"I understand," Zach said.

Embarrassed I'd gotten so worked up, I tucked a strand of hair behind my ear. "Sorry. Didn't mean to rant."

"Come here." He tugged me back down, so I was snuggled alongside his body again, and pulled the covers up. "You have the right to do anything you want with your life. If you want to use a sperm donor to have a baby, go for it."

"Well, I don't *want* to. I'm just worried about waiting around too long, looking for my average Joe. What's taking him so long?"

"Is it selfish of me to say I'm glad you haven't found him yet?"

"Yes." I smiled. "But I don't mind. If he was here, you wouldn't be. And right now, all I want is you."

When I woke up, he wasn't next to me. I sat up, wondering if he'd taken off without saying goodbye. I sat up, clutching the blankets to my chest. It was still dark. I reached over and tapped my phone screen to check the time and discovered it was just before four.

Was he gone already?

Outside, I heard a car door slam, followed by the closing of my garage. I relaxed a little—he was just moving the cars.

He entered the bedroom a minute later and dropped onto the edge of the bed. "Hey."

"Hey." I smiled shyly at him. "I thought maybe you'd snuck out without saying goodbye."

"Nah. I wouldn't do that to you. I just wanted to get your car back in the garage."

"I could have moved it."

"It's all done." He tugged a strand of my hair. "I better go. I need to make that flight, and the longer I sit here looking at you, the harder it will be to leave."

I nodded. Swallowed hard. "Okay."

"Friends?" He held out his hand.

"Friends." I shook it. It was chilly from being outside.

He looked at our clasped hands for a moment, then gently pulled his away. "So what will you do today?"

"If I can find the energy, I'll go to my strength training class at nine."

"Strength training, huh?"

"Yes." I flexed my bicep. "You mean you couldn't tell?"

He laughed and felt the muscle. "Very impressive."

"Then I'm meeting my sister Winnie's boyfriend at the jewelry store. He wants my opinion on the ring he's going to propose with."

"Sounds like a busy day."

"I'll still find time to think about you."

He grinned. "Come on. We've been friends for like three minutes straight. We're doing so well."

"Sorry." I grinned back, even though my heart was sinking. Was this the last time I'd ever see him? "Well . . . be safe."

"Always." He leaned over and kissed my cheek, then rested his forehead on my temple. "Don't be a stranger, okay? And don't you dare settle for that slowpoke average Joe."

I nodded, since I didn't trust myself to speak. A moment later, he was gone.

Squeezing my eyes shut, I swallowed the lump in my throat and told myself it was stupid to cry over losing something that had never been mine in the first place.

Downtown was busy, and I had to park two blocks down from the jewelry store. My feet felt heavy as I trudged up the sidewalk, just like they had at class this morning. In fact, the coach kept coming over to me to ask if I was okay. I'd said I was fine, just tired. It was half true, anyway.

When I caught sight of Dex standing right outside the door, looking like he was about to pass out, I had to smile. "Hey," I said as I approached. "What are you doing out here?"

"I was sweating in there," he said.

"Why? Are you nervous?"

He looked at me like I was crazy. "Fuck yes, I'm nervous. I can't screw this up, Millie."

I gave him a quick hug. "You are not going to screw this up—it would be impossible to screw this up! Winnie is head over heels in love with you, and this is going to make her the happiest she's ever been."

"You think so?" He rubbed the back of his neck.

"I know so. Now come on, show me the rings you've picked out. I'm dying!"

He held the door open for me, and I went into the shop, where gems and precious metals glittered and gleamed under sparkling clear glass. A dark-haired woman in a suit with a name tag that read Kirsten recognized Dex and came right over. "You're back. Have you decided?"

"Almost." He gestured at me. "This is Winnie's sister, Millie. I just wanted to get her opinion before deciding for sure."

"Of course." Kirsten smiled at me. "He's chosen some gorgeous rings. Give me one minute to collect them, and I'll meet you at the back counter."

"I can't wait." Excited, and beyond grateful for this happy distraction, I hooked my hands through Dex's elbow and gave his arm a squeeze. Together we wandered back to the display case showing off rings in every imaginable size, color, and style. My eyes roamed over diamonds and sapphires and emeralds and rubies set in gold and platinum. Classic solitaires nestled among more extravagant cluster, cathedral, and halo settings. There were stones cut in every possible way—round, pear, oval, marquise, cushion. Some were small and discreet, some were as big and round as doorknobs. "I can see why it's overwhelming," I said.

"Well, a lot of these are out of the question because of budget," he said with a shrug. "I wish I could afford a massive rock, but I just can't."

"Listen to me. Winnie does *not care* about a massive rock. She only cares that you are the one who'll put it on her finger."

"Here we are." Kirsten appeared and set a black velvet cushion in front of us with three diamond rings inserted into a horizontal seam.

"Oh, Dex," I whispered, covering my mouth with both hands. I felt like the wind had been knocked out of me.

The ring on the left was a round solitaire on a plain platinum band—elegant, modern, simple. The one in the center was emerald-cut and set between two baguettes—sleek and stunning. But it was the one on the right that set my heart fluttering. I just knew instantly it was Winnie's. The stone wasn't as big as the other two, but it was princess-cut and set on a delicate band of pavé diamonds.

"The round cut is the most popular with brides these days," said Kirsten. "It shows off maximum brightness. The emerald cut produces a sort of 'hall of mirrors' effect that's really breathtaking. And the princess cut—"

"That's the one," I said, pointing at it. "I'm sorry, I didn't mean to cut you off," I said to Kirsten. "But I just have this feeling about that ring."

Dex laughed. "That one is Hallie and Luna's favorite too—probably because of the princess thing."

Kirsten smiled. "It's a beautiful stone."

"Can I try it on?" I blurted.

"Of course." Kirsten pulled it from the velvet and handed it to me.

I began slipping it on my finger, then I looked at Dex. "Is this okay?"

He smiled. "Sure."

I held my breath as I worked it onto my finger, then held my hand out to admire it. "God. It's so beautiful. But it's your decision, Dex. Don't let me make it for you."

"You don't think she'd want the biggest diamond?" he asked, gesturing at the solitaire.

I shook my head. "No. I don't."

"Okay. Then I guess the decision is made."

"Wonderful." Kirsten beamed. "We'll have it sized, cleaned, and ready for you in a few days."

Reluctantly, I worked the ring from my finger and gave it to Kirsten, who said she'd be right back with the paperwork.

"You've got her ring size and everything?" I asked Dex.

He nodded. "I had the girls sneak a ring from her jewelry box to me, and I brought it in. Then they snuck it back into the box without her noticing it was gone. Operation Cat Burglary, they called it. Luna wore cat ears. Hallie dressed in all black."

I laughed. "I can picture it perfectly. Have you decided when you'll pop the question?"

"I think Christmas morning. The girls thought it would be fun to put the ring box in her stocking—they're going to make her a stocking to hang at our place this year."

"Oh." I fanned my face as my eyes filled. "That's so sweet."

"Now they just have to keep it a secret until then. Which will be hard because they're so excited. They love her so much."

I gave up trying not to cry and dug a tissue out of my purse to dab my eyes. "You're all going to be so happy, Dex. Everything about this proposal is perfect."

"She deserves perfection." He hesitated. "But she'll have to settle for me."

I laughed and gave him another impetuous hug, patting him on the back. "You're all she wants, I promise. And I can't wait to call you my brother."

Sixteen

Millie

AFTER SAYING GOODBYE TO DEX, I DECIDED TO GO IN TO work, even though I usually took Mondays off. I didn't want to face my empty, silent house, even though I usually cherished a chilly fall afternoon curled up with a cup of tea and a book or a few episodes of Antiques Roadshow. But even that didn't sound appealing.

Sitting at my desk, listless and unmotivated, I was staring out the window at a bleak gray sky when Felicity texted. **Did you see the rings???**

Rather than text back, I called her.

"Well?" she answered breathlessly. "How did it go? What did they look like? Did he buy one?"

I had to laugh. "It went great. They were all stunning, and yes, he bought one. The perfect one."

"What does it look like?"

I described it. "He's going to propose Christmas morning. The girls are going to help."

"I'm so excited for her. For all of them!"

"Me too."

"You okay? You sound sort of down."

"I'm fine." I tried to perk up my voice. "Just a little tired. I didn't sleep much last night."

"Dare I ask why?"

"You could. But you probably don't need to."

"So it's still going on? He's still here?"

"No, he's gone. He flew back to San Diego this morning." I glanced out the window again.

"Oh. Well, that's probably best."

"Yeah." I cleared my throat. "Listen, I should go, I'm at work and I've got a bunch of stuff to do."

"Oh, sorry! I thought you had today off. In fact, I was going to tell you that Hutton said to come over any time if you want help with a business plan. He was serious when he offered to help you out."

"Thank you. I'm definitely going to take him up on it."

After hanging up, I tackled some chores I'd been avoiding—I cleared out my inbox, reorganized my desk, cleaned the windows, dusted the furniture, and rearranged my bookshelves. When my stomach began to growl, I ordered some lunch and ate it while I scrolled through websites of wedding gown designers on my laptop. Looking at them restored some of my enthusiasm.

When I was finished, I saw that I'd missed a phone call from a downstate area code, but the caller had left a message. I figured it must be the owner of the bridal salon I'd reached out to yesterday, and quickly accessed my voicemail to listen.

"Hello," said a woman's voice. "This is Alison Obermeyer from Bellissima Bridal returning your call. I'd be happy to chat with you about my business, and I'm available until five p.m. today. If that doesn't work, I do have some mornings open this week. And if you're in the area, feel free to pop in! Hope to talk soon."

I returned her call, and she was so friendly and forthcoming with information, I found my spirits lifting even more.

"Best thing I ever did," she said about leaving her job as an administrative assistant and opening the shop. "After my disappointing experience trying to find a wedding dress as a plus-sized woman, all I wanted to do was make sure no one ever felt that way again. Every bride deserves to feel beautiful, and I love that I get to play a role in that."

"That's what I want to do too," I said. I told her about my background and my career, and about conversations I'd had with local brides who had struggled to find a dress that showed off everything they loved about their bodies. "Shopping for regular clothes is hard enough, not to mention dealing with critical mothers or fat-shaming doctors or tiny airplane seats or any of the other ways bigger women can be made to feel bad about their bodies. Finding the perfect wedding dress should make a woman feel celebrated, not humiliated."

"Exactly," said Alison. "And I know we've only been talking for thirty minutes and I already forgot your last name, but I think you should go for it—open that shop. I'm here to answer any questions and give advice if I can."

I laughed. "Thank you so much. I'd love to come see your salon."

"Please do! We're open Tuesday through Saturday, but if a Sunday or Monday is best for you, just let me know. I'm usually there on my off days too."

"I'm going to check my schedule and see what this week looks like," I said. "I'm so excited, I'd like to come down right away."

Alison laughed. "Do it. Sometimes a dream won't wait."

After rearranging a few meetings, I booked a hotel room in Detroit for Wednesday night and made the drive down that afternoon. I met a friend from college for dinner in Corktown and went back to my room around nine, got ready for bed, and slid between the sheets. I'd just turned on my Kindle when my phone vibrated with a text.

I glanced at it and gasped—it was a message from Zach.

Guess what I'm doing?

My heart hammered as I picked up my phone and studied it. There had been no word from him since he'd left my house Monday morning. Not that I'd expected him to reach out—in fact, I sort of figured he wouldn't. I almost hoped he wouldn't. How else was I going to get him out of my head?

But I replied to his text. **What?**

Watching Antiques Roadshow.

I laughed out loud as I typed. **Really?**

My phone hummed. He was calling me.

Chewing the inside of my cheek, I considered not taking the call, but then decided I would. We could practice being friends.

"I thought you deleted my number," I said instead of hello.

"I did. Turns out, you can undo that move." He sounded all stuffed up.

"Uh oh. Are you sick?"

"Yeah," he said. "It's just a cold. Probably picked it up on the plane home—the guy next to me was coughing the entire flight. Hang on." He sneezed three times in a row. *Loud.*

I laughed. "You sound demonic when you sneeze."

"I know." He blew his nose. "Jackson sent me home from work because he couldn't stand the racket."

"Awww. Are you okay?"

"I'll be fine. I'm just bored. I hate sitting still."

"So you decided to try a little Antiques Roadshow?"

"I was channel surfing and came across it. I thought of you."

"And?"

"And now I can't turn it off. This lady found the creepiest fucking doll I've ever seen in some dilapidated barn on her family's property. This doll literally looks like it's about to murder you. Turns out it's from 1880, and it's worth like twelve grand."

"Haha! Told you!"

"The guy before her had this helmet worn by his great uncle, a Naval officer during World War II who was in charge at Utah Beach on D-Day. He saw it on a table when he was a kid at his grandma's house. She was using it as a flowerpot."

"Stop it."

"It had dirt in it!"

"What did it turn out to be worth?"

"Forty grand."

I gasped. *"Wow. Really?"*

"Oh, yeah. D-Day stuff is always valuable."

"Are you into military history?"

"A little. I like the World War II stuff. When I was a kid, my grandpa would tell me about when he was in the Navy at that time. He wasn't at Normandy or anything, but he still had good stories."

"Did you write them down?"

"No. But I should."

"You definitely should! Before you forget them."

"Because I'm so old?"

I laughed. *"Exactly. Soon you'll be senile, and you won't even remember your name."*

"But I'll remember you."

My face warmed. *"Thank you."*

"So how are you?"

"Good. I'm in Detroit, actually."

"Oh yeah? What are you doing there?"

Settling down a little deeper beneath the covers, I told him about my phone conversation with Alison Obermeyer and the invitation to visit her shop. "I'm meeting her there at eight before it opens," I said.

"Are you excited?"

"Yes. I have this feeling that my life is about to change," I confessed. "It's this feeling in my belly—like when you're coming down on the Ferris wheel but your stomach stayed up at the top."

"Is it a good feeling? Do you *want* your life to change?"

"I think so. Yes." I plucked at a loose thread in the comforter. "I'm happy with my life now, but I think I've gotten into a bit of a rut. And to get out of it, I need to make a conscious effort to dream bigger and go for things."

"I agree. Trust your gut and be brave." He sneezed twice in a row, and I made a sympathetic sound.

"You poor thing. If I was your neighbor, I'd bring you some chicken noodle soup."

"That sounds good. You know how to cook?"

"I know my way around the kitchen," I said. "I'm not as good as Frannie, my stepmom, or my sister Felicity, but I enjoy it. And I love making soup on cold days—chicken noodle, pumpkin, minestrone . . ."

He groaned. "I wish you were my neighbor too. All that sounds delicious."

"Do you cook?"

"Depends how you define 'cook.' I'm very good at the microwave. I know what all the buttons are."

I laughed. "How about pots and pans? Own any of those?"

"I think I lost them in the divorce. My best real food-related skill is ordering takeout. I think that's what I'll do tonight."

"What will you order?"

"You made me want chicken noodle soup. I'll try to find some. Although I'm sure it won't taste as good as yours." He blew his nose again.

"Maybe not, but it will be good for you. Got any ginger tea?"

"Is that a real question?"

"Yes," I said, laughing. "You should drink some ginger tea with honey."

"I'm fresh out of ginger tea. And honey."

I sighed. "Fine. But make sure you're hydrating."

"Yes, Mom."

"And get enough sleep! You won't get better without rest."

"You were more fun in person. I'm starting to regret calling you."

I giggled. "I'm going to bed, but I'll check in on you tomorrow."

He coughed. "Okay. Goodnight."

"Night." I ended the call and touched my phone to my chin.

It was definitely easier to be friends with him when he wasn't right next to me. And that cold sounded awful.

But I still wished he was here.

"So how did it go?" Winnie asked. I had her on speaker as I headed north on I-75.

"It was fantastic!" I was bubbling over with excitement. "Her shop is so beautiful, and she's such a cool person. I loved her."

"That's awesome! So did you decide?"

"Pretty much," I said. "It makes my stomach all jittery to

say it out loud, but after talking to her, I'm more convinced than ever that this is what I should do."

Winnie squealed. "So what next?"

"Several things. I want to reach out to all the designers who are sending dresses and veils for the March show and tell them what I'm doing. Hopefully, they'll all want to be stocked in my salon."

"I'm sure they will!"

"I need to look for a space."

"Frannie said she knows a commercial realtor, remember?"

"She's my next call." I took a deep breath. "And then I need to let Aunt Chloe know I'm leaving. Were you serious about taking over for me?"

"Yes, but I'll need to give notice at Abelard, and I don't want to do that until we know for sure Chloe would be on board with hiring me. She might have someone else in mind for the job."

"Are you kidding? She'd never hire someone else if you wanted that position. You're amazing at what you do, and you're family."

"Still, you approach her and let me know. She's the boss."

"I'll talk to her right away," I promised.

We hung up, and I placed the call to Frannie, who said she would contact the real estate agent right away. But first she wanted to hear all about how the visit to Bellissima Bridal had gone. I told her everything I'd just told Winnie, with even more exuberance.

"Oh Mills, that's wonderful. I'm so excited for you."

"Thanks. I really feel this in my bones—it's the right move for me."

"I think so too."

"I'm nervous about talking to Chloe, though," I admitted.

"Don't be. Chloe will understand following your passion, believe me. Go see her tomorrow."

"Gah, that makes me so nervous. You don't think I should wait until I have some things in place first?"

"I think the sooner you tell her, the better, both for her sake *and* yours—this is going to make it feel more real."

"You're right. I'm just scared."

"Of course you are. But you're brave too. And you've got all our support."

After we hung up, I began mentally sorting through all the tasks I'd have to complete in order to get a new business going. In addition to finding the perfect physical space and all the renovations that would be necessary, there was the matter of writing up a business plan and bank account, licensing and registration with the county and state, setting up vendor accounts, outfitting the shop with display spaces and mirrors and seating. Plus computer hardware and software—there were plenty of unsexy things about this business I'd have to deal with.

I needed to hire employees, first and foremost a talented seamstress. I had some talent and experience, but not with wedding gowns—and there was no room for error with those dresses. Alterations had to be perfect.

And money . . . I remembered Hutton's offer to help me with a loan and a business plan. Then there was marketing and promotion. I'd have to get the word out about my shop—the ideal time would be at the fashion show. Would I be open by then? I needed a website and social media.

What was I even going to call this shop?

As exhilarated as I was, I also felt overwhelmed. I decided to drive straight to Hutton and Felicity's house—Winnie's unbridled enthusiasm was wonderful, but I needed some voices of reason in my head too. Both Hutton and Felicity had experience running their own businesses, and they were good with practical details and problem-solving.

It was dark when I pulled up, but I saw lights on in their

house. I shot Felicity a quick text. **Hey. You guys home tonight?**

Yes, she replied within seconds. **What's up?**

I need business plan help. I'm in your driveway. Can I come in?

LOL of course, she messaged.

Grabbing my shoulder bag off the passenger seat, I hurried to their front door. Felicity pulled it open before I could knock. "Hey! Come on in."

"Thanks." I inhaled the savory aroma of whatever they'd had for dinner. "God, that smells good."

"Eggplant lasagna! You want some? We just finished eating, but there's plenty left over."

"That sounds fantastic, thanks."

"Hutton is at the table." She shut the door behind me. "Go sit and I'll bring you a plate."

Two-and-a-half hours later, I left with twelve pages of handwritten notes for my business plan, assurance from Hutton that he would be glad to loan me start-up money once I had certain things in place, and a light-bellied feeling that was equal parts motivation and fear. Starting a business was not for the faint of heart.

Late that night I was lying in bed, wide awake and wondering if I should just stay where I was. I liked my job. I was good at it. Did I want to risk so much for a dream?

Sighing, I grabbed my phone and checked the time—after midnight. Normally I was fast asleep by now. Should I doom scroll? Or read? Get up and make some chamomile tea?

Tea reminded me of Zach, and I wondered if he felt any better today. I recalled promising him I'd check in and realized I hadn't done it.

Hey, I said. **You feeling any better?**

His reply was quick. **A little. How was your day? Want to call and tell me about it?**

I hesitated for a half-second, then remembered how nicely we'd behaved last night. We'd proven we could be trusted, even if I wasn't over my crush on him. I dialed his number.

"Hey, you," he said, his voice still gravelly.

I smiled. *"Hi. How are you?"*

"I'm okay." He coughed.

"You don't sound okay."

"Yeah, this stupid thing moved into my chest. But let's talk about you. It went well today?"

"Yes." I told him all about the meeting with Alison, how inspired I'd been touring her shop, how many ideas I'd gotten for what I could do to make my salon my own, and the business plan I'd created with Hutton.

"Who's Hutton again?"

"My sister Felicity's husband."

"She's the middle sister?"

"Yes. And they were best friends in high school but never dated until this summer." I laughed. "It's actually a great story." I recounted it while he listened, occasionally laughing or coughing. "And they tied the knot at Cloverleigh Farms just a few weeks later," I finished.

"Wow," he said. "And he's a billionaire?"

"Yes, but don't ask me what he does exactly. It involves the words *math*, *algorithm*, and *cryptocurrency*. I've never understood it and whenever someone tries to explain it, I zone out."

Zach laughed. "I probably would too. Although I always liked math."

"You did?"

"Yeah. Definitely my best subject at school. Not that I ever did much homework, but I was a good test-taker."

"Interesting."

"What about you? What was your best subject?"

"I liked English and history. I was a fast reader, which helped because until I quit dance, I didn't have a lot of time for homework."

"You mentioned you were serious about dance once before. Was it hard to quit?"

"So hard," I said. "I agonized over it."

"How old were you?"

"Fifteen. But it was the right decision for me. Once I got over feeling like a failure, I realized I was much happier. That's when I took up sewing and got really interested in fashion design."

"You can sew too?"

"Yes. I make a lot of my own clothes."

"You're a woman of many talents, Millie MacAllister. Some of them I can talk about, and some of them I can't." He sneezed.

I giggled. "Bless you. Did you get your soup last night?"

"I did."

"How about the tea?"

"Ah . . . I failed at tea."

"Do you have any aromatherapy candles?"

He laughed, which made the coughing worse.

I sighed. "I'll take that as a no. Just make sure you keep drinking liquids and getting enough sleep."

"Thanks," he said when he could talk again. "Speaking of which, isn't it late for you?"

"It is. I tried to sleep but couldn't. I think I'm nervous about this business thing. I don't want to make a mistake."

"What does your gut say?"

"That it's right."

"Then it is. You've got good instincts, Millie MacAllister. Trust them."

I smiled. "I appreciate that."

"And keep me posted."

"Okay. I hope you feel better. Drink some tea!"

He laughed, and the sound warmed my body. "Goodnight."

"Goodnight." I set my phone back on the charger and rolled over, pulling the blankets up to my shoulders.

I remembered falling asleep with his arms around me and waking up in the cozy warmth of his embrace. I thought about his voice, sometimes deep and serious, sometimes quiet and confessional, sometimes teasing and playful. I breathed in, hoping for a trace of his smell, but smelled only fabric softener and remembered I'd washed the sheets.

If only the feelings I had for him would fade as easily as his scent.

Instead, it felt like they were growing stronger.

The following morning at work, I spoke on the phone with the commercial real estate agent Frannie knew, a woman named Maxima Radley. The name sounded vaguely familiar, and Frannie said that was because it was Maxima who helped her start her own bakery years ago. I loved that, and so did Maxima.

"This is fate," she said after I told her what I was looking for. "I'm going to find you the perfect spot. I already have one in mind."

"You do?"

"Yes. It's an address right on Front Street. It's a historic building with a ton of charm. It was originally a hatmaker's—a millinery—but more recently it was a gift shop."

"I think I know the one you mean," I said, recalling the vacant storefront from my last few visits downtown. "Front Street would be perfect. But that's probably pretty high rent."

"Well, it's not a huge place," said Maxima. "In fact, you'd probably only have room for a couple dressing rooms, assuming you need a large mirrored area for fittings."

"I would."

"And there wouldn't be a ton of room for racks or anything."

"I can use rolling racks if needed," I said, recalling what Alison had said about making the most of space. "And when I start out, I won't have a ton of inventory."

"Let's just go see it. It has a lot of the things you're looking for—high ceilings, tall front windows, exposed brick walls, and the location is excellent."

"Okay," I said. "It does sound amazing."

"I'll be honest and say it does need some work. But that might keep the rent down. I'll contact the building owner and a few others and get back to you with possible appointment times."

"Sounds good, Maxima. Thank you."

After we hung up, I mustered my courage and sent an email to Chloe, asking her if she had any time to chat with me today. Before hitting send, I chewed my thumbnail for a moment. For some reason, this one thing felt like my biggest step so far—it meant actually leaving something behind. Once I left Cloverleigh Farms, I couldn't turn back.

Then I remembered Alison's words: *Sometimes a dream won't wait.*

I hit send.

Chloe's grin appeared before I even finished my prepared opening. "Oh my God," she said, her eyes lighting up. "This is an amazing idea and you have to do it."

"Really?" I was on the edge of my seat. "You're not upset?"

"Of course not! Yes, you're an outstanding event planner and I love having you at Cloverleigh Farms, but you're family too! I want what's best for you."

"Thank you," I said, relaxing into the chair across from her desk and placing a hand on my chest. "I was so worried about upending things around here."

She waved a hand dismissively. "Don't be silly. You said Winnie might be interested in the job?"

"She definitely is. If you're up for hiring her, she would leave Abelard. She said she could do it on good terms."

"The position here is hers if she wants it," Chloe said. "Just have her give me a call. Do you have any idea about a timeline?"

"I don't," I admitted. "I'm at the very beginning of this process."

"We'll make it all work." She smiled again. "I love this for you. I really do."

Back in my office, I closed the door, leaned against it, and allowed myself a little fist pump of triumph. Obviously there was a long road ahead, but I felt like I was on my way. I still had work to do here, though, starting with a wedding rehearsal this evening.

I decided to make myself a quick cup of tea in the kitchen before going over all the details one last time, and while I was waiting for the water to heat up, I got an idea that made me smile all over again.

Seventeen

Zach

"Hey, Zach. Delivery for you."

I looked up from the conference table and saw Gwyn, the front desk receptionist, enter the room carrying a white plastic grocery bag.

"What's this?" I asked.

"I don't know. It just arrived." She set it in front of me. "Jackson said to tell you he'll be here in a minute. He's finishing up a call."

"Okay. Thanks." I studied the bag for a second, then untied the handles. As soon as I peeked inside, I smiled. Then I pulled out a box of ginger tea, a plastic bear filled with honey, and a box of something called Assorted Aromatherapy Shower Bombs.

Shower bombs? What the fuck?

"Hey, Gramps." Jackson strolled into the room, laptop under his arm, and dropped into the chair across from me. "Gwyn said you got a delivery."

"Nothing." Quickly, I shoved the items back in the bag.

"Come on, let me see." He snatched the bag from my hands and looked into it. "Awww. A care package! Who's it from?"

I set my jaw and folded my arms over my chest.

"What do we have here? Tea." He placed the box of tea on the table. "And honey—isn't that sweet?" He held up the bear and made it dance a little, then set it next to the tea. "And . . ." He pulled out the red box. "Aromatherapy shower bombs? What the hell are those?"

"I have no idea."

He flipped the box over and read in an overdramatic voice. "The *ultimate* in self-care. Shower fizzies with essential oils in six stress-melting, pleasure-inducing scents: peppermint, vanilla rose, eucalyptus, lavender, coconut, and jasmine honeysuckle." He looked at me and raised his eyebrows. "Pleasure-inducing? Who sent you this box of pleasure?"

"None of your business," I snapped.

"Let me guess. Your secret girlfriend."

I rolled my eyes. "She's not my girlfriend. She's just a friend."

"I don't have any friends that send *me* fizzing pleasure scented like coconut."

I stood up and grabbed the bag from him, stuffing everything back inside it. "She knows I'm sick. She's being nice."

"How does she know you're sick?"

Sitting down again, I set the bag at my feet. "Because we've talked on the phone a couple times this week. And before you come at me, it's nothing inappropriate. We're just friends."

Jackson held up his hands. "I didn't say anything."

"But I know what you're thinking, and you can just stop thinking it."

A few other Cole Security employees entered the room, putting an end to the discussion, which I was glad about. What I'd told Jackson was true—Millie and I *were* just friends, and our conversations the past two nights *had* been totally appropriate.

My thoughts about her after we hung up were a different matter entirely. In fact, given how hard I was finding it to put her out of my head, I knew talking with her every night was probably a terrible idea.

And yet I called her as soon as I got home, even though it was after one a.m. her time.

"Hello?" She sounded sleepy.

"Hey," I said, dropping onto my couch. "I'm sorry for calling so late. I just got home from a job. Did I wake you?"

"It's okay. How are you feeling?"

"Better today. I think it was the tea and honey someone sent me."

She laughed, a lazy, sexy sound that sent a bolt of heat through me. "Wonder who that could be."

"I don't know. They also sent me a box of shower bombs, which sound terrifying."

"Did you try one yet?"

"No. But I drank some tea."

"Next time you take a shower, use one of those bombs. They smell really good. And the steam will be good for the congestion."

"You use those bomb things?"

"Yes. My favorite is the jasmine honeysuckle."

"Does it smell like you?"

She was silent a few seconds. "It might."

Now I was picturing her in the shower. Great. I cleared my throat and steered back to a safer topic—gratitude. "Thank you. Really. That was sweet."

"You're welcome. I've been worried about you."

"I'm fine."

"But when you're sick, it's nice to be taken care of, isn't it?"

"By you, it would be."

Then she went silent.

I exhaled. *"I'm sorry, Millie. I keep saying shit I know I shouldn't."*

"No, it's okay. I'm doing the same. Being just friends is hard after you've . . . been more."

"Let's try again—how was your day?"

"Good." She told me about speaking to a commercial real estate agent, and her voice grew more animated as she gave me some details about one of the places she was going to see tomorrow morning. *"I'm also seeing some on Sunday, and a couple early next week, but I really have my hopes pinned on this one building."* She sighed. *"Which is probably a mistake, because it's got the steepest rent, and it's not even the largest space."*

"Well, no harm in looking, is there?"

"There's harm if I fall in love with it! What if I get in there and it's the perfect fit, but I can't have it?"

"If it's the perfect fit, I bet you'll find a way to have it."

"Yeah," she said, but she sounded a little sad. *"Maybe. I hope so."*

"I should let you get back to sleep. I'm sure you're tired."

"I'm a little tired," she admitted. *"We had a wedding tonight, and it ran later than usual. That's one thing I won't miss—the late nights at work. Being busy pretty much every Friday and Saturday. Makes it hard to have a social life."*

"Yeah." But suddenly I thought of her out on dates or having cocktails with her sisters or friends in a bar, every guy in the place staring at her. I clenched my teeth. *"Let me know how it goes with the building."*

"I will." She paused, then laughed. *"I was about to tell you to let me know how it goes in the shower, but . . ."*

I laughed too. *"My shower will be lonely."*

Her laughter faded. *"God, Zach. This is even harder than I thought it would be."*

"I know."

Neither of us said anything for a few seconds.

"Goodnight, Zach."

"Night."

I went straight to the bathroom and turned on the shower. She'd said her favorite was the jasmine honeysuckle, so I unwrapped that tablet and placed it on the tile. As I undressed, I thought about her. While I stood beneath the spray inhaling the sweet floral scent, I thought about her. With my hand wrapped around my cock, working up and down its hard length, I thought about her.

I didn't know how to stop.

After I got out of the gym on Sunday, I noticed a text from her. It was ridiculous the way my heart raced when I saw her name.

I SAW MY SHOP! read her message. As soon as I got behind the wheel, I called her.

"I saw it!" she said, sounding out of breath. "I saw my shop!"

I smiled at her excitement. "Yeah? Which one?"

"The historic building. It needs work for sure, but the moment I saw it I had a feeling, and then when I stepped inside I got chills. I just knew."

"You gotta trust that feeling. What kind of work does it need?"

"I need to tear everything out that's in there now and configure it the way I want it. I'll need to put in dressing rooms, a riser and mirrors for fittings, a seating area, a reception counter, new lighting. I love the original floors, but they need to be refinished, some painting needs to be done, and there was a plumbing problem that damaged one wall, but my dad thinks it could all be done within a month or so. He came with me to see it, which was good because I'll need his help for a lot of the work. He's really handy."

A jolt of envy shot through me. I was handy too. If I was there, I could do things for her—the floors maybe, or the painting, or construct those fitting rooms. Install her computers. And a security system. I could carry heavy boxes or lift furniture or even just keep her company. She wouldn't need another man.

Great, now I was jealous of her dad. As if I wasn't officially an asshole before. "A month or so? That's not bad."

"Not at all. And January will be the perfect time to open. Now I'm reaching out to designers to see when I might be able to get sample dresses and veils. And did I tell you I spoke to my boss at Cloverleigh about leaving?"

"No. How did it go?"

"Amazing. I was so nervous, but she was really supportive and understanding—she agrees that I should do this."

"So when will you stop working?"

"Probably at the end of October. My sister Winnie will take over for me here, and she wanted to give her boss at least a few weeks' notice."

"You sound so happy," I said, picturing her smiling face. Why was it making my chest hurt?

"I am. Thank you for telling me to trust my gut. I kept hearing your voice when I was walking through the space, encouraging me to go for it."

"I want to see you," I blurted.

She was stunned silent. "Huh?"

"I want to see you." The words tumbled out quickly. "I have another job in New York this week. Meet me there."

"Zach, I—"

"Please, Millie. I can't stop thinking about you. I feel like I'm losing my mind."

"I can't stop thinking about you either," she whispered.

"We're not hurting anyone. No one will know. We'll just blend in with the crowd in Manhattan. Or hide out in my hotel room. I don't care—I just want to see you again."

"What days will you be there?"

"I leave tomorrow and I'll be there until Friday. Even if you can only come out there for one night. I'll buy your ticket. Whatever it takes. Just come."

She was silent for a moment. "Okay," she said. "Okay, I'll come."

On Monday evening, I heard a knock on my hotel room door. I knew it was Millie because she'd texted me to let me know she'd arrived just minutes ago. But the knock surprised me because I'd left her name at the front desk and instructed them to give her a key.

My pulse quickened as I went to the door and pulled it open. But that was nothing compared to what my heart did when I saw her standing there in the hall.

"Hi," she whispered with a shy smile.

"Get in here." I grabbed her wrist and pulled her into the room, and it was almost like our first night together all over again. Our bodies came together, mouths seeking, hands clutching. She dropped her bag and I kicked the door shut. Within minutes, clothes were flying and we tumbled onto the mattress. And with only slightly more patience and finesse than I'd managed to have on her living room floor, I indulged in her body like I'd been dreaming about every night since we'd been apart. I couldn't believe it had only been a week.

When it was over, I rolled to my back, and we lay panting on top of the comforter, side by side. Somehow my left hand found her right, and I wrapped my fingers around hers. "God, I'm glad you're here."

"Me too." Her head turned toward me. "I almost didn't get on the plane."

I brought her hand to my mouth and kissed her knuckles. "Why?"

"I lied to my sisters. I never do that."

"I'm sorry."

"It's okay." She smiled. "It's so good to see you. And be with you. I'm not going to think about anything else."

"Good. Hey, didn't they give you a key down there?"

"Yes. I just didn't feel right using it."

I laughed, turning onto my side. "Why not?"

"I don't know." Her grin was shy and adorable. "It's your room."

"It's *our* room." I pressed my lips to hers. "And for the next two nights, I'm only leaving it when I absolutely have to."

"I wish I had more time. But I have to be back Wednesday afternoon."

"It's fine. We'll make very good use of the time we've got."

We ordered room service and watched Antiques Roadshow while we waited for it to be delivered. Sitting there with her, wearing thick hotel robes, my back propped against the headboard, her back resting against my chest, our bare feet crossed at the ankles side by side . . . I couldn't remember the last time I'd felt so at ease with someone. Or with myself.

"Ooooh look at that necklace," Millie said dreamily.

I studied the necklace on the screen and listened to what the appraiser was saying about it.

"This is a fourteen karat white gold vintage lavaliere-style diamond pendant from the 1920s," he told the woman who'd

inherited it from her aunt. *"The pendant is in beautiful condition, only slightly worn, with an intricate Art Deco filigree design."*

"I love Art Deco jewelry," she said with a sigh. "So pretty."

"It would look gorgeous on you," I told her.

Turns out, the thing was worth over a grand, which made Millie laugh. "Guess I'll have to sell some wedding gowns first."

After we ate, she wandered into the huge marble bathroom and started filling the tub. "I'm going to take a bath. Want to join me?" she called over the running water.

"Yes," I said, jumping off the bed. From the bathroom doorway, I watched her slip out of her robe and hang it on a hook.

"Even this *bath*room is amazing," she said, slipping into the water. "Who the heck is your client?"

"Can't tell you." I ditched my robe on the tiled floor and got into the tub behind her. Wrapping my arms around her, I filled my hands with her breasts. "I mean I could, but then I'd have to kill you, and I'm really enjoying your company at the moment."

She laughed. "Gee, thanks."

"So where does your family think you are?"

"Here," she said. "I told them I was flying to New York. I made up some meetings with a couple designers."

I could hear the guilt in her voice. "Do you feel bad about that?"

"Kind of. But I keep telling myself this isn't anyone's business but ours. And we aren't hurting anyone. And we're being careful not to get caught."

"All true." I kissed the top of her head.

"But I should tell you that my sisters know about last weekend."

I went still. "They do?"

"Yes. But I trust them completely. They won't say

anything. And at the time I told them, I thought we were putting an end to this."

"We tried, didn't we?"

"I guess so. Not very hard, though." She sighed. "Let's talk about something else."

"Okay. Tell me more about your new business."

"Like what?"

"What will you call it?"

"I've been thinking about that." She tapped my wrists. "I don't want it to have a name that sounds like any other bridal salon—I want it to be really personal, because my vision is personal. And I don't really want it to have anything in the name that designates it as size-specific. I plan to cater to plus-sized brides, but there might be a day in the future when the business grows enough to be completely inclusive."

"Smart to think ahead."

"And I've been thinking a lot about my brand," she went on. "It will be elegant and feminine, luxurious but accessible, sexy but in a classy way, cozy but still fancy."

"You just described yourself," I told her.

She laughed. "You think so?"

"With one hundred percent accuracy."

"It's funny you say that because Frannie suggested I call it Millie Rose—Rose is my middle name."

"Millie Rose. I like it. Rolls off the tongue."

"I like it too, the more I think about it. I like the M sound at the beginning, the lilt of the L. And *rose* is a romantic word."

"I just like saying your name."

"Well, I have to think about this stuff, you know? But I do think my name has sort of a pretty, old-fashioned charm to it. It's funny, I used to hate it."

"Yeah?"

"Totally. My first name is really Millicent. Growing up, I didn't know any Millicents or any Roses. It was my great-grandmother's name, but I never met her. I wanted a name like Madison or Samantha or Chelsea. Millicent Rose just sounded like an old lady to me." She looked at me over her shoulder. "Did you like your name growing up?"

"I liked that it started with a Z. I thought that was cool." A memory surfaced. "My little sister Poppy couldn't say her S's or Z's though. She had a lisp, so when she said my name— *thack*—it always made me laugh. I would try so hard to get her to say it right, and she never could."

"Aww. Tell me something else about her," Millie said softly.

No one ever asked me about Poppy anymore. Most days I would have said that was how I wanted it, since talking about her was painful, but I wanted her to be remembered too. "She loved butterflies. She was fascinated by them and always wanted to chase them." I chuckled. "Moths too. I don't think she knew the difference. She just thought they were brown butterflies."

"Did she look like you?"

"Nope. I looked like my dad. She had blond hair she used to wear in pigtails and big blue eyes."

Millie took one of my hands and fit her palm to mine.

"I dream about her sometimes," I confessed.

"Do you?"

"Yeah."

"Are they . . . good dreams?" She laced our fingers together.

"Yes. She's still a child, exactly how I remember her, but I'm always an adult. She wants to hold my hand, just like she always did."

"That's so sweet."

I studied our interlocked hands for a moment and admitted something to her I'd never said to anyone. "I think she's the reason why I never wanted kids."

"What do you mean?"

"Losing her was so painful. I never wanted to feel that again."

Millie shivered.

"You're cold." I worried I'd said too much. "Should we get out?"

"In a sec." She turned over, putting us chest to chest, and pressed her lips to my collarbone. "Thanks for talking about her."

"You're welcome."

Another kiss, on my jaw this time, then a seductive smile. "Want to take a hot shower with me?"

"Definitely."

"Are you sure? I sing in the shower, you know. And I'm not good."

"Oh yeah? What's your favorite song to sing in the shower?"

"It changes. This morning, it was 'Beautiful Day' by U2."

"A classic." I rubbed my thumb over her lips. "And today is beautiful."

We said goodbye on Wednesday morning before I left for work.

"I wish I could take you to the airport," I told her. "Are you sure you don't want me to get a Cole Security car for you?"

"I'm sure," she said, zipping up her roller bag. "I'll just grab a cab. Let's not risk anything to link us together."

I laughed. "It's not like Cole Security cars have a logo on the side, Millie. They're totally discreet."

"Even so," she chided. "I'll feel better on my own."

"Okay." I took her in my arms and held her tight, her head tucked beneath my chin. "Thanks for coming here."

"I enjoyed every moment."

"Think about Vegas, okay?" I was headed there on another job in a few weeks, and I'd invited her to meet me.

"I will." She tipped her head back and our lips met one last time.

I held the door open for her and gave her arm one final squeeze, then watched as she left the room and headed down the hall toward the elevator. "Be safe," I called quietly.

She glanced at me over one shoulder and blew me a kiss, all my instincts told me not to let her go.

Eighteen

Millie

November

MY LAST FEW WEEKS AT CLOVERLEIGH FARMS FLEW BY. October was booked with weddings every weekend, and when I wasn't busy preparing for them, I was getting everything in order to ensure a smooth transition for Winnie. Mr. and Mrs. Fournier at Abelard said they were sorry to lose her, but they totally understood her decision to move over to Cloverleigh Farms.

During my weeknights and days off, every moment was spent preparing to launch my new business. Even mundane things like securing my tax identification number from the state gave me a thrill. I hired a website and graphic designer, opened a bank account, finalized the terms of the loan from Hutton, signed the lease for my dream space, hired a contractor, switched the utilities into my name, and scheduled interviews with potential employees.

On my last day at Cloverleigh Farms, my co-workers threw me a little farewell celebration in the bar at the inn, complete with a cake made by Frannie's bakery that said Good Luck, Millie with Cloverleigh's signature four-leaf clover on it. I was moved by all the kind things everyone said, all the hugs and well wishes, and by all the encouragement from women who heard about the shop I was opening and said, "It's about time."

During the party, my dad caught me wiping tears from my eyes. "What's this?" he asked. "Second thoughts?"

"No," I assured him. "I'm just overwhelmed by everyone's support. And I feel like I'm saying goodbye to a chapter of my life, you know? I have a lot of happy memories in this place."

He wrapped an arm around me and kissed my head. "You'll always have a home here."

I tipped my head onto his shoulder, my heart too full to find words.

Starting the very next day, I dedicated every hour and all my efforts to turning Millie Rose from a vision in my head into reality. During the first week in November, I picked up the keys and drove straight to my new business address. My sisters surprised me later that afternoon by showing up with a bottle of champagne—we popped the cork and poured three glasses.

Goosebumps blanketed my skin as I turned around inside the empty space.

"To Millie Rose—the shop and the woman!" shouted Winnie.

"To chasing your dreams!" added Felicity.

"To all the brides who will find their wedding gowns here," I said, lifting my glass. "I cannot wait to be part of your story."

We clinked glasses with shining eyes.

"I have keys to my shop!" I told Zach on a video chat later that night, dangling them in front of the phone. "It's really happening!"

He laughed, relaxing on his couch. "So now what? The renovations begin?"

"Yes. I have so much work to do." As I talked, I made dinner, moving back and forth from the fridge to the pantry to the counter while my cats watched me like observers at a tennis match. "My family is going to help me as much as they can, but I also ended up hiring some guys to fix the plumbing issue, tear out the previous tenant's interior, and build what I need. Then my dad can help me with the floors and the walls. And my sisters are going to help me with the furniture and decor. I have stock arriving in December, so I need to work fast!"

"What about employees? Need me to do any background checks?"

I giggled. "Not yet. I have some interviews scheduled for tomorrow, and guess what? One woman who answered my online ad is a seamstress with tons of experience! Her name is Diane Tucker. She's worked in a bridal salon outside Nashville for fifteen years, but her husband just retired and they're moving up here to be closer to their daughter and grandchildren."

"Sounds perfect."

"I know. She's definitely the most qualified candidate I'm interviewing. I hope I can afford her." I sliced some lemons on a cutting board.

"What are you making for dinner?"

"Lemon chicken. Frannie's recipe."

"My stomach is growling."

"Awww. Come over. I'll feed you."

"I wish I could. I'll probably end up with takeout again."

He listened to me babble on about light fixtures and fabric textures and wood floor stains and paint colors and even hanger styles, asking the occasional question but mostly just letting me talk. Sometimes I'd stop meal preparations to run over to my laptop and make a note about a call I needed to make or a task I feared I'd forget to handle or an idea I wanted to run by the contractor.

"I'm sorry, Zach, I'm totally monopolizing the conversation." I grabbed a spatula from a drawer and flipped the chicken breast over in the pan. "How are you? How was your day?"

"I'm fine," he said. "Nothing new or exciting here. And I like hearing you talk about your shop. I wish I could see it."

"Me too."

"I wish I could see *you*. Have you given any more thought to meeting me in Las Vegas next weekend?"

"Of course I have. I think about it all the time." I glanced at my cats, as if they might hear and judge me. "I'm just nervous. Where will I say I'm going and why?"

"Las Vegas is the wedding capital of the world, isn't it? Say you're going for research."

I laughed. "There *is* a veil wholesaler out there. I guess I could say I'm going out there to look at stock."

"Perfect. I'm booking your ticket. I'll be there Thursday to Monday. What days work for you?"

"I can get away for a weekend. Friday to Sunday. And I'll see if I can visit that wholesaler on Saturday."

"I'll make sure you have a car too. And a driver if you want one."

I smiled as my stomach fluttered with excitement. "Then I guess I'll see you next Friday."

The ticket Zach purchased for me was first class. The hotel was five star. The bed was king-sized and made up with 600 thread count sheets that felt like satin against my skin.

We spent a *lot* of time in them.

The hotel room door had barely closed behind me and

Zach was striding toward me, his eyes dark and hungry. I tried to say hello and his lips consumed mine with a kiss. I tried to pull back and look at him—my eyes were desperate to get their fill after two weeks apart—but his arms were locked tight around me. I tried to unbutton his shirt, eager to feel his bare chest under my palms, but he wouldn't let me get him naked until he'd pulled every stitch of clothing off me and gotten his hands and lips and tongue on every inch of my skin.

He was still fully clothed, his face buried between my thighs, my fingers fisted in his hair, when I had my first orgasm, leaning back against a mountain of pillows like a queen.

Only then would he allow me to undress him, and I took my time—savoring every new part of his body revealed to me as I peeled off his clothes piece by piece. I removed his shirt and brushed my lips against the hair on his chest. Ran my tongue along the lines of ink on his biceps and ribs. Caressed the ridges of his abs with my nose, breathing in his scent. I pulled off his jeans and boxer briefs and pushed him onto the bed, kneeling between his legs. I ran my hands up his legs, appreciating the firm muscles of his calves, his thick, powerful thighs, the V lines bracketing his erection, which rested on his abdomen, massive and heavy and hard.

I traced those V lines with my tongue. I watched his stomach muscles flex and his cock twitch with anticipation. I rubbed my lips against his crown and swept them down the thick, veined shaft, relishing in every texture of his skin.

He lay back against the pillows like I had, watching me, his jaw slightly open, breaths coming fast, chest rising and falling. He groaned when I finally took him into my mouth, his fingers threading into my hair. "God, I've thought about this," he rasped as I took him to the back of my throat. "Every fucking night. My good girl." His hips were already lifting off the bed, and I could taste him on my tongue—salty and masculine. I would have finished him off that way, but he lifted my head and turned me beneath him.

"I have to get inside you," he growled. "I can't wait a second longer."

I didn't argue, just as anxious as he was for the heat and friction and the feel of his body deep inside me. I clung to him fiercely, wanting to be closer even when it was impossible, surrendering to the longing for him that never seemed to abate, crying out as he drove us both off the edge, falling to pieces beneath him.

You can't keep doing this, said a voice in my head. *You're out of control.*

I ignored it, let it be swallowed up by the sensation of his weight above me. His rapid-fire breathing. His warm, damp skin against mine. The final shudder and pulse of his body.

As my heartbeat slowed, my eyes filled with tears. Embarrassed and confused, I pretended I had to use the bathroom. "I'll be right back," I whispered, my throat thick with emotion.

He rolled off me, and I quickly slipped from the bed and hurried into the bathroom, where I splashed cold water on my face and took several deep breaths. When I had control of myself, I stared at my reflection and issued that girl a warning.

No. Just don't.

I knew what I was doing when I agreed to come here. I knew what this was and what this wasn't. I knew where this could go and where it couldn't. No one was suffering any delusions or making any false promises. The truth was always right in front of my face. And as long as I kept it in plain sight, I'd be fine.

I fluffed my hair, wiped the smudged eye makeup from beneath my eyes, and went back into the room. The sight of him, rugged and gorgeous and looking concerned, wasn't good for my heart.

"Hey," he said, his forehead wrinkling. "You okay?"

"Of course."

"Come here." He opened his arms to me, and I crawled onto the bed and snuggled up against his side. "That's better."

"Do you have to work tonight?"

"No. I'm doing building security risk assessment here. We work during the day." He kissed my head. "What should we do? Gamble? See an Elvis impersonator? Go clubbing?"

"Clubbing!" I laughed. "You're talking to a woman that gets in bed almost every night by nine. We are too old to go clubbing. They'd probably turn us away at the door, Grandpa."

He inhaled sharply. "Oh, you are *begging* for punishment, aren't you?" He put his hand in my hair and tightened his fist, making me wince. My scalp tingled with pleasure and pain as he tipped my head back. His eyes narrowed. His voice deepened. "Aren't you?"

"Yes."

He clenched his hand tighter. "Yes, what? Where are my good girl's manners?"

"Yes, please."

His fist relaxed slightly. "That's better. Now I think you better lie across my lap so I can teach you a lesson."

Grinning, I did as requested—my body was up for some hurting tonight, but at least if we played games, my heart was safe.

For now.

The following morning, I drove the car Zach had gotten for me over to Marigold Bridal Wholesale, where I'd scheduled an eleven o'clock appointment.

Marigold was family-owned, and I was greeted by the

Songs, a friendly husband and wife team who led me on a brief tour of the factory before ushering me into the showroom.

I couldn't help but get excited by all the gorgeous tulle and beading and lace. The Songs' daughter, Nicole, introduced herself and showed me what was new, what was popular, what was evergreen, and what she suspected the trend-setting brides would be wearing next year. I saw veils with every possible edge—corded and pearl and horsehair and ribbon and soutache—as well as every variety of length and style, from birdcage to flyaway to waist to chapel to cathedral. Colors ranged from white to ivory to champagne to moscato to blush. There were hair accessories too.

"The cool girls are still going for birdcage," said Nicole, "but I also think a lot of trendy brides will forego veils this year and do things like bows, barrettes or clips, and even some caps or hoods."

"Oh, the big satin bow is cute, isn't it?" I took it off a display shelf and turned it over in my hand.

"Definitely." She grinned. "Want to try it on?"

"No, that's okay." I laughed as I replaced it. "I'm a little old for a big bow, I'd feel silly. I think I'd go more traditional."

"Traditional brides are going for drama," said Nicole. "Look at this." She took a floral-embroidered veil from the wall and brought it over. "Isn't it gorgeous?"

I gasped, gently touching the edge. "It is."

"Face the mirror. Let me show you what it looks like on."

Turning around, I faced the middle of three full-length mirrors with ornate silver frames. I'd worn my hair half-up today, and Nicole centered the veil's comb where my barrette held my hair back. "Look at that," she said, adjusting the sides so they cascaded down in front of my arms. Then she knelt and spread the chapel-length veil in a semi-circle that fanned out like a peacock's feathers on the floor at my feet. "Stunning, right?"

"It is," I whispered, staring at myself in the glass. My clothes—a black, cap-sleeved, belted jumpsuit worn with leopard pumps—didn't really scream bridal attire, but it was easy to imagine the dress that would complement this veil—something long and sleek and embroidered, with a deep V neck or maybe strapless, and a hint of a mermaid shape. The hair on my arms stood on end.

"It suits you." Nicole smiled at me in the mirror and stood back, her arms folded. "Are you married already?"

"No."

"Engaged?"

I shook my head.

"Well, if and when the time comes, maybe you'll choose something like this."

"Maybe." My throat was dry. I glanced down at my left hand, which seemed extra naked right now. "Right now, I'm just trying to get my store going. I don't have much time to date."

"I totally understand," she said, removing the veil from my head. "And there's no rush, you know? Live a little. Have fun. When it's meant to be, it will happen."

I smiled and nodded, rubbing the fourth finger of my left hand. "I hope so."

That night, Zach and I braved dinner out at a small, off-the-beaten-path Italian restaurant. Seated at a table for two in a dark corner, candle flickering on the table between us, we enjoyed a Saturday night date just like any other couple.

Looking across the table at Zach made my heart quicken. He was so handsome in his navy dress shirt with the cuffs rolled up. Every woman in here watched him walk through the room. I still recalled seeing him for the first time at the hotel bar, the way he caught my attention and wouldn't let it go. How incredible that the hot stranger from two months ago was the man out with me tonight. The one looking at me like I was the only woman in this restaurant, maybe even this city. The one reaching across the table to take my hand.

I smiled at our clasped fingers and gasped in mock surprise. "Mr. Barrett! What if someone saw? My reputation would be ruined forever."

His lips tipped up. "I figure we're safe here. Holding hands isn't exactly scandalous behavior in Las Vegas."

"I suppose you're right."

"And it's hard for me to be near you and not touching you. Especially when I have to let you leave tomorrow morning."

My smile faded. "Don't talk about it. We've got the rest of tonight."

"Tell me more about today. You liked what you saw at the wholesaler?"

"Yes. I really liked the owners and the quality of their products. I ended up placing a pretty big order." Heat crept into my cheeks. "I even tried one of their veils on."

"Playing dress-up on the job, huh?" He looked amused.

"Yeah. It was really pretty." I glanced down at my left hand, the one he held. "But it was just for fun."

The server arrived with our entrees, and I took my hand back and repositioned my napkin on my lap.

"Can I ask about *your* wedding?" I asked when we were alone again.

He shrugged. "If you want to."

"Was it big?"

He picked up his whiskey. "Yes."

"What did you wear?"

"A very uncomfortable tuxedo." He took a sip. "Or maybe it was me that was uncomfortable."

I reached for my fork and poked at a seared scallop on my plate. "What kind of venue was it?"

"A country club. Whatever one her parents belonged to." He set his glass down. "We were married outside, and the reception was inside. I had very little to do with any of it. It was hot and I sweated a lot. That's mostly what I remember."

I began eating my dinner as I pictured the details—Zach looking gorgeous but tense in his tux, hundreds of guests in white chairs on a sunny country club lawn, a bride in a big white dress being walked up the aisle by her father. I wondered about her, about what had gone wrong with them.

"So what was she like? Your ex-wife."

He studied me for a moment. "Why do you ask?"

"I don't know. I'm curious. I mean, she's on television, right? I assume she's attractive."

"I haven't seen her in over a year. On TV or in person."

"But you must remember what she looks like."

"She had dark hair and blue eyes." He took a bite of his steak. "She also had a loud voice and long middle finger she liked to give me. *That* I remember."

I hid a smile. "Did you guys fight a lot?"

"In the end we did. Or at least, she would try to pick fights and I'd refuse to have them. I didn't see the point."

I nodded and ate a bite of my dinner. I still wasn't certain what I was digging for.

"I don't mean to blame Kimberly for everything. Like I said, I knew going into it the marriage was a mistake. I never wanted to be anyone's husband."

"So what made you do it?" I asked.

"Believe me, I've asked myself that question a million times. I still don't have a good answer." He focused on cutting his steak. "For a long time, it was like I was married to the Navy. But when that was over, my life changed. Guys around me were getting married, having families. I figured I'd try it instead of being alone." He glanced up at me. "I probably sound like a real dick."

"No," I said quickly. "You sound honest."

"Believe me, she didn't like being married to me any better than I liked being married to her. When I'd travel for work, instead of coming home and finding someone who was glad to see me, I had someone determined to punish me for being gone."

"Really?"

He shrugged. "She was an only child, and her parents had spoiled her rotten. She was used to feeling like the center of the universe."

I laughed. "She never would have lasted in my house. Growing up with four sisters means you're always sharing attention. We never had a chance to be spoiled."

Zach picked up his drink. "I'll spoil you," he said. "Right here at this table if you want me to."

I met his eyes and felt my core muscles tighten. "Maybe we should go back to the room first."

"I'll get the check."

My flight left early the next morning, and Zach insisted on taking me to the airport. He drove an unmarked black SUV with tinted windows and spotless black leather interior.

"Wow," I said, running my hand over the smooth seat. "Is your car at home this clean?"

"Pretty much."

"My car is the opposite. You would think a bomb went off."

He laughed. "I noticed that when I moved it at your house."

"Don't judge! It's not dirty, there's no trash in it or

anything. There's just a lot of *stuff* in it—fabric samples, clothing, shoes, water bottles. It's weird, because inside my house, I'm a stickler for neatness. I like everything in its place, nice and organized. My car is . . . another story."

"No judgement. You'd probably take one look in my kitchen and think a fifth grader lived there."

"Why?"

He shrugged. "It's just kind of empty. I don't own much kitchen stuff, and what I do own is pretty random. Nothing matches. Lots of plastic."

I laughed. "Now I know what to get you for Christmas."

He was quiet for a moment. "Mason keeps asking me to come out to Michigan at Christmas. I turned down his Thanksgiving invitation."

My stomach tensed at the mention of Mason. I tried never to let myself think about him, or I felt too guilty. "Have you spoken to him much?"

"Once or twice since the wedding."

I nodded, staring at my feet. "Will you visit them?"

"I haven't decided. What do you think I should do?"

"I'm not making that decision for you, Zach." I shook my head. "No way. I feel bad enough that I'm complicating your relationship with your son."

He reached over and took my hand. "Don't feel bad. I take full responsibility for my decisions. You've done nothing wrong."

I closed my eyes a moment. "Let's not think about that. Where will you go for Thanksgiving?"

"Probably to Jackson's. He and his wife are nice enough to invite me to their family dinner every year. What about you?"

"I'll go to my parents' house. Frannie always does the turkey, but we all pitch in and help."

He pulled up at the curb in front of my terminal and put

the SUV in park. His hand stole to the back of my neck. "I wish you didn't have to go."

"Me too."

Leaning across the center console, he pressed his lips to mine, then whispered against them. "Chicago. I'm there on a job the first week in December, and I'll stay through the weekend. Meet me."

"God, Zach. I want to. You know I want to."

"Then say yes."

I swallowed hard. Every night we spent together only brought us closer. Every kiss made it harder to part. Every goodbye was an inevitable reminder that we had no future.

We couldn't keep this up forever. Being apart from him was starting to hurt too much. And what possible excuse could I come up with for a trip to Chicago right when I was trying to get a business off the ground? This had to stop.

But when I opened my mouth, that isn't what came out.

"Okay," I said. "I'll work it out."

Nineteen

Zach

WHEN I ARRIVED HOME AFTER BEING IN LAS VEGAS WITH Millie, the silence in my apartment felt oppressive.

I was tired, but I didn't feel like sleeping. I was hungry, but I didn't feel like eating. I was lonely, but the only company I wanted was Millie's, and I couldn't have it.

If she lived here, maybe she'd be in the kitchen making something for us to eat, or maybe I'd have brought dinner home for the two of us. Maybe I'd have called her and said, *I'm on my way, what would you like?* Or maybe when I got home, she'd be waiting for me in bed. Instead of giving me the cold shoulder because I'd been gone for work again, she'd reach for me, tell me how much she missed me, make me feel happy to be home again.

I dropped onto the couch and rubbed my face, at a loss to understand what the hell was the matter with me. Once my divorce was final, I'd sworn that was it—I wouldn't get tangled up with anyone again. The occasional good time here or there was fine, but no relationships. No commitments. No feelings.

But it was hard to deny I felt something for Millie beyond

sexual attraction. I didn't just want sex from her. I wanted to *be* with her. All the time.

Too fucking bad.

Scowling, I got up from the couch and stalked into the kitchen. *You can't be with her, so quit pining like a jackass teenager.*

I yanked open the fridge and stared at the pathetic contents—some leftover takeout, ketchup and mustard, eggs I didn't remember buying, and a few apples. After checking the sell by date on the egg carton (long past), I chucked them down the disposal and ran it, wishing I could toss in my feelings too.

What was I even doing with her? How long could I expect her to keep running around the country to meet me for a night or two, lying to her family about where or why, knowing that there was absolutely no future for us? She'd told me what she wanted—a husband. Children. A family. She wanted kids so badly she was considering donor sperm so she could have them on her own, sooner rather than later.

The thought of some guy's stuff anywhere near her made me want to throw a kitchen chair through the window. I had to lean on the edge of the sink and take several deep breaths to calm down.

But it wasn't fair, what I was asking of her. The lying and the secrecy. Spending time with me she should be dedicating to her business. Giving me her attention instead of looking for the one who could give her what she wanted. I knew in my bones how unfair this was.

And yet, I wasn't ready to give her up.

In a cupboard I found a random can of chili that hadn't expired, dumped it into a bowl, and stuck it in the microwave. One more weekend, I vowed as I waited for it to heat up. One more secret meet-up and then we would break it off.

She texted me as I was rinsing my dishes. **Are you home yet? Want to call me?**

I hit her name in my recents.

"Hello?"

I smiled at the sound of her voice. "Hey, gorgeous. How was your day?"

"Good! My dad took the day off and we started painting."

"Oh yeah?" I took my phone into the bedroom and sat on the mattress.

"Yes, and remember that woman I told you about? The seamstress with all the wedding dress experience and the amazing references? She accepted my offer!"

"That's great."

"I'm *so* relieved. I still have a few people to interview for the sales positions, but that's the job I worried about the most."

"So everything is coming together."

She laughed. "It might be a little too soon to say that, but things are off to a good start."

"I'm happy for you."

"Thanks. How was your trip home?"

"It was fine."

"What's wrong?"

"Nothing," I said. "I'm just tired."

"Same," she said with a sigh. Then she added softly, "And I miss you."

"I miss you too."

I couldn't remember the last time I'd said those words, or even experienced the feeling. I wasn't in the habit of missing people—and that was on purpose. But later, after I'd showered and climbed into bed alone, her absence gnawed at me like a physical ache.

I scowled into the dark. This was *not* supposed to happen.

On Thanksgiving, I went to Jackson and Catherine's house, even though I feared feeling like a fifth wheel at their dinner table. But their house was warm and welcoming, and it smelled delicious when I walked in. I handed Catherine a bottle of wine and kissed her cheek. "Thanks for having me."

"Of course." She smiled. "Go tell Jackson to make you a drink. I kicked him out of the kitchen because he kept getting in my way."

"You don't need any help with dinner?"

She shook her head. "I've got the girls. You men can be on dish duty after we're done."

"Sounds good."

I found Jackson in the family room watching football. "Hey," he said from his leather recliner. "How about a beer?"

"Sure."

"They're in the fridge over there." He gestured to a wet bar along the wall. "Help yourself. I'd get up, but I don't feel like it."

I grinned and grabbed a bottle from the small beverage fridge beneath the counter. Popping off the cap, I sank onto one end of the couch.

"So what's new?" he asked, lowering the volume on the flatscreen.

"Not much."

"You've been quiet lately."

"Have I?" I tipped up my beer.

"Yeah. Are you going to tell me what it is that has you so preoccupied or should I guess?"

I set my jaw and shrugged.

Jackson laughed. "Okay, we'll play this game. I think it's the girl back in Michigan. The one who sent you the care package. I think you're still hung up on her."

"I'm not *hung up* on her," I said defensively, although that's exactly what I was.

"But you're still thinking about her."

I took a long pull from the bottle and decided to be up

front with Jackson. *"If I was just* thinking, *there wouldn't be a problem. Or at least, it wouldn't be so big."*

"You mean you've seen her again?"

"Twice," I confessed. *"She met me in New York in October and in Vegas this month. We're meeting up next weekend in Chicago."*

"Jesus, Zach." He rubbed a hand over his jaw. *"Why are you doing this?"*

"I don't even know." I shook my head. *"It makes no sense. She's too young for me. She's my son's ex. Every time we meet up, she has to lie to her family about what she's doing. And when I go visit Mason and Lori at Christmas, we won't even be able to see each other. If we do, we'll have to pretend there's nothing between us—and I'm not sure we'll be convincing."*

"Barrett, this is fucked up." Jackson pinned me with a stare.

"I know," I said irritably. *"That's why we're going to end it."*

"When?"

"In Chicago."

He cocked his head. *"So what is that, like your final hurrah?"*

Another shrug.

"And she's on board with that plan?"

"She will be when we discuss it," I said carefully.

"And what happens if she isn't?"

Unable to sit still anymore, I jumped up and started to pace. *"She agrees this is wrong, Jackson. She hates the lying as much as I do."*

"So come clean about it."

"We can't. Not only will Mason despise us both for lying, but she really doesn't want to be known in her small town as the woman dating her ex's dad—who's also about to be a grandpa. Fuck." I stopped pacing and chugged some beer. *"I*

thought this was just a temporary thing, you know? I thought maybe I was just panicking about getting old. About never feeling young again."

"It does have a whiff of midlife crisis about it," Jackson agreed.

I'd have laughed if I wasn't so distraught. "She deserves better, Jackson."

He studied me silently. "You really care about this girl."

"It doesn't matter," I insisted. "If things were different, if I were ten years younger . . . who knows? But things are what they are, and I'm forty-fucking-seven and sterile." I shuddered at the sound of the word.

"How old is she?"

"Thirty-two."

"Oh. So she's not *that* young."

"No. She's looking for a guy who wants to get married and have kids. That's not me. I never wanted to get married in the first place, I was crap at it, and having kids is impossible anyway."

Jackson nodded. "She knows that, right?"

"She knows about the vasectomy, yes. I'm not leading her on. I wouldn't do that."

"I believe you."

I sank onto the couch again, defeated. "But I'm not an idiot. I know this can't continue. I'm wasting her time. I'm being selfish."

Jackson was quiet for a moment. "Even beyond that, I don't think you should be lying to your son. If you're truly going to build a relationship with him based on mutual trust and respect, this is not the way to start."

"I know." It was nothing I hadn't said to myself a thousand times.

"You know secrets like that don't stay secret, Zach. Not in a small town. If you continue to see her, Mason *will* find out.

You'll be the long-lost father who slept with his ex and then tried to cover it up. Not really going to win you many points in the dad department."

"I never wanted to be a dad," I said angrily, as if it mattered.

"And I never wanted to babysit a bunch of ex-Navy SEALs, but here we are. I've been where you are, man. I've kept things hidden because I thought it was the right choice. I thought I was protecting people I cared about, so I know better than anyone—it's a road that leads to a very steep cliff. Either come clean, or break it off."

I let his words sink in. "I'll talk to her."

Twenty

Millie

THE DAY AFTER THANKSGIVING, I woke up early and went into the store. I stopped for coffee at a chain donut shop instead of Plum & Honey, which made me feel terrible, but I couldn't face Frannie. All day yesterday, I'd felt like I was wearing a giant neon sign that said LIAR on it. My stomach was so upset, I'd hardly enjoyed the meal.

Several times, family members had asked me if I was okay, and I nodded and smiled and said yes, I was fine, just preoccupied with the shop. Since that was such an understandable reason for my distraction, everyone believed me. In fact, they got excited and asked tons of questions and volunteered to help out if I needed extra hands this weekend. I was expecting both of my sisters to show up this morning, possibly my dad and Dex as well. Even Dex's girls piped up and offered their services if I needed anyone to try on dresses and see if they'd fit short brides.

I'd thanked them and said I was pretty sure the dresses were only going to fit grown-up ladies, but they were welcome to come visit the shop and try on a veil or two. They'd exchanged a look of pure joy.

Smiling at the memory—they reminded me of the MacAllister sisters at that age—I let myself into the store and looked around. There was still a ton of work to do, but the builders had finished, the floors were done, and the new lighting had been installed. It was amazing progress for just three and a half weeks.

I sipped my coffee and grimaced—it was awful, weak and stale. But I told myself I deserved it for keeping my distance from Frannie. It hurt my heart to keep something so big from her, to refrain from asking her advice. I could use it. Same with my sisters. I wasn't used to hiding my feelings this way.

When the door opened behind me, bringing in a gust of cold air, I turned in surprise.

Felicity entered, carrying two white cardboard cups. "Morning," she chirped with a smile. Then she saw the coffee in my hand, and her face fell. "Oh, shoot. You already got coffee this morning."

I eyed one of the cups in her hand. "Is that from Plum & Honey? Because this isn't, and I can't even drink it."

"Yes. Here." She handed me the cup. "Why'd you go someplace else?"

Walking over to the reception desk, I ditched my old coffee on the marble counter and eagerly inhaled the aroma coming from the Plum & Honey cup. "I took a different way downtown, that's all."

"Oh." She came over and set a large purse on the counter, then pulled a white bakery bag from it. "I brought breakfast too."

"You're an angel." I glanced at the pink velvet circle settee with the tufted back that had just been delivered on Tuesday, the only seating I had in there so far. "We just can't get anything on that upholstery."

She laughed. "Let's sit on the floor."

We dropped down on the newly refinished pine floor,

stained a gorgeous dark walnut, and leaned back against the couch. Facing the front of the shop, we stretched out our legs and Felicity placed some scones on the bag between us. Outside the windows, snow flurries drifted to the ground.

"So how are things?" Felicity asked.

"Good. Great. I'm on track to be open by the first of the year."

"That's awesome." Felicity sipped her coffee. "But I meant with you personally."

I took a bite of scone and wondered if I should confide in Felicity. It would feel so good to have someone to talk to about Zach. But would she guilt me about it? Or would she understand? "I'm fine," I said gingerly.

"I know you're fine, but I have this feeling something's going on with you that isn't just about the shop."

I took a small sip from my coffee cup. "If I tell you," I said slowly, "do you promise not to judge? Or say anything to anyone else?"

She held out one pinkie, and I hooked it with mine.

"Okay." I inhaled deeply. "I'm having a sort of . . . affair with Zach."

"I figured that might be it. You've been traveling so much—you're seeing him on those trips?"

"Yes."

"So it's serious?"

"Yes and no." I struggled to explain it. "My *feelings* are serious, but what we're doing can't be. That's the problem."

"And the more time you spend together, the more you feel."

"Exactly."

"Well, he's not a lost puppy," she pointed out, a tinge of hope in her voice. "Is Mason the issue?"

"Mason is a huge part of it. Zach gave Mason his word that nothing happened between us."

"But that was before there really *was* something, right? I mean, couldn't you just explain to Mason that you tried not to act on your attraction, but you just . . . couldn't help it?"

"'Couldn't help it' might explain one time," I said. "But the last three months? If we admit the truth to Mason now, it means revealing that we've been carrying on since the wedding behind his back. People will talk about me, and it won't be nice. I'm trying to get a business going in this town. I want people to associate my name with professionalism and romance, not a tawdry scandal."

She sighed. "Yeah. It would be juicy gossip."

"We would hurt Mason, destroy his relationship with his father, make Zach look like a jerk, ruin my reputation . . . and for what? It's not like there's any possibility of a future."

"None at all?"

"No." I set my coffee down and tried to fight the tears that sprang to my eyes. "He has a grown son and an ex-wife."

"I didn't know about the ex. Are there other kids?"

"No. He had a vasectomy years ago."

"Oh." Then, a little softer. "*Oh*."

In the silence, the hopelessness of it all seemed to pile up around me.

"Wait, can't a vasectomy be reversed?" Felicity asked, sitting up taller.

"It can, but the success rate of pregnancy afterward is only about fifty percent or so, given how long it's been since he had it done. I Googled it."

"Hmm." She leaned back again. "Fifty percent doesn't give you great odds."

"Nope. So there's really no point in suffering Mason's anger and small-town scorn. Zach cannot be the one." The lump in my throat continued to swell. "No matter how perfect he is for me in every other way."

Felicity sighed. "I'm sorry, Mills. I don't know what to tell you."

"Tell me I'm an idiot to fall in love with him."

"I could, but I don't think it will help." My sister scooted closer and put an arm around me.

A tear slipped down my cheek, and then another. Annoyed with myself, I wiped them away. "This is stupid. I knew going in what this was."

"Sometimes our hearts don't communicate with our heads."

"Hearts are dumb," I said angrily.

We sat in silence for a moment, watching the snow grow a little thicker. "So what now?" she asked.

"We're meeting in Chicago next weekend."

"You *are*?" She sounded surprised.

I remembered Zach's words the night he showed up at my house after telling me he couldn't see me again. "Believe me, Felicity, if I could stay away from him, I would."

"But isn't it just going to make it harder to end things if you keep seeing him like that? Why torture yourself?"

I sniffed as my eyes welled again, then picked up my coffee. "Like I said. Hearts are dumb."

Twenty-One

Zach

WE DIDN'T HAVE THE TALK. We spent the entire weekend she visited me in Chicago hiding out in my hotel room, steaming up the windows while the wind howled and the temperature dropped and the snow swirled around in the streets below. In fact, the blizzard was so bad, she stayed in Chicago an extra night—she'd driven down to the city, and I didn't want her on the roads until the plows had cleared the snow from the highway.

Which meant I had a whole extra day to bring up calling it quits, and I still didn't do it.

We talked about plenty of other things . . . our childhoods, our favorite songs and movies, our biggest regrets and accomplishments, our greatest fears.

"Snakes," she said with a laugh. "Definitely snakes. But spiders are up there too. Really any bugs. That's why I'm never going to Japan."

"Japan?"

"Yes! I read that country has the worst bugs in the world. There's some kind of giant centipede that sounds terrifying, and also a giant hornet that has flesh-melting venom."

I laughed. *"Are you making this up?"*

"No! I read about it."

"Well, I've been to Japan, and I've never seen those things."

"Consider yourself lucky." She picked up her head from my chest and looked at me. "So what's your biggest fear? I assume it's not bugs."

"It's not bugs."

She poked my chest. "Tell me."

I played with her hair, threading my fingers into it and slowly combing through the thick, gold strands. "I've always had the same fear since I was a kid."

"What is it?"

"Someone dying on my watch."

She didn't say anything. She just put her head on my chest again and wrapped an arm and leg over me. But I didn't need words from her. What she was giving me was far better— her trust.

Maybe she hated giant bugs, but she'd once told me without even realizing it what her greatest fear was. *I want him to need me*, she'd said. *I never want to be scared he'll leave.*

I kissed the top of her head and held her tight.

Maybe tomorrow we'd end things.

Of course, we didn't.

There were moments of silence between us, times when we were just lying next to each other, or eating room service, or hiding at a corner table in the hotel bar our last night there, hoping no one we knew would wander in. During those moments I knew in my gut I should bring up what had to happen next. But I never did it. I couldn't bring myself to ruin the mood or take the smile from her face.

And the next morning, she woke up with a cold—her nose

pink and stuffy, her eyes bloodshot, her voice hoarse. She must have sneezed fifteen times inside two minutes.

"Maybe you shouldn't leave today," I told her as she blew her nose again.

"I have to," she said, sounding miserably congested. Already, her poor nose was red and raw. "I have dresses being delivered in the morning."

I frowned. "I'm going to run down the street to the pharmacy to get you some cold medicine."

"Zach, it's okay. I'm fine."

"Hush." I shrugged into my coat. "Don't leave until I get back. That's an order."

Half an hour later, after she'd dutifully taken the meds I'd brought back, I walked her down to the lobby. I even held her hand.

"Someone might see us," she whispered in the elevator.

"I don't care," I said. I gave the valet her ticket and waited with her while her car was brought around. Then I cradled her face in my hands. "Drive carefully. If you get drowsy, you pull over, okay? And let me know when you get home."

"I will." She tried to smile. "Have a safe flight."

I frowned again—this was not sitting right with me. "I wish I could take you back myself."

"You can't."

I exhaled through my nose and studied her face, more pale than usual, her brown eyes tired. My heart was in a vise. "Fuck it. I'm driving you."

"What?"

"Give me ten minutes. I'll tell the valet to hold your car here."

"Zach, this is crazy! You cannot drive me home!"

I was already heading for the elevator. "Ten minutes!" I yelled back at her. "Don't move."

"Okay. But don't look at my car!"

Millie was right—her car was a mess. It looked like she'd emptied the contents of her closet into the back seat. And when I opened the trunk to stow our bags, it looked like she'd hit a rummage sale with a wad of cash. "Jesus," I said. "Is that an air fryer?"

"I told you." She sneezed again and dug a tissue from her purse.

I made some room and stuck our bags in there, pulling a sweatshirt from mine that she could use as a pillow. Then I opened the passenger door for her. "Get in."

She was too sick to argue.

I tipped the valet and got behind the wheel, asking her for her address.

"I'll just give you directions," she said, stifling a yawn. "You gotta get on I-90."

"You're going to sleep," I told her, handing her my phone. "Just type your address in here first."

She sighed but did as I asked, then folded her arms over her chest. "I'm not going to sleep. I don't get enough time with you as it is."

But we weren't even out of Illinois before she was out like a light, her seat tipped back, her head resting on my balled-up sweatshirt. I smiled and kept the radio volume low, making sure not to change lanes too abruptly or speed up aggressively. I wasn't in a rush.

The roads were decent, but it still took just over five hours to get to Millie's house. She woke up as I was pulling into her garage.

"We're home already?" She rubbed her face and blinked in disbelief.

"Yes. You slept the entire way home. Good job."

"I'm sorry." She reached over and rubbed my leg. "Thanks for driving me."

"You're welcome. No apology necessary. I did not feel right about putting you behind the wheel."

We hurried from the garage into the house through the back door, which led into her kitchen. Her cats came over to greet her, and she bent down to pet them. "Hello, my loves. Did you miss me?"

"Does someone feed them for you while you're gone?" I asked.

"Yes. My sister Winnie. She brings Dex's daughters with her."

I nodded. By now I knew the who's who of Cloverleigh Farms by heart. My stomach growled loudly, frightening her cats, who ran for cover.

Millie straightened up and came over to me, rubbing my belly. "You poor thing, you drove straight through without eating. Let me feed you." She went over to the fridge and opened it.

I pushed it closed. "No. You are going straight to bed."

She arched a brow. "Trying to get me in bed already?" Then she was seized by a sneezing fit.

Spying a box of tissues on the counter, I brought it over to her. "Believe it or not, no. I'm not thinking about sex right now."

She blew her nose and tossed the tissue in the trash. "I can believe it. I am *not* sexy at the moment."

"Upstairs. Now." I took her by the shoulders and steered her from the kitchen, through the center hallway, up the stairs, and into her bedroom. Then I gently sat her at the foot of the bed and knelt down on the rug. Untying her boots, I pulled them off her feet, peeled off her socks, and stood up again. "Are you keeping those clothes on?"

She shook her head. "I want pajamas."

"Where are they?"

"Second drawer on the left."

I dug in the drawer and pulled out something soft and white. "This?"

"That works." She sneezed again. "And the plaid flannel pants."

Bringing the items to her, I helped her out of her jeans, sweater and bra, and into the pajamas without even laying a hand on her. Proud of myself, I turned back the covers on her bed and watched her crawl in. "Are you hungry?" I asked, pulling the blankets up to her waist.

She nodded. "Yes. And thirsty."

"Water or tea?"

"Tea. It's in the pantry. With honey, please."

"You got it. What sounds good to eat? Don't worry, I'm not going to cook. I'll order in."

She laughed, which turned into a cough, and settled back on the pillow. "You can choose. I don't think I can taste anything anyway."

"Okay. I'll be back in a minute with tea."

Down in the kitchen, I noticed a kettle on the stove—the old-fashioned kind—which made me smile. I filled it with water, turned on the gas beneath it, and hunted in the pantry for tea. Her cats watched me suspiciously.

While I waited for the water to boil, I ordered some Italian food for delivery. A few minutes later, I brought her a glass of ice water and a mug of hot tea with honey, and set it on her nightstand.

"Thanks," she said. "I'm sorry to make you go down again, but can you also bring up that box of tissues?"

"Of course." I hustled back to the kitchen, snatched the box off the counter, and returned to her room, setting it on the nightstand.

"You're the best." She sipped her tea. "Sit with me for a minute?"

"You need rest."

"Come on, just for a minute." She patted the bed beside her. "I feel awful you're missing your flight."

"Don't." I lowered myself onto the mattress and leaned back on one arm, my hand on the far side of her legs. "I'd rather be here with you than go back to that empty apartment."

She smiled. "You need a cat or something."

"I'd like to get a dog. But it wouldn't really be fair to have an animal when I'm gone so often."

"Do you think you'll always travel so much?"

"Hard to say. I suppose at some point, I'll have to slow down. Give up the danger."

"Is what you do for work really dangerous?" She looked worried.

"Sometimes. But I'm careful."

"Would you ever want to do something else?"

I shrugged. "Sometimes I think about opening a whiskey bar or something. If I ever got tired of what I do now. Or of being away from home so much. But . . . I don't even really know where I'd do it."

"Not San Diego?"

"I could," I said. "I've been based in San Diego for the last five years. But I don't know if it's where I'll stay for good."

"Why not? Don't you like it?"

"I do." I searched for words. "There's just something about it that doesn't feel like home."

"Is there a place that does feel like home? Maybe Cleveland?"

I shook my head. "Not really. I think I've moved so much since joining the Navy that I never really got attached to any one place."

She nodded. "I get that."

"Did you ever consider moving away from here?"

"If I'd have gone into fashion design, I probably would have. New York, probably. Or maybe even Paris or Milan." She smiled. "But I feel like even if I'd moved to one of those far-off cities, this would always be *home* to me. Because it's where my family is. Where my heart is."

"Yeah." I leaned over and kissed her forehead. "I ordered some lunch for us. Or dinner. It's after three, so I don't even know what this meal is. I got Italian."

"Perfect." She set her mug on the nightstand as I rose to my feet.

"You rest. I'll let you know when it gets here."

"Okay. And Zach?"

Already at the doorway, I turned around. "Yeah?"

"Thank you for this." She touched her heart. "It means a lot to me. It feels a little strange because I'm not used to being the one taken care of, but . . . I like it."

I smiled at her and tapped the doorframe. "Good."

When the food arrived, I went up and peeked at her, but she was asleep. I ate sitting at her kitchen table alone, under the watchful gaze of her cats. "Relax," I told them. "I'm here for good, not for evil."

While I was eating, Millie wandered down to the kitchen, looking mussed and sleepy, a blanket wrapped around her. "Hi."

"Hey." I got to my feet and pulled a chair out for her. "Sit down. How are you feeling?"

"A little better, I think." She shuffled over to the table and sat down.

"You don't sound much better." I brought her a plate

and fork. "What would you like? I have two different pastas, some chicken, some meatballs, a salad, some sausage and peppers . . ."

She started to laugh, then coughed into her elbow. "This is enough food for ten people."

I grinned. "I was hungry when I ordered. Point at what you like, it's all good."

She indicated what she wanted, and I put everything on her plate, then brought her another glass of water and a napkin.

"Thank you. Did you rebook your flight?" she asked.

"Not yet." I sat down again and started back in on my seconds. In all honesty, I wasn't in any hurry to leave.

Once we said goodbye this time, that was it. It had to be.

"Not that I want you to go," she went on. "I just don't want anyone to see you. And I'm sure you have things to get back to."

"Not really," I said.

She looked over at me in surprise. "No jobs?"

"Nothing this week." I lifted my water glass. "I could stay a couple days."

Her jaw stopped chewing and she set down her fork. Swallowed. Studied her hands in her lap. "Zach. It's not that I don't want you here. I do. But . . . is this wise?"

"I could stay inside," I said, although I had a feeling she wasn't just talking about being seen.

She picked up her fork again and took a small bite of a meatball. "I have to work this week."

"That's okay. I could see you when you got home. Unless you're busy after work too."

"No," she said. "If I had time, I was going to get a Christmas tree."

"A real one?"

She nodded. "I was going to ask my dad if he could help

me cut one down one day after work." A little grin appeared. "I'm not all that handy with a saw."

"I could do it." I sat up a little taller, eager for this opportunity to show off how fucking handy I was. "I happen to be amazing with a saw."

She laughed. "What if someone sees us at the tree farm?"

"I'll wear a disguise," I told her. "A mask over my face."

Still laughing, she shook her head. "That's terrifying. No."

I thought for a moment. "Could we go to a tree farm a little ways out of town?"

"I guess we could."

"What night do you want to do it?"

"I have those deliveries tomorrow that I think will keep me busy all day. Maybe Wednesday?"

"That's fine."

"And you're sure you don't mind staying that long?"

"I'm positive. What am I going back to in San Diego?"

Her cheeks grew pink. "I don't know."

I realized I didn't either.

After tucking her back into bed, I went down to the kitchen and called Jackson.

"Hey," he said. "You back in town?"

"No."

"You're still in Chicago?"

"Uh, no." I leaned back against the sink. "I'm in Michigan."

A pause. "Interesting."

"I drove Millie home. She wasn't feeling well, and I didn't want her light-headed behind the wheel," I said defensively.

"So you're at her house now?"

"Yes."

"Do I even need to ask if you had the talk you were supposed to have?"

I closed my eyes. "No."

"No, I don't need to ask, or no, you didn't do it?"

"Yes."

He exhaled. "Okay, then. So you're there. Are you going to see your son and have the talk with him?"

"No."

"I'm a little confused, Zach. What are you doing?"

"I'm going to spend a couple days here lying low, and when she feels better, we'll have the talk. Then I'll leave."

If I said it, maybe it would happen that way.

Jackson chuckled. "Okay. Whatever you say."

Twenty-Two

Millie

"THIS ONE?" ZACH GESTURED AT THE BALSAM FIR. I studied it critically through softly falling snow. Took a sip of my hot chocolate. "No. There's something weird going on at the top."

He gave me a look. "This is like the tenth tree you've rejected."

"I know, but I have to look at it every day. I want it to be perfect."

He grit his teeth and walked up the row a little more, bow saw in one hand, blue plastic tarp in the other. "How about this one?"

I walked around the tree in question. Poked in its branches to check for animals. Leaned in and sniffed it. "It doesn't have a scent."

"Yes, it does. You have a cold—you can't smell."

I shook my head. "This isn't the one."

He exhaled, his breath making a little white puff in the icy air. "It's a tree, Millie Rose. Not a wedding dress."

"Let's keep looking." I nudged him forward with one elbow, and we turned up the next row.

"How about this one?" He pointed the saw toward another tree. "It's nice and full at the top."

I took a step back and looked it up and down. "It is. I like it." Putting my nose in its branches, I inhaled as deeply as I could. "And I can smell it!"

"Is this the one?"

I nodded enthusiastically. "This is the one."

"*Finally.*"

"Hey, you're the one who said you wanted to come with me."

"I didn't know how particular you were going to be." He pulled the tape measure from his pocket and double-checked it would fit.

"I can't help it. The tree sets the whole tone for the holiday."

He grumbled as he got down on his knees to examine the trunk.

"Don't be grouchy around my tree." I poked his butt with the toe of my boot. "You'll give it bad juju. I want a jolly tree."

"One jolly tree coming up."

Honestly, I had no idea how sexy cutting down a tree could be until I watched Zach sawing through the trunk of that evergreen. My insides did all kinds of twisting and tightening as he crouched down and gripped the handle of the bow saw, his arms and back muscles flexing. Could I see them beneath his winter clothing? No. But I knew what they looked like, and I had no trouble picturing him performing the task with no shirt on.

Since it was only about thirty degrees, though, we were both layered up with sweaters, coats, and gloves. My cold was getting better, but I still had a packet of tissues stuck in my pocket, and I wouldn't let Zach kiss me in bed.

Which he said was fine, because there were plenty of other places on my body he enjoyed putting his mouth.

The first night at my house, we actually didn't mess around at all. But falling asleep next to him was pure bliss, and waking up next to him the next morning was enough to make me smile even though I was still all stuffed up. It was a long day at work, and when I got home, I was tired but also bursting with excitement, because my first sample dresses had arrived, and I'd spent the day unpacking them, steaming them, hanging them up. When they were all displayed, I got tears in my eyes.

Zach had listened to me prattle on about it while he measured my living room ceiling and doorways with a tape measure so we'd know what size tree would fit. We'd had plenty of leftovers from the night before for dinner, so we warmed them up and ate sitting at the kitchen table again. Afterward, we did the dishes together and went upstairs, and it struck me how *normal* this felt. How sweet and ordinary—and yet it thrilled me to the bone.

This is what it could be like, I thought. *And it's exactly what I want.*

When the tree was all wrapped up and tied to the roof of my car, we hit the road for home. The ride was about ninety minutes, since I'd chosen a farm way outside town in order to avoid the odds we'd run into anyone I knew. But I didn't mind the extra hours spent with him—it was dark and cold and snowy outside, but the interior of my car was warm and cozy, and Zach's hand rested on my lap. I'd vowed to stay in the moment, focus on the present, and let myself enjoy what time we had left.

Let my heart play pretend.

We were approaching town when I remembered I didn't have a tree stand.

Zach groaned. "I asked you yesterday, and you said you did."

"I'm sorry, I forgot that it broke and I threw it out. We

can just hit the hardware store in town. I'll go in alone." I directed him to the store, and he pulled into a parking spot in the lot out front.

"I'll be right back," I said, unbuckling my seatbelt.

He put a hand on my leg. "I hate that I can't go in there with you."

"Zach, it's just a tree stand. They're not very heavy." I flexed my bicep. "I work out, remember?"

"It's not that. I just . . . want to do things for you. And there aren't that many things I can do."

I put my mittened hands on either side of his face, leaned over, and lightly kissed his lips. "You're a sweetheart."

"Will you at least let me pay for it?"

"No! You already bought the tree." I patted his cheek. "I'll be out in a minute. You stay here and don't talk to anyone."

He clenched his jaw and stared straight ahead, one wrist draped over the steering wheel. I grabbed my purse and hopped out of the car, humming a Christmas tune as I hurried into the store. After asking an employee where I might find a tree stand, I was directed to the seasonal section at the back of the store. I was looking for stands when I heard someone say my name.

"Millie?"

I looked up and saw Winnie's best friend Ellie Fournier and her fiancé Gianni Lupo coming toward me. Over his thick gray sweater, Gianni was wearing a baby sling on his chest with their two-month-old daughter, Claudia, in it.

I smiled. "Hi, guys. How's it going?"

"Good." Ellie was pushing a cart with some holiday decorations in it. "Just doing some shopping since Gianni had a night off and the baby has decided she only likes falling asleep when someone is wearing her and walking around."

"I don't mind." Gianni grinned and patted the baby's butt through the wrap. "I like it, actually."

I peeked at her little face. "Ohhh, she's so sweet," I whispered. "Look at those eyelashes."

"You should see her eyes when they're open," said Gianni. "Prettiest blue eyes you've ever seen. Aside from yours, of course," he added, leaning over to give Ellie a kiss on the cheek.

Ellie laughed. "Of course. So what brings you out?" she asked me.

"I'm looking for a tree stand. I got a tree today."

"Nice." Gianni smiled. "We're planning to do that soon too."

"I hear your new shop is coming along," Ellie said. "Winnie talks about it nonstop. I can't wait to come in and see it."

"Come any time," I said. "I'd love to show you around."

The baby started to fuss, and Gianni bounced her a little, swaying back and forth and making gentle shushing noises. Ellie looked on appreciatively. "Turns out, Gianni is like the baby whisperer. Who'd have thought?"

"Not me." He grinned. "I had no idea how much I'd love being a dad. But it's the best."

Envy squeezed my heart as I gave them a little wave. "Well, I won't keep you. Nice seeing you—the baby is beautiful."

"Thanks. Bye, Millie."

They passed me by and I moved up the aisle, finally locating the tree stands. But instead of grabbing one off the shelf, I stood there for a moment, fighting sadness.

You're being ridiculous, I told myself as tears blurred the red, green, and white boxes in front of me. *Are you going to cry every time you see a new family?* After a couple deep breaths, I picked a tree stand I hoped would work and went up front to pay for it.

That's when I spotted Mason and Lori at checkout.

Immediately I dropped my eyes to the floor and spun around, heading back in the direction I'd come from, as if I'd forgotten something. My heart rattled around in my ribcage, and my pulse beat like a drum in my head.

I lingered in the paint aisle, perusing brushes and rollers and rolls of tape without actually registering any of it. After five minutes, I snuck to the end of the row and peeked at the registers from behind a stack of paint cans. They were gone.

Breathing a sigh of relief, I paid for my tree stand and bolted out of there.

"I was starting to get worried," Zach said when I got back in the car. "What took you so long?"

"Don't ask," I said, slouching down in my seat. "Just get us out of here."

The following day at work, Frannie surprised me with an afternoon visit. She brought me a cup of coffee, which I accepted gratefully. "Thanks," I said, inhaling its delicious aroma. "I could use a pick-me-up."

"You sound better. How's the cold?"

"Almost gone. I think it was just a two-day thing."

She smiled with relief. "Good."

"Let me show you what's new," I said eagerly, motioning for her to follow me to the back. "The sewing machine arrived, the dressing rooms are finished, and the painting is finally done. Best of all, I actually have some dresses!"

After I gave her a tour, we ended up by the front windows, where two dresses were displayed on either side of the double front doors. She gushed over them both, turned to face me, her blue eyes bright. "Oh, Millie, it's so beautiful. I'm so happy for you."

"Thank you."

Just then, the door to the shop opened and Lori poked her head in. Behind her stood Mason. "I know you're not open for business, but would it be okay to take a peek?"

"Sure," Frannie said. "Come on in."

They entered the shop, bringing a gust of cold air with them. "We were just downtown doing some shopping, and I saw the sign was up and the lights were on, and dresses were in the window!" she said excitedly. "I told Mason we had to stop in."

I smiled at them both, squelching the guilty feeling in my belly. "I'm glad you did."

"It looks great, Millie," said Mason, looking around. "You must be so proud."

"Thank you. I am."

"It's like a *dream*." Lori's eyes shone as she took it all in. "If I wasn't already married, I'd come here to shop for a gown first thing. It's so elegant and feminine and pretty."

"Tell all your friends that," encouraged Frannie.

"Oh, I will." Lori clasped her hands together under her chin. "When will you start taking appointments?"

"I'm hoping by the first of the year."

"That's perfect!" she squealed. "Right after the holidays!"

"Mmhm." I thought of Dex and Winnie, who'd be engaged by then.

"Speaking of holidays, you're both coming to the Cloverleigh Farms Christmas Eve party, right?" Frannie asked them.

"Definitely," said Lori, tucking her arm through Mason's and giving him a sentimental smile. "That's where we met last year, so it's special to us."

"That's right." Frannie laughed. "Hard to believe just one year later, you're Mr. and Mrs. now."

"Thanks to Millie." Lori beamed at me. "We owe her a lot—not only for introducing us at that party, but for managing to get us a Saturday wedding date at Cloverleigh Farms on four months' notice."

I held up my hands. "There was a cancellation. It wasn't me, it was just meant to be."

"Still," she said. "We'll always be grateful."

"My father, Zach, will be in town that night," said Mason. "Would it be okay to bring him too?"

"Of course!" Frannie tossed a hand in the air. "The more, the merrier!"

Panic seized me, resulting in a coughing fit. I turned away from the group and walked toward the front desk, where I had a bottle of water. "Sorry," I managed.

"Millie is just getting over a cold," Frannie explained, as I guzzled water.

"Sorry to hear that," Mason said.

"It's okay." I tried to breathe normally. "I'm on the mend."

"Well, we'll let you get back to work," said Lori. "Just wanted to see the place—congrats again, Millie!"

"Thank you," I called weakly, returning Mason's wave and watching him hold the door for his wife and then follow her out.

When they were gone, Frannie looked at me. "Are you okay?"

"Yes. I just needed some water."

"Okay. You just look really pale all of a sudden." Her expression was concerned. "Make sure you're getting enough sleep, okay?"

"I will."

When I got home, Zach had dinner waiting and a fire going in the fireplace. My tree stood in the corner, tall and fragrant, ready for lights and ornaments. Our plan was to decorate after we ate.

It was on the tip of my tongue to tell him about seeing Mason and Lori, but I couldn't bring myself to mar the festive mood with anything unsettling. I'd already broken down in tears once this evening, right after Frannie left the store. And as soon as I got home, I'd run right upstairs under the guise of taking off my work clothes to make sure my face wasn't blotchy and tearstained. The puffy and slightly red eyes I could blame on my cold, but I quickly applied some concealer and wiped away all traces of running mascara.

Downstairs, we ate the Mexican food Zach had ordered, then decorated the tree. Zach poked affectionate fun at the clumsily handmade ornaments I had from when I was little, and I needled him about not having a tree at all for the last few years.

"Who are you, Ebenezer Scrooge?" I teased.

"I think I lost Christmas in the divorce, along with the pots and pans." He caught me in his arms from behind and buried his face in my hair. "But I didn't even care."

"Maybe you can get a tree this year," I suggested. "There's still time."

"I don't know. It wouldn't be as fun without you there to help me decorate it. And what if I chose a grouchy tree? I might ruin Christmas altogether."

I laughed, but the sound faded when I thought about this afternoon. "I heard you're coming here. For Christmas, I mean."

Behind me, he went stiff. "What?"

"I saw Mason and Lori today. They were downtown, and they came into the shop."

"Oh."

I turned within his embrace to face him. "Mason asked

if he could bring you to the Cloverleigh Farms Christmas Eve party."

His eyes closed. "Fuck."

"I didn't realize you'd decided to come."

"It's hard for me to say no to Mason. He really doesn't ask much of me, all things considered."

"I know." I toyed with the buttons on his shirt. "You can go. I'll stay home. I'll say I don't feel well."

"Millie, no. That's your family's Christmas party. I'll make up an excuse why I can't attend."

I shook my head, feeling us coming apart at the seams. "Lies and excuses. Making things up. Near misses at the hardware store—or anywhere else we go! Zach, we can't keep doing this."

"I know." He swallowed, tightening his arms around my back. "I know."

"This is getting too hard." My voice caught, and I choked back a sob. "I think we have to stop. Because the longer this goes on, the more I feel for you. And the more I feel, the more hope starts to build that some way, some*how*, we can be together. And we can't."

He tipped my chin up. "You're so much younger than I am, Millie. Even if Mason didn't have a problem with us, and we got over what everyone in town would think, you want things I can't give you."

"That's what I mean. And yet I keep pretending—I'm like a kid who just wants to believe in Santa Claus even though I know darn well there's no fat man in a red suit who slides down every chimney in the world on Christmas Eve."

"I wish there was. I really fucking wish there was."

"This is the reality we were always going to have to face. It's not your fault or my fault. It's just the way things are, Zach, and they won't change."

He wrapped me in his arms again, pulling me tighter to

his broad, warm chest. "I think about you every minute of the day. I wish I could be the one, Millie Rose."

"Maybe in another life, you could have been." Tears leaked silently from my eyes.

He kissed the top of my head. When he spoke, his voice was gruff with emotion. "I'm not sure I'd have deserved you in any life, but I sure as hell would have tried."

Of course, because neither of us was good at being apart, we went up to my bedroom and spent our last night together exactly the way we'd spent our first—only instead of fast, frantic fucking and fun games, we went slow, taking our time, savoring every single moment because we knew it was goodbye.

Afterward, we lay wrapped in each other's arms, my head on his chest, loath to fall asleep and face the inevitable dawn of the day we'd have to part for good.

"I want to tell you something," he said, breaking the silence.

"What?" I whispered.

"You once asked me why I got married. And I didn't answer honestly."

"Yes, you did. You said you didn't want to be alone, so you thought you'd try it."

"That wasn't the whole truth."

I picked up my head and looked at him, his features vague in the dark. "What's the whole truth?"

He tucked my hair behind my ear. "I liked the idea that someone might . . . belong to me. That there was someone I had to protect and provide for. But I didn't want to love anyone so much I couldn't live without them. With her, that was never a danger. But with you . . ."

My heart stopped. "With me?"

"With you, it is. With you, it's been a danger all along."

Once again, the tears threatened to undo me. I put my head down again, listening to his heart beat while he held me close.

I love you too, I mouthed. But like him, I didn't say the words aloud.

Maybe that would make it easier.

Twenty-Three

Zach

IN THE MORNING, I WOKE UP BEFORE MILLIE AND CALLED A CAR to take me to the airport. When it arrived, I texted the driver to give me one minute.

Slipping into her bedroom one last time, I bent down and kissed her forehead.

Her eyes opened. "Are you leaving?"

"Yes. The car is here."

She propped herself up on one elbow. Beneath her beautiful brown eyes were dark circles. I knew she'd hardly slept. "Okay."

"Take care of yourself, Millie MacAllister." I straightened up, even though my body felt like caving in.

A tear slipped from the corner of one eye, and she nodded.

"Go after everything you want. You deserve it all," I whispered, my voice caught somewhere in my throat.

"So do you," she said. "Have a safe trip home."

Home.

I thought about the word as I kissed her lips one last time, as I watched her eyes refill with tears, as I forced myself to walk away from her.

I thought about the word on the flight back to California,

on the drive back to my apartment, as I walked through my front door.

I thought about the word as I went through the motions of my life—work, gym, sleep. As I ate meals for one while I hunted for episodes of Antiques Roadshow. As I fought the compulsion to pick up my phone and call her, just to hear her voice. As I stared at the empty corner of my apartment where a Christmas tree would have fit if I'd had the energy or motivation to go get one. But everything seemed empty without her.

Every day at work, I listened to my colleagues talk about plans for Christmas and New Year's . . . family gatherings, fun vacations, letters to Santa, decorating the tree. Cards arrived in my mailbox from former Navy buddies showing off family photos—kids with gap-toothed grins, teenagers with acne and reluctant smiles, dogs wearing reindeer antlers. Surrounding me was so much togetherness, my life felt like solitary confinement in comparison.

I considered telling Mason I couldn't come for Christmas after all, but he was so excited to see me again, I didn't have the heart to let him down. I had no idea how I was going to get out of that Christmas Eve party, but I supposed I didn't have to worry about it until I was there. A last-minute illness was probably the way to go.

Just to get out of the house, I went Christmas shopping, even though I could have just bought things online. I got Jackson a bottle of the scotch he liked, and I bought a box of chocolates for Gwyn. For Mason, I purchased some cool barware and a bottle of my favorite whiskey. I asked Catherine for help with a gift for Lori, and she suggested something warm and cozy for the winter. I thought maybe a Cole Security fleece, but Catherine said that was *not* what she meant, and she helped me choose a soft pink sweater instead.

I also went through the box of mementos I had from my grandfather, which I'd inherited after my mom died. There wasn't a ton of stuff, but I thought Mason might appreciate having one of his ties, some old photographs, a couple letters he'd sent home during the war. I remembered how Millie had told me to write down the stories he'd told me, and I thought maybe that was something I could do for Mason as well. That night, I sat down at my laptop and began typing them up.

And always, always, I thought of her.

On December twenty-second, the day before I left for Michigan, I was picking up some clothes from the dry cleaner when I noticed a jewelry shop next door. Had it always been there? I wandered over to the window and looked at the pieces on display.

I saw it immediately—and it hit me like a fist to the solar plexus, knocking the wind out of me. It was a necklace almost exactly like the one Millie had admired the day we'd watched Antiques Roadshow in my New York City hotel room. It wasn't identical, but it was damn close.

Before I knew what I was doing, I'd entered the store and asked a salesperson about it. Sure enough, it was a vintage piece, an Art Deco lavaliere in white gold with a diamond pendant.

"It's beautiful, isn't it?" The woman smiled. "The filigree is so pretty."

I stared at it, imagining it on Millie's neck, fastening the clasp as she held up her hair, seeing it on her and knowing I was the man who put it there. "I'll take it," I heard myself say. "Can you gift-wrap it?"

"Of course." She laughed. "Don't you want to know the price?"

"No," I told her. "I don't care about the price. I just want her to have it."

"Your wife is a very lucky woman," she said.

That night, Cole Security had a little party in the pub down the street from our offices. While Jackson and I sat at the bar with a couple beers waiting for our turn at the pool table, he asked me when I was leaving.

"Tomorrow," I said.

"You staying with Mason?"

"Nah. I got a hotel." I tipped up my beer. "I like my privacy."

"Are you going to see Millie?"

At her name, my heart lurched. "I told you, we ended things."

"I know what you told me, but I also know how miserable you've been for the last couple weeks. I've never seen you like this, not even after your divorce."

I shrugged. "What do you want me to say?"

"You know what?" Jackson shook his head. "I'm not sure. I know you did the right thing, it just sucks that it has to be this way."

"Yep." I took another long pull on my beer. "I bought her a diamond necklace."

Jackson about choked. He set his beer down and turned on his stool to face me. *"What?"*

"I saw it in the window of this jewelry store, and I knew she'd love it. I bought it for her for Christmas without even asking the price, and the woman working was like, 'Your wife is a very lucky woman.' I almost fucking lost it."

"Dude." Jackson folded his arms over his chest. "What *is* this? What are you hoping will happen when you give her a *diamond*?"

"I honestly don't fucking know." I stared at the bottle in my hand. "I just want her to have it. I want to give it to her."

Jackson stared at me silently.

"When we said goodbye, I told her to go after what she wants in life, I told her she deserves to get everything she wants. And she said, 'So do you.' But you know what the crazy thing is?"

"What?"

"I don't even know what that is." I looked at him. "What am I doing with my life? What do I want?"

He nodded slowly, then rubbed one finger beneath his mouth. "Is there any chance," he began, "that you'd *consider* having a family with her? Like, if the vasectomy could be reversed?"

I frowned. "Every once in a while, the thought occurs to me, and then I think, 'Are you fucking serious? You'd have a *grandchild* older than your own kid.' It's too messed up. And those reversals don't always work."

"What about adoption?"

"I'm not asking her to give up having her own child for me. No way."

"You don't think she'd like to be the one to make that choice?"

"Look, we already had this discussion, and you were the one who told me I had to break it off," I said testily. "I did the right thing."

"Okay, okay." He held up his hands. "I hear you. I just want to make sure you're doing the right thing for the right *reason*. We've known each other a long time, Barrett. You know my past and I know yours."

I looked away from him and clenched my jaw. "This isn't about the past."

But I had a hard time sleeping that night, wondering if, somehow, it was.

Twenty-Four

Millie

THE CLOVERLEIGH FARMS CHRISTMAS EVE PARTY WAS IN full swing.

Guests dressed in cocktail attire were milling around the inn's spacious lobby, which was fully decked out for the holidays. A towering evergreen stood in one corner, dazzling with white lights and gold ornaments. A fire in the huge stone fireplace warmed the room, and stockings for every employee hung along the wide wooden banister of the staircase. Carols played on the inn's sound system, a bar was set up at the reception desk, and long rectangular tables covered in white linen were laden with serving platters. Everyone was eating, drinking, chatting, and enjoying high spirits.

Except me.

I was doing my best to fake it, standing with Winnie and Dex near the tree, glass of wine in my hand, watching Hallie and Luna toss pieces of popcorn at each other's open mouths from farther and farther away. Every now and again, I glanced at Winnie's left hand and thought to myself, *By this time tomorrow, she'll be wearing that ring.*

But mostly I kept my eyes on the door, watching for Zach to come in. We hadn't spoken since he left my house over two weeks ago. Was he even in town? Maybe he'd decided not to come. Even if he was in town, the chances he'd actually show up at this party were slim to none. But Mason and Lori weren't here yet, so anything was possible.

Felicity wandered over and tugged my sleeve. "Hey. Come here."

I followed her around the corner, into the hallway that led to the bathrooms on one side and the inn's bar on the other, which was closed and dark. "What?"

"I'm just checking on you."

I shrugged. "I'm fine."

"You sure?"

"Of course I'm not sure. I'm checking the door every thirty seconds, terrified he's going to walk through it and equally terrified he won't, and I'll never see him again."

She put her hand on my upper arm. "I'm sorry. I can see how upset you are. Can I do anything to help?"

"Remind me that we did the right thing. That carrying on with him was only going to lead to worse heartbreak down the road. That someday I'll be as happy as you are with Hutton."

"All of that is true," she said.

"I know." I took a shaky breath. "I know it is."

"Come on, let's go get some more wine." She took my hand and led me over to the bar, where several bottles of wine were lined up. "Okay, what are you drinking? We've got pinot, we've got cab, we've got—"

"Oh, God." My entire body stiffened. "He's here."

She glanced over her shoulder toward the door.

"*Felicity*," I hissed. "Don't *look*."

"Sorry." She met my eyes again. "You look like you've seen a ghost."

I wasn't sure my knees wouldn't buckle. He looked so good. He was dressed in all black, like he had been the night we met, and it set off the touch of silver in his beard and dark hair. Our eyes met, and everything in the room went still. My vision went gray at the edges. "I think I'm going to slip away to the ladies' room for a minute."

"Okay."

Leaving my glass on the bar, I spun on my heel and made a beeline for the back hall. But instead of hitting the bathroom, I opened the door to the inn's pub and went over to the windows on the opposite side of the dark room. The moon was full tonight, and I looked at it as I pressed my palms to the cold glass, then placed them on my hot cheeks.

"Millie?"

I didn't turn around. I knew that voice. "Yes?"

"Can I talk to you?"

"In here?"

"I didn't think you'd want anyone to see us."

I forced myself to face him. "I wasn't sure you'd come."

"I wasn't either." He came closer, his hands in his pockets. "You look beautiful."

"Thank you." I looked down at the black, one-shouldered dress I wore, the same one I'd worn the night we met.

He closed the gap until he stood next to me at the window, bathed in the silvery light. "You're wearing the dress."

My heart thudded like a cannonball in my chest.

"You know I can't breathe when you wear that dress."

"Zach, I—"

"I have something for you." He took a long, narrow box from the inside pocket of his coat. "And then I'll leave you alone."

"What is this?"

"Open it."

With trembling fingers, I pulled off the ribbon and

unwrapped the package. It was a hinged leather box. I held my breath for a moment.

"Go on," he urged.

I opened the box and gasped. Resting on black velvet was the most beautiful necklace I'd ever seen, the diamond pendant and delicate filigree sparkling in the moonlight.

"Do you recognize it?" he asked.

I shook my head.

"It's just like the one from that episode of Antiques Roadshow." He couldn't keep the excitement from his voice.

"Oh my God. Zach." I covered my mouth with one hand. "You didn't."

"Can I put it on you?"

"No." I shook my head and closed the box. "I can't wear this. You can't give this to me."

"Why not?"

"Because we're not together anymore. I don't even know if we ever were."

"Please, Millie." He took the box from me, opened it up, and lifted the necklace from the velvet. Tucking the box back into his coat, he undid the clasp. "Let me give this to you and see you wearing it."

"But why?" I'd started to cry.

"You know why," he whispered. Stepping around me, he lowered his hands in front of my chest. "Lift up your hair for me."

I did what he asked, even though I knew I shouldn't, and let him fasten the clasp behind my neck. Then he pressed his lips to my bare shoulder. I closed my eyes, wishing this moment could have a different ending.

I heard a noise by the door and turned to see a shadow moving away.

Dropping my hands, I let my hair fall and turned to face

him. "You have to go," I begged. "Now, please. Before some-one sees us."

His eyes held mine, then dropped to my chest, where the diamond pendant glimmered. "Keep it," he said, his voice thick. "It was meant for you."

Then he walked out, leaving me alone to cry. I turned to the window and saw my reflection, the necklace and my tears shining like stars in the dark.

Twenty-Five

I MANAGED TO LAST ANOTHER TWENTY MINUTES OR SO, THEN I faked a headache and told Mason and Lori I'd see them tomorrow.

"Oh no." Lori looked distressed. "Are you okay?"

"I'm fine," I lied. "It's just been a long day."

We'd exchanged gifts at their house before coming over to the inn, and Mason had gotten choked up over the items that had belonged to my grandfather. Then he'd opened up the bottle of whiskey I'd bought him, and we enjoyed a drink while he and Lori listened with rapt attention to all the old family stories I told. Mason said he wanted to do more research on my grandfather's military record and even create a family tree that went back generations—he'd always been envious of kids at school with huge family trees when they'd been assigned projects about family history.

Lori adored the sweater, pulling it on immediately and rubbing the soft sleeve against her cheek, and I sent a quick text to Catherine to thank her for the suggestion.

They'd gifted me with a hooded sweatshirt from the high school where Mason taught, a bottle of wine from Cloverleigh

Farms, and finally, a card with a black and white picture inside. I held it up—it was an ultrasound image.

"It's a girl," Mason said, his voice full of pride.

My throat felt scratchy when I tried to speak, and I cleared it as I continued to stare at the figure on the paper. Her profile was clearly visible, and a tiny little fist was in front of her face. "Wow."

"We don't know what her name is yet, but we thought you might like to have a copy of her first photo," Lori said softly.

"Thanks." All kinds of feelings were swirling around inside me, including fear and the urge to run out the front door, but there was no denying the surge of protectiveness in my chest. This tiny little being was my blood. She would carry within her some of me, for better or worse. Some of my parents and grandparents before me. Some of Poppy.

My throat grew even tighter, my chest more full. I wasn't used to these kinds of emotions and wondered how the hell any father got through a day with this kind of maelstrom going on inside them.

And yet, I wondered if I'd made a mistake throwing away my chance to be one.

I let myself into my hotel room and fell back on the bed, feeling like I'd fucked up Christmas Eve for everyone. I'd made Millie cry, I'd disappointed Lori, Mason had been silent when I'd shook his hand before walking out. As for myself, I'd never been so fucking lonesome.

And tomorrow would be more of the same. I'd been invited to Lori's parents' house for Christmas dinner, but that wasn't until five o'clock, so most of the day would be spent sitting in this hotel room pondering all the terrible choices I'd made over the course of my life.

And what about that life? Was it half over? How much longer did I have? What had I done with it that would matter? What would I do with the time I had left? What did I *want*?

I was still lying there, on the verge of an existential crisis, when my phone vibrated. Thinking maybe it was Millie, I sat up fast and pulled it from my pocket.

It was Jackson.

"Hello?"

"Sorry to bother you on Christmas Eve. I know you're on vacation."

"It's fine. I might cut the vacation short anyway."

"Does that mean you're available for a job?"

"Sure."

"Good. You're the only one I'd trust on this. There's a woman and child involved."

My pulse sped up a little. "What's the job?"

"You'll pick them up outside Twin Falls, Idaho and drive them to Rose Canyon, Oregon."

"When?"

"Day after tomorrow. I'm leaving for Las Vegas in the morning, and I'll drive them to Idaho. You'll take it from there."

"Okay. Who's the client?"

"A British guy. He hired me to protect his wife and daughter upon his death—get them out of the UK and transport them to Rose Canyon without being tracked."

"Was the death suspicious?"

"No. A terminal illness. But he knew the end was near and for some reason felt they weren't safe. He gave me specific instructions to follow."

"*Are* they safe?"

"No." Jackson's tone was firm. "But beyond that, I don't have a lot of details."

"Understood."

"Book a flight to Twin Falls. I'll meet you there with further instructions."

"Got it," I said, glad to have a distraction and purpose.

"So what happened to your trip?" he asked. "Why are you cutting it short?"

"It's just time for me to go."

Silence. "Did you see her?"

"Yeah."

"And?"

I closed my eyes. "I gave her the necklace. I made her cry."

"In a good way? Like, happy tears?"

"No. In a sad, fucked-up, you-just-made-everything-worse way."

Jackson exhaled. "Well. Merry Christmas."

"Yeah." I rubbed my temples with a thumb and forefinger. "I'll see you in two days."

Twenty-Six

Millie

ON CHRISTMAS DAY, WE ALWAYS GATHERED AT OUR PARENTS' house for dinner—and this year we had something extra special to celebrate.

"To Winnie and Dex," said my dad, holding up his beer. "Congratulations!"

Next to him, Frannie slapped his shoulder. "That's it?"

"What else do you want me to say?"

"How about welcoming Dex to the family? Never mind, I'll do it." Frannie turned to the table and raised her glass of wine. "Dex, we're so happy to have not only you join our gang, but your darling girls too. Hallie and Luna, welcome to our family!"

"Cheers!" said Winnie, holding up her glass with her left hand, her diamond ring catching the light from the chandelier.

"And thank you," said Dex, lifting his beer.

Hallie and Luna beamed, holding up the Christmas mocktails Felicity had made for them and the twins, and I raised my wine. Around the table, my entire family toasted the engagement, and I took a moment to be fully happy for my sister, for Dex, and for his girls.

But the moment I set my glass down, the sadness that had been weighing on me throughout the day returned. I did my best to cover it up, but constantly felt like I was on the verge of tears. After dessert and coffee, I helped do the dishes, faked a huge yawn, and said I'd better get to bed since I planned to work the next day. Millie Rose was opening in exactly one week, and I wanted everything to be perfect. I hugged everyone goodbye, congratulated Winnie and Dex once more, wished everyone Merry Christmas, and headed for the front hall closet.

As I was buttoning up my coat, Felicity found me. "Hey," she said, sticking her hands in her cardigan pockets. "You okay?"

"No." I wound my scarf around my neck. "But I was hoping it wasn't obvious."

"It wasn't," she assured me. "I just know what's going on. But you left Cloverleigh so fast last night, I didn't get a chance to ask what happened. Did you talk to him?"

I nodded as I pulled on my hat. "Yes. And he gave me a diamond necklace."

Felicity stretched her neck forward like a goose. "He did?"

"Yes." Angrily, I yanked on my gloves. "It's gorgeous."

"But—but why?"

"I have no idea, Felicity!" I threw up my hands. "And when I asked him, he said, 'You know why.' Whatever that means."

Felicity's mouth opened, then she tucked in her lips and pressed them together. "I think it means . . . he loves you?"

"No, he doesn't," I said crossly. "If he loved me, he wouldn't have let me go so easily."

"But you said it was a mutual decision. It's not like he abandoned you."

"I know what I said, but it doesn't feel that way, okay?" My eyes filled. "This is why. This is why I don't date men who don't need me. It's too easy for them to walk away."

My sister made a face. "I don't know, Mills. It doesn't seem like this was all that easy for him. He bought you a diamond necklace. Can't you guys maybe . . . try again?"

"What's the point?" I asked, drowning in the hopelessness of it all.

"Love?" she offered.

"But if he doesn't love me enough to consider getting married or having kids, it doesn't matter. I want a family."

Felicity sighed. "Are you sure it's out of the question? Did you actually *have* this conversation?"

"Not exactly," I admitted, playing with a button on my coat. "I couldn't bring myself to come out and ask him if he'd ever have the vasectomy reversed. It seemed like too much when we've only been seeing each other for a couple months."

"So does a diamond necklace," Felicity pointed out. "Compared to asking a question, that's a *lot*."

"I just can't," I insisted. "What if the answer is no? I'll feel terrible and rejected. At least this way, it feels like a decision we made together."

"Okay," she said, giving me a hug. "It's your life. I just hate seeing you so sad at such a happy time of year. And I know all the Winnie and Dex stuff must be hard."

I hugged her back, grateful for the affection. "I'll be okay. Eventually."

Twenty-Seven

Zach

I FLEW OUT TO IDAHO THE DAY AFTER CHRISTMAS.

I sent Mason and Lori an apology text, explaining that an emergency had arisen at work, and I was needed on a job and promising to come back soon. I thanked them for the gifts and said I planned to put the ultrasound photo on my fridge where I'd see it every day. I wasn't sure I'd actually do it—did I really want that constant reminder of impending grandfatherhood?—but I hoped it would make them happy. I knew I was letting them down by leaving early. I felt even worse when I received no reply to my message.

After checking into a nondescript Twin Falls motel, I met up with Jackson at a place called The Anchor Bistro for a bite to eat. Over wings and nachos, Jackson went over the instructions with me for the job, which included providing the woman and her child with new identities.

"Give them this." Across the table in our booth at the back, Jackson handed me a large yellow envelope, which I assumed had documents with their new names on them.

I put the envelope on the seat next to me. "Where are they now?"

"Sleeping. They were exhausted." He took a drink of his coffee. "I've got them in a safe house, and it's being watched."

"How old is the kid?"

"Little. Maybe two or three."

My protective instincts went into overdrive. "Are they being tracked?"

"I have to assume someone is trying. The woman—her name is Sophie—is scared and confused. Her husband was obviously involved in something he didn't want her to know about, and we can't provide her any details—we don't even have them—but he took extensive measures to keep them safe."

"Does she trust us?" I asked.

"Probably not, but we're all she's got right now." He ate a wing and wiped his mouth with a napkin. "Move fast. She'll be ready at four a.m."

I nodded. "Got it."

Jackson hadn't been lying when he said the woman was frightened. She was visibly trembling in the front hall of the home where I picked her up. "It will be okay, Sophie," I told her, meeting her distrustful eyes. "My name is Zach Barrett. And you're safe with me."

"My daughter, Eden," she whispered in a British accent. "She's asleep upstairs."

"I'll put your things in the car while you wake her," I said. After loading two small bags into the back of the SUV, I went back inside to find the woman standing at the top of the steep staircase, carrying a sleeping child.

Nervous that she would fall, I took the steps up two at a time and reached for the girl. "Let me."

"But—"

"If anything happens to either of you, I'll get fired," I told her, transferring the child to my arms. Sound asleep, she didn't protest, her head resting neatly on my shoulder, my arms securely around her back. "And I happen to like my job. I'm good at it."

Sophie gave me a ghost of a smile.

We went out to the car, which idled in the dark under the watch of another Cole Security hire. He opened the passenger-side back door for me and went around to the other side of the car to help Sophie in. I carefully placed the little girl in the back seat and buckled her seatbelt.

Sophie slipped in beside her daughter and covered her with a blanket before looking up at me. "Thank you."

"You're welcome." I tucked the blanket around the little girl's legs.

"Do you have children, Mr. Barrett?"

I almost said no. "Yes."

"I can tell."

Swallowing hard, I reached into the front, where the yellow envelope rested on the passenger seat, then handed it to her. "These are for you."

Sophie looked at me blankly.

"The new identities," I explained. "And some cash."

Her eyes closed. "Right. This is all so strange and frightening." They opened again. "Tell me we'll be okay again."

"You'll be okay," I said. "You have my word."

She studied me for a moment. "I believe you."

A few minutes later, we were on our way to Oregon.

The drive was long, over twelve hours. We stopped a couple times to eat and get gas, and I was also careful not to speed— no need to call attention to ourselves.

At the gas station, Sophie asked if she could take Eden inside to use the bathroom, and I requested that she wait for me to accompany her inside the store. She nodded and dutifully sat in the back seat until I opened the door, locked the SUV, and followed them to the restrooms. I waited for them a little ways away, and when they came out, the little girl wanted a snack. When the mother said no, because she'd left her purse in the car, I offered to buy it.

At first, Sophie demurred, but when Eden started to cry, she relented. I watched the pint-sized version of her mother peruse the selection, her eyes wide and excited.

"American snacks are new to her," Sophie said, the closest thing to a smile I'd seen yet on her face. "She's never seen half this stuff."

"She can pick whatever she wants. As much as she wants."

Back on the road, Sophie caught my eyes in the rearview mirror. "How old are your children, Zach?"

"I have a grown son."

She looked surprised. "You seem young to have a grown son."

"Yeah. Life is unpredictable."

"It is," she said, her eyes drifting to her daughter, who joyfully shoveled bright orange Cheetos into her mouth. "And scary sometimes. But I guess . . ." She closed her eyes. "I guess sometimes you just have to believe everything happens for a reason, and trust the people you love to protect and guide you—even if they seem to be guiding you to a whole new life."

Her words stuck with me.

After delivering Sophie and Eden safely to Rose Canyon, I went back to San Diego and my silent, stuffy apartment. I'd done my job, but I remained on edge—as if I'd forgotten some detail or left something to chance. Multiple times, I checked in with Jackson to make sure everything was okay with Sophie and Eden, and he said they were fine.

I went to the gym to try to work off some of the restlessness, but it didn't help. I unpacked. Did laundry. Cleaned out the fridge (not much in there, anyway). I turned the television on, then off again. I picked up the thriller I'd bought in the airport, but I found myself stuck on the same page for long stretches of time, not seeing the text, not caring what happened, not invested in anyone in the story. The only person I cared about was Millie.

Was she still upset with me? Did she miss me? Had she tried to reach out? I checked my phone for the millionth time—nothing.

Frustrated, I put the phone down and went into the kitchen. Maybe I was hungry.

But once I got in there, all I did was open the fridge and stare at the empty shelves. When I closed it, the ultrasound photo caught my eye. I'd stuck it there, as promised, out of guilt. Neither Mason nor Lori had reached out to me since I'd abandoned them on Christmas Eve, and I wondered if I should try calling them. Or maybe send a screenshot of the baby's picture on display.

Baby.

In just a few more months, they'd have a baby. I imagined what that would be like, sharing something as monumental and transformative as bringing a life into the world. Keeping her safe. Feeding her. Teaching her to talk and walk. I pictured a tiny little thing on two chubby, wobbly legs, her little fists wrapped around my thumbs, taking her first halting steps.

But the child I imagined wasn't Mason and Lori's—she was my own, and the steps she took were toward Millie, who waited with arms outstretched. A crack in my heart began to widen as I imagined watching my little girl ride a tricycle or splash around in a puddle or—my throat closed—chase butterflies.

I'd missed all those things with Mason. For the first time, I felt cheated by that, but I knew I'd only cheated myself.

I'd denied myself the chance to be a father to a child, to watch him or her grow, to experience all the joys and sorrows that came with it. And to share it all with someone I loved.

I'd never have the opportunity to experience it again, unless . . .

Unless what?

Unless I had the guts to admit I'd been wrong. To open a door that I'd closed long ago. To undo a decision I'd made out of fear and obstinacy, and give myself a chance at a new life.

My vision swam, and I felt light-headed. When I could see clearly again, I grabbed my keys and ran out the door.

Fifteen minutes later, I found myself knocking on Jackson's door. One of his daughters answered it with a big smile on her face, which faded the second she saw me. "Oh, it's you," she said.

I had to laugh. "Sorry to disappoint."

"I'm waiting for my ride. Come on in." Then she yelled over her shoulder, "Dad! Mr. Barrett is here!"

I stepped into their foyer, and Jackson came jogging down the stairs. "Hey," he said. "What's going on?"

"I'm not sure."

He reached the landing and studied my expression. "Come on, brother," he said, throwing an arm around me. "Catherine is gone for the evening. Let's have some scotch and talk it out."

We went into the kitchen, and I took a seat at the island. After opening the bottle of scotch I'd gotten him for Christmas, he poured us each a couple fingers and set a glass in front of me. "Speak."

I turned the glass on the stone counter without even taking a sip. "I think I made a mistake."

"Zach, you didn't. Sophie and Eden are fine."

"That's not what I mean." I took a deep breath. "With Millie. I think ending things was a mistake."

"Okay." He leaned back against the counter across from me and took a sip of scotch.

"But when I think about what it would take to turn it around, I feel like I might pass out. It's . . . so much."

"Okay, let's go piece by piece. How much of your decision to end things was about Mason?"

"Some." I paused. "But I think I could talk to him. Get him to understand. I never felt right about keeping the truth from him anyway."

"Okay, and how much was about what people would say, or small town gossip?"

I shrugged. "I don't really care what people say, but I worry about Millie. If she could get past it, I could. People would probably find something else to talk about pretty fast."

"I agree. So now the family issue. Would you consider surgery to reverse the vasectomy if it came to that? Or are you at least willing to have that conversation?"

I took a deep breath. "I would have that conversation."

"Good. So now we go deep." Taking a step toward me, he leaned against the island with both hands. "How much of this is about unpacking your baggage?"

I opened my mouth to argue once again that this wasn't about the past, but as soon as I met his eyes, I closed it. Jackson knew me too well. "How do you get over it?" I asked him, because he'd suffered loss too.

"You don't. You accept it and move on with your life. And you haven't done that, Zach. Don't even bring up that bullshit marriage to Kimberly—I know what that was. That was you trying to go through the motions without actually feeling the feelings."

"I know," I muttered, dropping my eyes to the marble. "I know."

"Okay, so I have one more thing to ask you. You love this woman. And by the way, that's not the question, because I already know you do. You love this woman. So how could you possibly trust that someone else would take care of her like you would, or keep her as safe?"

"I couldn't," I said, looking up at him again. "No one would ever take care of her like I could. The thought makes me sick."

Jackson's arms went out. "So what the fuck are you still doing in my kitchen?"

I was awake all night trying to think of what should happen next. Obviously, I needed to go back to Michigan, but I needed to prepare. First, I'd have to have a conversation with Mason. I'd admit the truth, apologize, and explain that while I'd never meant for any of this to happen, I was in love with Millie and wanted to be with her. Since I knew Mason cared for Millie, I was hoping he'd want her to be happy—and I could make her happy.

I just had to convince her.

Not that I thought she'd deny it, but I wanted to do something to show her that I didn't just miss her or even just love her—I needed her in my life. Always.

As I tossed and turned, I kept thinking about what Sophie had said. *Sometimes you just have to believe everything happens for a reason, and trust in the people you love to protect and guide you.*

Trust the people you love to protect and guide you.

There was something about those words that embodied Millie and me, but I couldn't put my finger on what it was.

I fell asleep toward morning knowing the answer was there somewhere, but I still hadn't figured it out.

It was when I was getting dressed after my shower that it hit me. I caught a glimpse of my upper body in the mirror before I pulled on my shirt, and the sight of my tattoos never failed to remind me of the way Millie touched them—reverently, tenderly, curious about the story behind each one.

I knew what I wanted to do.

Twenty-Eight

Zach

On the afternoon of December thirty-first, I knocked on Mason and Lori's door.

It was Lori who pulled it open. "Zach," she said, obviously surprised. "What are you doing here?"

"Hi, Lori. Can I come in?"

She glanced behind her. "Ah. I don't know."

"Please. I know I hurt Mason's feelings, and yours too, by leaving so suddenly on Christmas Eve. I'm really sorry, and I'd like to make it up to you."

"That's not—I mean, you don't have to—" She sighed and closed her eyes for a second. "You should really talk to Mason."

"Is he here?"

"Yes," she said, backing up and opening the door wider. "Come in."

I entered their house, and she took my coat, hanging it in the closet by the foot of the stairs. "Have a seat in the living room," she said, still looking a little uneasy. "I'll tell Mason you're here."

As she headed up the stairs, I took a seat on the living room sofa and rubbed my sweaty palms over my knees. I had no doubt that I was doing the right thing, but I was nervous about how this was going to go—I was here without Millie's permission, and this involved her. But I didn't want to go to her without having done the honorable thing where my son was concerned. And even if Mason was upset, he wasn't vindictive. He wasn't the kind of person to spread ugly gossip.

Still, a lot was riding on this conversation. I had to do it just right.

The minutes ticked by, and Mason still didn't come down. I was beginning to wonder if something was wrong when I heard some heated voices from upstairs. Had I come at a bad time? Were they having a fight? I was thinking I'd come back later when Mason finally appeared on the stairs, visible from where I sat.

He descended slowly, his arms folded across his chest, and I could instantly tell something was way off. His jaw was set, and his eyes were devoid of their usual warmth. "Zach," he said.

I rose. "Mason. How are you?"

He shrugged. The air hummed with tension.

"Will you sit?"

He hesitated, but then lowered himself to the opposite end of the couch and sat back, his arms still crossed. I perched on the edge of the cushion.

"I'm sure you're surprised to see me," I said, "and I apologize for showing up without any notice. I'm also sorry about Christmas."

Another shrug. "It's fine."

"I'm here because I need to tell you something." I leaned forward, my body angled slightly toward his. I kept my focus on my hands, tapping my fingertips together between my knees. "This isn't easy for me to say, but—"

"I know about Millie, Zach."

I looked up at him sharply. "What?"

"I know about Millie. I saw you."

"When?"

"Christmas Eve. In the bar."

It sank in fast. The shadow at the door. "Oh."

"I mean, I'd suspected something before—at the rehearsal, actually. And if you remember, I asked you about it then."

"You did. And I wasn't truthful with you."

"Obviously," he said tersely. "What I don't get is why."

"I was ashamed," I said. "And so was she. We'd—we'd spent the night together in New York without realizing the connection. And when we figured it out, we just sort of panicked."

"I told you that night how important honesty was to me," Mason said, sounding less angry now and more hurt.

"And I didn't take that lightly." I sat up taller. "Mason, believe me. That night, nothing was more important to me than earning your trust and respect. Since the moment we got those test results back, all I've wanted was to do right by you."

"Why should I believe you? You clearly kept lying to me for months. You're just like my mother."

"Mason," Lori said quietly.

I hadn't even realized she was there, but now I saw her leaning against the entrance to the living room, arms wrapped around her middle.

Mason frowned. "Lori thinks I'm trying to get back at my mother by being mad at you."

"I just don't want this—this—misunderstanding to cost you an important relationship in your life," Lori said, wiping her eyes.

"It's not just a misunderstanding," Mason insisted with a headstrong expression and set of his jaw that I knew all too well. "My entire life, people who claim to care about me have deliberately withheld important information from me. It makes me feel like a fucking idiot."

"I'm sorry," I said. "You're right, and I'm sorry. I should

not have kept my feelings about Millie a secret. We thought we were protecting you, and that was wrong of us."

"Did you think I wouldn't be able to handle it? Because I can. I'm a grown man, Zach."

He looked like such a stubborn teenage version of me when he said it, it was almost funny. It was like looking in a mirror thirty years ago.

"I didn't reach out to you because I needed a daddy," he said. "I just wanted to know my family."

"I understand," I said. "And I should have treated you like a man and not like a child that needed protecting. To be honest, I'm still grappling with how to be a father to an adult son. I have protective instincts as it is, and somehow finding out I'm a dad has multiplied them."

"I get that." Mason's arms loosened a little. "I just don't want to be in the dark anymore. I want to feel like I'm part of a family—like I came from somewhere. The things you gave me at Christmas, the stories you shared, all that meant so much to me. I've never had those things."

"You will," I promised. "Going through all those old things brought back a lot of memories, and I want to share them with you. That's new for me—I've never really had anyone ask or care about my family history. I've never thought about passing things on to another generation. But now I am." Then I took a breath. "This thing with Millie . . . I need to know how you feel about it."

Mason was silent for a moment, taking it all in. Then rubbed the back of his neck. "It's hard to say. My feelings about it are all tangled up in my anger about you guys hiding it from me."

"I understand."

"So you and Millie are . . . together?" asked Lori, coming deeper into the room and perching on the arm of the couch next to Mason.

"Not exactly. We have feelings for each other, and we've seen each other a few times outside of town, but a few weeks ago we called everything off."

"Looked different to me on Christmas Eve," Mason said stiffly.

"Yeah." I felt heat in my neck. "Staying away from each other is harder than we thought."

"So it's serious between you?" Lori asked.

"It was. I hope it will be again."

"Why did you call it off?" she asked. "Because of Mason?"

"Mason was the biggest reason at the start," I said, "but there were a few other reasons too, although those have grown less important over time. To me, what matters right now is making sure, Mason, that you know I never meant to hurt or embarrass you. I know I was wrong to lie, and I want to be the kind of man you hoped your father would be."

Mason didn't say anything for a moment. "I guess that can happen. I just never thought my *dad* would date my ex-girlfriend."

"Mason," Lori chided, placing a hand on his shoulder. "You and Millie have been just friends for well over a year now. And you told me yourself you two were much better as friends."

"We are," he said. "It's just weird."

"It's definitely weird," I agreed, "and we understand that people might judge us."

"I mean, if you two have kids," Mason went on, "your baby would be younger than its niece."

I grimaced. "Yeah. I know. The math hurts."

"But you don't have to listen to what other people say." Lori's voice was firm. "And we'll support you. You're our family and Millie is our friend. Right, Mason?"

"Right." He looked up at his wife, then put an arm around her waist. "Right."

"So it's okay with you?" I asked. "Millie and me?"

"I guess so. Like Lori said, Millie is our friend. I want her to be happy." Mason shrugged. "If you make her happy, then you should be with her."

"I'm going to try," I said, an odd catch in my chest. "You know, Mason, I've learned a lot from you."

"You have?" He sounded surprised.

"Yes. I'm sure it wasn't easy to reach out to me after you found that letter. You had no idea how I'd react. You risked rejection or my being a total jerk about it."

"I was nervous," he admitted. "But I decided it was worth the risk."

"That took a lot of courage."

Mason shrugged, his mouth tipping into a crooked smile. "I get it from my dad."

I left Mason and Lori's house and drove over to Millie's. It was starting to get dark—going on five o'clock—and I had no idea if she'd be there or out for New Year's Eve already. When she didn't answer my knock, I experienced a moment of panic. What if she was out on a date? Or in the shower getting ready for a party? What if she was putting on one of those dresses that fit her curvy body like a second skin? What if some other guy thought he deserved to put his eyes or his hands or his lips on her tonight?

My blood started to boil. My breath came faster as I knocked again, harder this time. I rang the bell. I shifted my weight from side to side, sweating even though it was icy cold and starting to snow.

Finally, I gave up and went back to my rental SUV. Sitting behind the wheel, I wondered if I should call or text her. It would ruin the surprise, but what choice did I have? I didn't want to wait another day. But would she even tell me where she was if she was with someone else?

A thought occurred to me—maybe she was at the shop. It was opening in just a couple days, right? It was New Year's Eve, but Millie was the kind of person who'd work through a holiday if there were still things to get done. I drove downtown, hoping I was right.

When I passed Millie Rose, I saw lights on inside, and my pulse quickened with anticipation. I found a parking spot a couple blocks down and ran back to the shop, shouldering between couples and groups of friends on the sidewalk. Once or twice, I slipped on the freshly fallen snow, but I kept my balance and hurried on.

In front of her shop's double doors, I stopped and caught my breath. Ran a hand over my hair. I couldn't see her inside, but she had to be there. I tried the door on the right—locked. The door on the left was locked as well. I knocked on the glass and waited. Nothing.

Frustrated, I framed my eyes with my hands and leaned on the glass, trying to see better. That's when I spied her at the back of the store pushing a vacuum. Adrenaline shot through my veins, and I banged my fist on the glass hard enough to shatter it.

Startled, she finally looked up.

Twenty-Nine

Millie

HE WAS *HERE*?

My heart began to hammer louder than the music in my earbuds or the vacuum in my hand. I turned them both off and returned the vacuum handle to its upright position, then looked up front again.

He was still there, wearing a black coat and waving his arms like a madman.

I blinked, expecting him to disappear. After all, I'd been fantasizing about him showing up like this to surprise me, to tell me we'd made a mistake, to say he couldn't live without me, then we'd ride off into the sunset together . . . but it was so ludicrous, I never imagined it actually happening.

But there he was.

Plucking my earbuds from my ears, I stuck them into my pocket—realizing as I made my way to the front that I was *not* dressed for a ride into the sunset. I had on elastic-waist sweatpants and an old hoodie of my dad's that said USMC on the front. On my feet were fuzzy socks, and my hair was wrangled into a loose, sloppy bun on the top of my head. I touched it as I reached the front doors, then unlocked them. Pulled one open.

"Hi," he said, his dark eyes bright with excitement. His entire body seemed to radiate with heat and energy.

"Zach." I shook my head slightly. "What are you—"

But I didn't even get to finish my question, because he burst inside, crushing his lips to mine and throwing his arms around me. He kissed me breathless for a solid minute, my back bowing, my bun tipping to the side, one of my feet coming off the ground. Cold air and snow blew in through the open door, but I hardly noticed. His body was warm and solid, his arms were locked around me, and his mouth, oh God—I missed the way he kissed me so much, like he'd been searching for me everywhere.

Finally, we came up for air. "Zach," I whispered, shivering a little. "Can you shut the door?"

"Oh, sorry." He released me and did as I asked. Thankfully, the moment the door was closed, he reached for me again, taking my face in his hands as we walked deeper into the store, as if we were dancing. "God, I missed you. I forgot how beautiful you are."

"I look terrible." I felt my bun listing to one side and reached up to pull out the ponytail holder.

As soon as my hair tumbled to my shoulders, Zach slid his fingers through it, then bent his head to inhale its scent. "I missed the smell of your hair. I missed everything about you."

"I missed you too."

He looked down at me, his eyes searching mine. "I was an idiot to think I could just let you go. I can't. I want to be with you. I *need* to be with you."

His words made my heart sing with hope, but I told myself to tread carefully. "What about Mason?"

"I spoke to him earlier today."

"You did?"

"Yes. I'm sorry, I know I should have asked your permission before telling him about us, but I didn't want to show up at your door without clearing the way forward."

"What did he say?"

"He said he already knew." Zach's expression turned a little sheepish. "He saw us on Christmas Eve in the bar."

My stomach dropped, and I gasped. "I *knew* I saw someone by the door! That was Mason?"

"Yes."

"But he didn't say anything! He wasn't upset?"

"He was," Zach admitted. "But he held it in. I think he's conflict-avoidant. Or maybe he just deals with his anger by going silent. Either way, when I showed up at his house today and told him about my feelings for you, he told me he'd seen us together."

"Oh no," I breathed. "Poor Mason."

"Mostly he was mad that I hadn't been honest with him," Zach said, dropping his hands to my hips. "He said he's tired of people who should care about him keeping him in the dark. It makes him feel like an idiot."

"I get that."

"What's important to him is being part of a family. Feeling like he belongs."

I hated to bring this up, but it seemed like the right time. "Speaking of family, Zach, is there—are you—have you changed your mind about—" I struggled with how to phrase it.

He put a finger to my lips. "I know what you're asking, and the answer is yes. I'm open to wherever the future leads us."

"Really?" My eyes filled. "You'd consider having a family someday?"

"With you, I would. I want to make you happy, Millie. I want us to build a life together. And if that life includes a family, I'd be the luckiest man on earth."

"Are you sure?" I asked, wanting to believe him, but still

wary of heartbreak. I'd been so sad the last few weeks without him—what if he changed his mind again?

"Yes." He locked his arms around my lower back, setting his hips against me. "Listen, I wasn't looking for you. But when I saw you in that hotel bar, it hit me like a lightning strike—I had to have you. But once wasn't enough. I swear to God, you never left my head for a moment after that night we spent together."

"You never left mine either."

"And when I saw you again, it was the same thing—electrifying, like I'd been brought back to life. I started wanting things with you I've never wanted with anyone, because I *felt* things for you I'd never felt for anyone. I *told* you things about myself I've never told anyone. I trusted you with pieces of me I've never trusted to anyone else."

"I trusted you too," I said. "Immediately. The moment we met."

"I know you did." He smiled. "It's one of the things I love about you, because I know you don't trust easily."

I sniffed as a tear rolled down one cheek.

"No more crying." He brushed the tear with his thumb. "We're going to be together. My life no longer feels right without you. You know what I realized after Las Vegas?"

"What?"

"That home didn't even feel like home anymore. Home to me now is wherever you are, and no matter where I go, I will always make my way back to you. I want to show you something." He let me go and slipped out of his coat, tossing it onto the velvet settee behind me.

I watched him unbutton the cuff of his black shirt and roll it up, sucking in my breath at the new ink on his inner forearm. "You got a new tattoo!"

"It's a compass rose," he said. "A navigational tool for sailors, but also a symbol of discovery."

I studied the beautifully rendered design, the skin still tender and pink around it. "I love it," I whispered.

"I got it for you." His voice was quiet but firm. "You're my north, south, east, and west, Millie Rose. You ground me, you guide me, you inspire me. And I'm madly in love with you."

The tears were flowing freely now, but I didn't even care. I threw my arms around his neck and buried my face in his chest, blubbering like a baby. "I love you too," I sobbed. "I'm so happy."

"Are you sure?" He chuckled as he stroked my back. "This is a lot of crying for 'happy.'"

"Yes, I'm sure." It took me a minute or two to stop, but eventually I let go of him and hurried into the bathroom so I could blow my nose and clean up my face.

When I came out, he was looking around. "The shop is beautiful, Millie. I'm in awe of what you've done."

"Thanks," I said. "I'm really excited, but also nervous. I open in just two days. I've got appointments already!"

He smiled as he took me in his arms again. "Don't be nervous. You've got this. Tell me what I can do to help you. I'm all yours."

I tipped my head back and looked up at him. "What I could really use is a distraction. Got a date for New Year's Eve?"

He lowered his lips to mine. "I do now."

I'd been invited to a party at my Aunt April and Uncle Tyler's house, but we decided to skip it and have a night in. I sent a quick text to my sisters saying I wouldn't be there but I was fine, better than ever actually, and I'd explain in the morning. I wished them both a Happy New Year and said I was positive this was going to be the best year ever for all the MacAllister girls.

Audrey and Emmeline would graduate from high school.

Winnie and Dex were getting married this summer. Hutton and Felicity were building a gorgeous new house. And me? I smiled as I headed for home, Zach's headlights in my rearview mirror.

I'd found love—the greatest plot twist life has to offer.

We stopped on the way home and picked up some groceries and champagne, planning on making dinner and ringing in the new year with a cozy indoor picnic for two in front of the fireplace. But as soon as Zach got the fire burning, he came into the kitchen and wrapped his arms around me from behind, kissing my neck.

"I can't use a knife if you're going to do that," I said, giggling as I tipped my head to one side.

"Then put down the knife." He took it from my hand and set it on the counter.

"Aren't you hungry?" I asked as he led me into the living room, where he'd spread out a blanket in front of the fireplace. The curtains were closed, the fire was crackling, and the only lights came from the tree we'd decorated together.

"I'm starving," he said, lifting my sweatshirt over my head. "But only for you."

We undressed each other quickly and tumbled onto the floor, where we made up for lost time, luxuriated in the moment, and let dreams of the future enrapture us. When he was buried deep inside me, his skin golden in the firelight, I reached up and touched the silver in his hair, the edge of his jaw, the back of his neck. "I love you," I whispered as he moved above me. "You're all I've ever wanted."

"I love you too." He pressed his lips to mine. "You're all I'll ever need."

Epilogue

Millie

March

"SHOOT!"

Winnie stopped her dramatic strutting on the rented catwalk and looked over at me. "What's wrong?"

I stared at my cell phone in dismay. "Olivia, one of the models, just had to drop out. Her dad had some kind of health emergency, and she has to fly to Houston right away."

"Oh no!" Winnie carefully hopped down from the three-foot-high runway that bisected the room full of tables for ten, all of which were sold out for this afternoon's show.

"He's going to be okay, but I'm down a model, and I can't get ahold of the agency to find a replacement." I set my phone on a table and rubbed my temples. "What am I going to do? It's nine already, and the show starts at two!"

"Do you have any friends who'd fill in for you?"

"None that are the right size."

"What size does the model need to be? Could you fill in?"

"Me?" I shrank back. "No way—I'm strictly behind the scenes."

"But I'll be here behind the scenes. And wouldn't that be

better than cutting dresses from the show?" Her eyes lit up and she clapped her hands. "Come on, it will be fun! Remember that fashion show you were in with Dad when you were a kid?"

I laughed. "When I forced him to wear the homemade T-shirt covered with glittery pink and red hearts?"

"Yes!"

"That was the extent of my modeling career, Winnie. I'd probably fall flat on my face walking this runway in wedding gowns." I frowned and dropped into a chair. "Although I hate to think of those dresses not being in the show—they're some of my favorite looks. I don't understand why the agency isn't getting back to me." I reached for my phone to try them again, but Winnie took it away from me.

"I think the best plan is to do it yourself. The chances of finding the perfect model last-minute are slim to none, and at least if you fill in yourself, you might have time to do some quick alterations if necessary."

I chewed the inside of my cheek. "I can't do them myself. I'd need Diane."

"Get her on the phone right now." Winnie handed my cell back to me.

"She's at the shop," I said, placing the call. "We're fully booked with fittings. She might not answer."

But she did, and she said if I hurried over to the store and put on the dresses in question, she'd see what could be done. She wasn't sure she could rework all four of the dresses to fit me in time, but she thought at least one or two might be possible.

"Go," said Winnie. "I've got things covered here."

"Okay. I need to run home and grab some heels and undergarments." I grabbed my bag and hurried for the door, waving at Winnie. "Call me if you need anything."

"I will!"

If I hadn't been so distraught, I'd have noticed the sneaky, satisfied little smile on her face.

Zach

My cell phone buzzed just after nine a.m., right on schedule. "Yeah?"

"Done," Winnie said breathlessly. "She just left, and she's headed over to the shop."

"And she doesn't suspect anything?"

"Not a thing. I was *very* good in my role." She laughed. "Keeping this scheme a secret was much harder for me than convincing her!"

I laughed. "Thanks for your help."

"My pleasure. Are things all set with my dad?"

"Yes. He'll stay out of sight until Felicity gives him the cue. I'll be the one to tell Felicity when to get him, which I'll do after you give me the signal."

"Got it."

It had been Winnie and Felicity's idea to involve Mack in the plan, and even though Millie's dad still made me a little nervous, I went to him and asked if he'd like to take part. I knew how much it would mean to Millie.

It took some convincing from his younger daughters, but eventually he agreed. When he shook my hand that day, he said he was happy for me, and told me he knew his daughter would be in good hands—even if I was a Navy man and not a Marine. "I once told her she deserved the best," he said, "and I think she found it."

I'd never forget the morning I met him and Frannie for the first time. It was New Year's Day, and Millie insisted we attend the usual January first gathering at her parents' house.

I tried not to show it, but I was terrified—this guy, a former Marine, was about to hear that his daughter had fallen for a man closer to his age than hers. How would he take it?

Luckily, after a few sidelong glances and some stiff conversation, he'd warmed up to me. I didn't blame him for being wary—I wouldn't trust my daughter to just anyone either, especially if she had a heart like Millie's, huge and giving. Frannie had been welcoming from the moment we met, and her sisters were great too. Eventually, there was some teasing about the whole situation, but they always did it affectionately.

"Perfect." Winnie squealed with delight. "I just cannot wait to see her face! This is the best plan ever, and we totally pulled it off!"

"Not yet we didn't," I reminded her. "This was only part one. You're sure that dress she really loves can be done in time?"

"Diane has already been working on it. She pretended to have an issue with a seam the other day and asked Millie to put it on—she says it's all under control."

"Good." I took a deep breath. "I'll see you later."

"Okay. And Zach?"

"Yeah?"

"Good luck."

After we hung up, I went over to my leather laptop bag and pulled out the small hinged box, opening it up to reveal the ring I'd chosen—an Art Deco-inspired style with an emerald cut diamond in the center and two smaller ones on each side, set in shiny platinum. The stones caught the light coming in from the bedroom window and sparkled the way I hoped Millie's eyes would when she saw it.

The last two months had been the happiest of my life. I'd moved in with her a couple weeks into January, and although I still traveled a lot for work, coming home to her was even better than I'd imagined.

Jackson had said there was no problem with me using Michigan as a home base. For now, I was keeping my job with Cole Security, but Millie and I talked a lot about the whiskey bar idea, and she'd introduced me to a family member of hers who'd opened up a microbrewery here in town. He was a great guy and offered to talk to me about business any time.

All of Millie's extended family was great, actually—I'd met a ton of them by now, and they were a close, welcoming bunch. I saw Mason quite a bit too. Lori was due any day now, and the two of them were beside themselves with excitement. I was happy for them, even if I wasn't thrilled about being a grandpa at my age.

But life was good.

And it was about to get better.

Millie

"You're sure you can do it in time?" I fretted.

"I'm positive. It already fits you near perfectly." Diane stuck one more pin in the dress I had on, a stunning gown that fit snugly over my upper body and flared out beneath the hips. It had long sleeves and an illusion bodice, and the lace was Chantilly. None of the other dresses Olivia had been slated to wear could be altered in time, but this one was my favorite, so I was really hoping it could be in the show. Diane stood up and patted my shoulder, checking my reflection in the mirror. "Gorgeous. I'm sorry none of the other dresses fit, but I promise this one will be done."

"Okay. Thank you so much." I stepped off the riser, holding the dress off the floor. "I'm just going to run home and do my hair. I'll swing by to pick up the dress when I'm on my way back to the show."

"Sounds good." Diane smiled and followed me to the dressing room. "I'll help you take it off."

At home, I raced frantically up the stairs and jumped into the shower. Zach was already gone—he'd left about an hour ago for the airport to catch a flight to Denver. A job had cropped up last-minute, and he'd offered to turn it down so he could be at the show, but I'd told him it was okay. He was so supportive of me and my work in every possible way, from taking care of dinner on my late nights to maintenance work in the shop to giving the best foot rubs ever if I'd been standing all day.

I missed him when he was gone, but his homecomings were always a thrill. We'd been talking more often about the day when he might stop working for Cole Security and start a business around here, but I never put any pressure on him. Nor did I question when he might schedule his reversal surgery. We weren't exactly taking things slowly (had we ever?), but he'd upended his life and moved across the country for me. It was enough for now.

After my shower, I blew out my hair, curled it, and pinned up the back, leaving some pieces in the front to frame my face. We had a makeup artist for the show, so I left my face bare, stuck my heels in my bag, and pulled on sweats and sneakers.

As I was tying my shoes, I caught a glimpse of my tattoo and smiled. It was an anchor, placed on my inner forearm so it would mirror the one Zach got for me. I liked looking at them side by side—the compass a symbol of guidance, the anchor a symbol of stability. Whenever I saw it, I was reminded of Zach, not just because he'd been a sailor, but because his presence in my life was solid, strong, and comforting.

When he held me, I was home.

Back at the venue, there was a surprise—Olivia, the model who'd texted me that she had to cancel her appearance, was there.

"My dad is doing much better," she told me. "I ended up not having to leave town. I just texted you."

"I'm so glad," I said. "But shoot! I didn't get your message in time and one of your dresses was altered to fit me."

"No big deal." She smiled and patted my arm. "You wear it. I'm sure it's stunning on you. I'll just model the other three looks."

As the makeup artist was finishing with me, Winnie came over, a clipboard in her hand. "Couple things," she said. "We switched the order of the show. You're going to be last."

"What?" My heart started to thud. I didn't love last-minute changes, and I already felt like I had whiplash today. "Why?"

"It just works better." She was already walking away from me. "But don't worry, everything is going smoothly and there's a packed house out there who can't wait for the show. I'm going to get it started."

Within a couple minutes, the music began, the announcer came on the mic, and the first model stepped in front of the curtain. The cheers that erupted from the audience nearly brought tears to my eyes. And I wasn't the only one.

"I saw someone crying!" said one of the models as she hurried by to get into her next dress. "Like, in a good way!"

"Really?" My heart was pounding with joy and exhilaration. "That makes me so happy!"

But as we neared the end of the show, I began to get nervous. I was in my dress, which fit like a dream, and one of the assistants was pinning a veil to my hair. "You look beautiful," she said. "You ready?"

"I think so." But I wasn't prepared for what I saw when I turned around. "Dad?"

"Hi, sweetheart." He came toward me dressed in a black tuxedo, his hair neatly combed, his blue eyes shining. Winnie was beside him.

"You look amazing," I said, laughing in spite of my nerves—or maybe because of them. "But what are you doing here?"

"We thought it would be a nice touch," Winnie said gleefully. "A little throwback to your first fashion show."

"I like my outfit better in this one," he said as he offered me his arm.

"Me too." With my heart still jumping, I put my hand on the inside of his arm. "This is so sweet, Dad. Thank you. I'm less nervous with you at my side."

He smiled. "I'll always be here for you."

A moment later, we were being ushered out onto the catwalk. The crowd cheered, and I squeezed my dad's arm as we slowly made our way to the end of the runway, at which point we were supposed to pause, then turn around and walk back. I was wondering if anyone had explained that to him when suddenly I saw a familiar face at the back of the room.

My jaw dropped.

Zach was moving toward us, also dressed in black tie, his dark eyes locked on mine. The end of the runway had two steps, which he ascended without ever looking away from me. Beneath the music, I could hear the surprised whispers in the audience, who were watching the drama unfold with rapt attention.

My father nodded. "She's all yours, Zach."

"Thank you, sir." They shook hands, and my father went down the steps and took a seat next to Frannie and the twins, who were all in the front row on the left side. Felicity was there too, her phone in front of her like she was recording this.

The volume of the music was lowered, and I looked at Zach. I could feel my heart in my throat. "What's going on?"

But instead of answering, he went down on one knee.

The audience went wild, and Zach waited until the room quieted a little before speaking. "Millie MacAllister, you captured my heart the moment I saw you. And I never want it back." Reaching into his pocket, he pulled out a small box and opened it up. Within the black velvet interior, a ring sparkled and shone in the lights. "Will you marry me?"

For a couple seconds, I was too stunned to even answer. And when the word *yes* came out, it was only a whisper.

"Louder!" yelled Winnie.

"Yes!" I shouted to the ceiling. "Yes!"

The crowd erupted once more, and over the speakers, the DJ blasted "Beautiful Day" by U2. But I barely registered any of it because Zach was sliding that gorgeous ring onto my shaking finger. He squeezed my hand and stood up, and I lifted my face to him. When his lips rested lightly on mine, I swear I felt the earth move. When he took my hand and kissed my knuckles, my heart nearly burst. When I glanced down at the ring, it was blurry through my tears.

The other models returned to the runway for a final bow, and the audience members jumped to their feet, whistling and applauding. I looked at my family and touched my heart—they'd taught me to believe in myself. I looked at the man beside me and took his hand—he'd taught me to trust in love. And I looked around this room, where I'd run around as a child with a million dreams, so full today of joy and hope, and felt my bones reverberate with the celebration of life and love and possibility.

The future was bright.

THE END

Did you love Zach and Millie's story? Want a peek into their future? Subscribe to my mailing list by going here: www.melanieharlow.com/subscribe-for-a-tempt-bonus-scene and the first thing you'll get is a TEMPT bonus scene!

Be a Harlot

Want new release alerts, access to bonus materials and exclusive giveaways, and all my announcements first? Subscribe to my twice monthly newsletter!
harlow.pub/mh-news

Want to stay up to date on all things Harlow day to day, get exclusive access to ARCs and giveaways, and be part of a fun, positive, sexy and drama-free zone? Become a Harlot!
harlow.pub/harlots

Want a chance to become a Top Fan and win exclusive prizes? Check out my Facebook page!
harlow.pub/ap

Want to be notified about freebies and sales? Try Bookbub!
harlow.pub/bb

If you love audiobooks,
you can find audio versions of my books here!
www.audible.com/author/Melanie-Harlow/B00DXOYC1S

Also by

Melanie Harlow

Want a reading order? Go here:
www.melanieharlow.com/reading-order

Acknowledgments

As always, my appreciation and gratitude go to the following people for their talent, support, wisdom, friendship, and encouragement . . .

Melissa Gaston, Kristie @read_between.the_wines, Brandi Zelenka, Jenn Watson, Hang Le, Jan @janbookshelf, Corinne Michaels, Anthony Colletti, Rebecca Friedman, Flavia Viotti & Meire Dias at Bookcase Literary, Nancy Smay at Evident Ink, Julia Griffis at The Romance Bibliophile, Michele Fight, Stacey Blake at Champagne Book Design, Erin Spencer at One Night Stand Studios, the Shop Talkers, the Sisterhood, the Harlots and the Harlot ARC Team, bloggers and event organizers, my readers all over the world . . .

And once again, to my family. You're everything to me.

About the Author

Melanie Harlow likes her heels high, her martini dry, and her history with the naughty bits left in. She's the author of the Bellamy Creek Series, the Cloverleigh Farms Series, the One & Only series, the After We Fall Series, the Happy Crazy Love Series, and the Frenched Series.

She writes from her home outside of Detroit, where she lives with her husband and two daughters. When she's not writing, she's probably got a cocktail in hand. And sometimes when she is.

Find her at www.melanieharlow.com.

Printed in Great Britain
by Amazon

14034634R00180